"Your kindness matters."

Rayna gestured for him to take the coat she'd gathered up and folded with care. He couldn't seem to make his feet move forward.

For a brief moment he inhaled her sweet warm woman scent that made him think of lilacs and spring breezes and lark song. Desire stirred in his blood, for he knew she would smell like that all over. Knew her smooth skin and soft curves were made for a man to caress and cherish.

Unaware of his thoughts, Rayna lifted her right hand to stroke her loose hair away from her eyes. It wasn't a seductive movement. It might as well have been, for the blood roaring in his ears.

"I need to finish my errands. Good day to you, Daniel."

She walked away, and it felt to him as if she took all the light with her, leaving him in utter darkness.

* * *

Montana Wife

Harlequin Historical #734—December 2004

Praise for Jillian Hart's recent books

High Plains Wife

"Finely drawn characters and sweet tenderness tinged with poignancy draw readers into a familiar story that beautifully captures the feel of an Americana romance."

—*Romantic Times*

Bluebonnet Bride

"Ms. Hart expertly weaves a fine tale of the heart's ability to find love after tragedy. Pure reading pleasure!"

—*Romantic Times*

Cooper's Wife

"...a wonderfully written romance full of love and laughter."

—*Rendezvous*

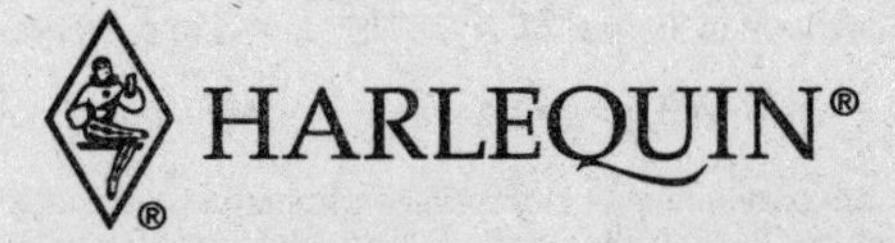

TORONTO • NEW YORK • LONDON
AMSTERDAM • PARIS • SYDNEY • HAMBURG
STOCKHOLM • ATHENS • TOKYO • MILAN • MADRID
PRAGUE • WARSAW • BUDAPEST • AUCKLAND

ISBN 0-373-29334-8

MONTANA WIFE

This edition published by arrangement with Harlequin Books S.A.

www.eHarlequin.com

Printed in U.S.A.

Available from Harlequin Historicals and JILLIAN HART

Last Chance Bride #404
Cooper's Wife #485
Malcolm's Honor #519
Montana Man #538
Night Hawk's Bride #558
Bluebonnet Bride #586
Montana Legend #624
High Plains Wife #670
The Horseman #715
Montana Wife #734

Chapter One

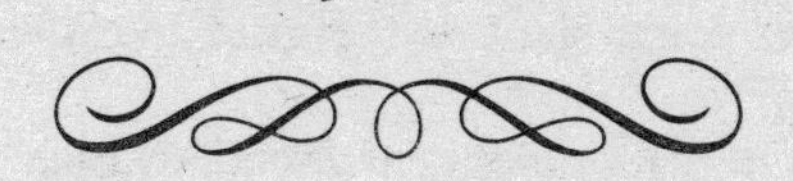

Montana Territory, 1883

Rayna Ludgrin twisted the lace handkerchief in her hand, the delicate material shockingly white against her black dress. This was a nightmare, the kind that felt so real that when you awake in the dark of night, there's that moment of confusion before realizing it's only a dream.

She was ready to wake any time now. Ready for the scorching-hot sun to fade into darkness, for day to wane into night and for the cemetery to vanish so she could rouse to the peaceful shadows of her bedroom. So the webby remains of this bad dream could taper away and her husband could be alive and sound asleep beside her, as he was meant to be forever, flung on his back and snoring like a freight train barreling down a straight stretch.

She blinked, still in the chair at the graveside with the blistering sunlight tight on her face.

''Let me take you home now.'' Betsy's black-gloved hand caught hers.

The service was over, and so should the dream be, too. Rayna stood up from the hardwood chair someone had brought earlier from inside the church. Betsy, her dear friend, guided Rayna around the corner of the grave where a pine casket lay with Kol inside.

But if this was a dream, why could she see the green grass and breathe in air tainted with the sharp scent of earth? How come she felt the grief like the breeze on her skin?

"That's it," her other dear friend, Mariah, was at her other side, clutching her other arm. "Step up here. That's right. Betsy, she needs to lie down."

"I'll run up and ready her bed," another voice said from somewhere beyond the haze of her despair.

Footsteps dashed off, or was that the uneven thump of her own shoes on the porch steps? Rayna was confused, but from the moment Dayton's daughter had knocked on her door with the news of Kol's collapse and death, time had stood still.

He's not dead. He can't be dead. The force of fear and grief and loss expanded like a soap bubble beneath the whalebones of her corset.

Her eyes snapped open and she was sitting in bed in the dark. The hot sun and green cemetery had vanished. The peaceful stillness of night surrounded her. So, she'd been dreaming, after all, but Kol's death was still a reality.

A faint glow from a setting moon gleamed on the lace curtains breezing at the window, illuminating the patchwork quilt on the bed. The quilt she'd made during Kol's courtship. The patches she had cut and sewed with care, every stitch of her needle made with all of the love in her heart for Kol and with the hope for a happy future as his wife.

The harsh rasp of her breathing was the only sound in the room. The hope chest tucked beneath the window, the chair in the corner, the graceful curve of her looking glass by the wardrobe were all as they should be. See? Everything was fine.

But it wasn't.

She didn't have to look beside her to see the truth. She could feel the empty place where no man lay sprawled on his back. Hear the silence instead of the rhythmic snoring that had disturbed her sleep for the past fifteen years. There was no comforting warmth in her bed.

She was alone.

The faint hues of the interlocked circles on her quilt, representing wedding rings that by day were a cheerful calico patchwork, were shades of gray in the night. Cold prickles, as sharp and as merciless as needles, stabbed behind her eyelids.

No amount of wishing would bring her dear Kol back. He was dead and buried. His heart had failed him while he'd been helping the neighbors with their harvesting. He was never coming back.

Ever.

Rayna wrapped her arms around her waist, as if she could hold in the pain and the sorrow lodged in her heart.

''Ma!'' A little boy's fear vibrated in that single word. ''Ma, Ma!''

She was out of bed and across the hall faster than a bolt of lightning could travel, on her knees beside her youngest son's bed before he could cry out again. Hans was in her arms, that sweet smell of little boy, the warm, solid dearness of him.

She was grateful that he was safe and tucked against

her heart, his sobs shaking through her as if they were her own. She would give her life to make his pain stop.

"Mama's right here, my baby." She pressed kisses to the crown of his head where the cowlick just like Kol's stuck up at all angles. "Mama's here. It's all right."

"I d-dreamed about P-Papa."

"So did I." She rocked him, her dear, precious child, cradling him tight, trying to will all the pain out of him and into her. But he cried all the same.

Helpless, she could only comfort him until his sobs quieted into tears and, finally, aching silence.

She laid him on his bed and tucked the sheet snug around his chest. He was lying as if asleep. He wasn't. She could tell. How did she make this better? This was no cut knee to bandage or no broken toy to fix.

She sat on the edge of his feather mattress and sang the lullabies her mother had sung to her in Swedish, her first language. She no longer remembered what the words meant, but the songs were melodies of love and comfort, and so she sang until her throat turned hoarse and her son relaxed into a dreamless sleep.

Only then did she rise, blow a kiss to his brow and steal from the room. She left his door ajar so she could hear him should he stir again.

Her bare feet whispered on the polished floorboard and emptiness accompanied her to her room. The moon had set and there was only stardust to guide her to the window as she brushed the lace curtains from the sill and gazed out at the seed-heavy fields of wheat.

Wheat that had to be cut before the grain fell from the stalks. But how? *Kol, how am I going to do this without you?*

You will find a way, you always do. That was his

voice she heard in her thoughts, words he would often say to her. Remembering him renewed the pain of his passing. Made the ache within her explode and leave only pieces of her heart as she buried her face in her hands.

She had children. A homestead. Responsibilities. Yes, she would find a way. What hurt to the depths of her being was having to make her way without Kol.

It wasn't being alone that troubled her the most. No, what broke her from the inside out was realizing the night would end. Dawn would come. She would have to live that day, while Kol could not.

Unable to climb into her lonely bed, she sank to her knees on the unforgiving floor. She buried her face in her hands and cried for the life Kol would not have.

For the care she would never be able to give to him. She cried for the man she'd vowed to cherish until death parted them.

Death *had* parted them. The love had not.

It was too soon after the funeral and Daniel Lindsay knew it, but what was he going to do? Let the opportunity go to someone else? No. His conscience troubled him, but it didn't keep him from rapping on the Ludgrin's front door even though two whole days hadn't passed since the funeral.

Life went on; it was the sad truth. He couldn't say he knew what it was like to lose a loved one. He'd never had any family that he remembered to lose—

The glass handle turned and the door squeaked open. A round-faced little boy gazed up at him with sad eyes. Daniel pegged the little guy to be about seven or eight years old, too damn young to be without a father. This, Daniel sorely knew.

"Is your mother home?"

His solemn eyes blinked. The breeze batted at his white-blond hair sticking straight up at the crown. "Ma's out back."

Out back? Probably tending to the livestock. Kol might be gone, but the cattle still needed fresh water. "I'll go look for her."

"She's hard to find cuz the wheat's so tall. I gotta watch her from the window upstairs." The boy pointed straight through the roof.

His chest ached for the tyke, who was anxious to keep track of his mother as if he could lose her, too. Daniel couldn't help feeling sorrow, for he knew something about loss. He'd grown up in a string of orphanages. He knew what it was like to wish for a family lost. It was sad this son of Kol's would know the sting of loss the rest of his life. No kid should have to live with that. It left scars on the man Daniel was to this day.

How would it affect the little Ludgrin boy?

The door squeaked closed as he knuckled back his hat and followed the wraparound porch to the steps leading to the side yard.

Flowers bloomed everywhere, fat roses and yellow climbing flowers that smelled good enough to eat. There wasn't a weed in sight, and that said something about the care Rayna Ludgrin took with her house and, he hoped, with her life.

Would she be fair? Would she listen to what he had to say, even if it wasn't the most appropriate time to be saying it?

As he opened the white, hand-carved gate and clicked it shut behind him, he could see the care Kol had taken, too. Kol had been a good man. Judging by the look of the place, he'd been a good husband. The barn was newly painted, the roof in good repair. Every joint in the split-rail fence solidly hewn. The cattle looked well fed. The sleek, matched bay horses were groomed and their brown-velvet coats gleamed with fine health.

Surely his wife wouldn't want to see all her husband's hard work fall to ruin. It wasn't as if she could harvest the hundred and sixty acres herself.

Where was she? Daniel looked around, in case he had somehow missed her. He was alone in the shade of the fruit trees. She wasn't at work in the ripe acre-size garden. Nor was she in the pasture where the livestock drowsed in the hot afternoon sun.

How far out back had she gone? Daniel wandered past the fence line and called out a greeting before he stepped foot inside the barn. Only the faint echo of his hello in the rafters and the beat of his boots on the hard-packed earth answered.

She wasn't here, either.

A fresh new trail of horse hooves and the deep rut of wagon wheels marked the dusty path. Daniel followed them, wandering from the barn and into golden fields where the fat, seed-heavy heads of wheat spread for miles in every direction.

There, about a quarter of an acre due south, rose a cloud of chalk dust, a brown smudge hovering above the fields of gold. Someone was harvesting the Ludgrin's wheat. Someone had beat him here. He'd waited too long. Cursing, he walked faster. Who had beaten him to the draw? Who was harvesting Kol's wheat and for what price?

He shouldn't have waited an extra day, shouldn't have waited at all. When he thought of Rayna Ludgrin, pale and fragile at the funeral, he was at a loss. He couldn't trouble the grief-stricken woman, not at her husband's gravesite. He wasn't a heartless person.

Neither, he figured was she. Although she'd suffered a terrible tragedy, she had to be starting to realize what she was up against. She had crops ready to drop in the fields. There were financial consequences that came from that. It had to be overwhelming to face her husband's death and the responsibility that went along with farming all alone, all at once.

It was only natural that a person in that circumstance would want help. She'd said yes to the first man to approach her. Why wouldn't she? It only made sense. Daniel felt like a clodpate for waiting. He'd meant it as a show of respect, but apparently that hadn't been necessary.

As did many women he'd come across—most, in fact—Rayna Ludgrin probably only cared that a man was providing for her. Doing the hard work for her.

Yep, he knew that about some women. His low opinion of the gender was one of the reasons he'd never married. It was hard to find a smart woman who was kind and industrious.

He removed his hat and wiped the sweat from his brow. What he ought to do was to accept defeat, turn around and get back to his wheat. Why his boots kept heading deeper into Ludgrin's fields instead of back toward his own, he couldn't rightly say. Maybe he wanted to see who had beaten him to the gun.

It wasn't any of the Dayton grandsons, because he'd seen them hard at work on the Dayton land on his way over. Who did that leave? The rest of the surrounding ranchers all worked together, buying one harvester between them and working as a team to bring in all the crops. An effort that Daniel had been invited to join but had turned down. He'd learned his hard lesson long ago. It was better to be alone than to trust someone else. Best to stand on his own two feet.

The tall rows of dense endless wheat gave way before him. Instead of the bright paint of a newfangled harvester, he saw the tailgate of a wagon. A hand scythe lay propped against the rear axle. The cutting implement was so old the blade was rusted at the joints and the wooden handle was cracked.

Daniel followed the wide swath where fallen, plump-headed wheat stalks lay on their stubble. The clearing was sizable, the same breadth as the town square. And cut by hand, too.

Whoever was doing this had to be plumb crazy. Or desperate for a little extra cash. That was probably it. Mrs. Ludgrin had no notion of how farming was done, like many women he'd come across. So she'd been sweet-talked by someone in town who thought he'd cut what he could and pocket the profits for himself.

White anger seared through him at the injustice. Some men were swine, he already knew it, and whoever was taking advantage of the widow was going to get an earful. Kol Ludgrin had been a fine neighbor, and he would expect Daniel to keep an eye out for Rayna's well fare—

He stalked around the wagon, expecting to find some no-account sitting in the shade, taking a swig from a flask, no doubt. Daniel's hand was already at rest on the holstered Colt .45 at his hip, just in case he needed it. A man had to be prepared.

The glare of the high-noon sun flashed in his eyes. Blinded, he knuckled his Stetson low so the hat brim shaded him from the brilliant sun.

It was a woman, dressed in a pair of trousers and a man's short-sleeved work shirt, upending a jug of water over her head. She was half turned to him; she couldn't have heard his step over the water streaming down her gold locks.

The liquid dampened the cotton along the nape of her neck, touching her ivory skin. His heart stopped beating as that lucky rivulet of water trailed the curve of her shoulder and meandered down the outside swell of her breast. Her uplifted arm gave him a fine view of her dark nipple puckered against the thin white cotton.

Don't look, Daniel. What are you doing? That beautiful sight was not meant for his eyes. Heat spit into his veins and he took a step back. Not all the heat that burned through him was lust.

Embarrassed, he pulled his Stetson lower and cleared his throat. "Excuse me, ma'am."

The water jug slipped from her fingers and hit the ground with a thud.

"Mr. L-Lindsay." Rayna glanced down at the shirt sticking to her like a second skin and stepped diplomatically behind the rails of the wagon bed. "I d-didn't expect anyone to find me out here or I would have, uh, dressed more appropriately."

"Don't worry, ma'am." His face blazed as hot as the sun, no doubt she knew what he'd seen. "I didn't expect to find a woman doing this work."

"The wheat will not harvest itself, will it?"

He stared at a rock in the earth. "You cut all this?"

"My older boy was helping me, but he went to town on an errand." Even though the side rails of the wagon bed hid her and Mr. Lindsay averted his gaze, Rayna felt more naked than clothed as the sun warmed the damp fabric hugging her uncorseted figure.

Goodness, what he must think of her! "I have a

wagon wheel in need of repair—I sent Kirk since I could cut wheat faster.''

''By *hand?*'' The way he said it, with that left hook of his dark brow, made her feel foolish.

She'd worked since just before noon and had made hardly a dent in the acres of gold that rustled around her, undulating like a slow tide on a mile-wide lake. So much wheat, it was overwhelming. Her responsibilities weighed on her each time she looked up from her cutting.

How was she ever going to cut it all? Not by wasting her time talking with another man come to swindle her. ''I would appreciate it if you'd be on your way. I have a lot of work to do until dark falls.''

''Why aren't Kol's friends helping you?''

''Because they are busy bringing in their own crops, I imagine.'' She fought to keep the edge from her voice. Every muscle within her exhausted body shrieked with a sharp, ripping ache as she lumbered around the tail of the wagon and took the scythe in hand. The worn wooden handle scraped against her dozens of blisters, popped and weeping.

With her back to him, she didn't need to worry about propriety. ''Please, be on your way, Mr. Lindsay. I'm of no mind to give away the wheat my husband worked hard to sow.''

''Give away?''

''I'll harvest it myself before I hand over this crop for free, so listen up and take your leave, like the others who came to my door this morning. I may be a woman, but I am far from stupid, and I'll not be robbed blind. I have my boys to think about.''

''Do you mean other ranchers around here have wanted your wheat. For *free?*''

''Not only for free! Most insisted upon a generous fee for the privilege of harvesting it.'' She sent the sharp curving blade through the tender stalks and they fell with a tumble of chaff.

What was in the hearts of some men that they came like vultures, looking for quick money? It made her angry, that's what it did, and the heat of it flashed like a flame in the center of her stomach. It was a good thing! She wasn't as aware of the pain in her raw hands and the gnawing ache in her spine as she swung the scythe.

More chaff tumbled like rain to the earth as the stalks fell, lost amid the stubble. Would she lose half the wheat before she could get it into the wagon?

Frustration burned behind her eyes, gathering like a thunderstorm, and the pressure built within her. ''That'll be all, Mr. Lindsay. Don't you have a crop to bring in?''

''That I do.'' His shadow fell across her. The worn leather toe of his boot blocked the next swing of her scythe. ''I have come to bring in yours, too.''

''Thank you, but I am declining your offer.''

''There's no reason.'' He did not move but stood as solid as granite as she swung the blade around him.

His wide hand settled on the wood, stopping her. Daniel Lindsay was a big man, tall and broad. Standing as he did, towering over her, he was intimidating.

Would another seemingly kind neighbor bully her? Kol had been the first to help any number of their neighbors over the years and without a single expectation of payment or compensation, no matter the crisis.

Was this how his generosity was to be returned? ''I'll thank you to let go.''

''It's not right, you laboring this way.''

When she expected hostility or scorn, Daniel Lindsay's words were kind. ''I have my harvester waiting alongside the road. May I have your permission to take down a section of fence so I can harvest this wheat? I'll get you the best market price I can at the station.''

''You'd do that?'' She knew her mouth was hanging open, but she couldn't seem to close it. He'd come here to help her? When so many hadn't? ''I imagine you'll want to be paid for your trouble, the way Mr. Dayton did.''

His dark eyes narrowed. ''What did he offer you? A right to half the wheat?''

''Half? He said I could keep a quarter of the value he got at the mill.''

''That swindler. He'd cheat Kol Ludgrin's widow?'' Daniel Lindsay's hard face turned to stone.

Rayna swallowed. She released the scythe and crossed her arms in front of her breasts. He wasn't looking at her, but she felt vulnerable. Angry, he was, and an imposing man while doing it. ''I would appreciate it if you would be on your way.''

''No.'' He strode away, taking her scythe with him. There was a clunk as he tossed it in the back of the wagon bed. ''Kol helped me bust sod that first spring I came here. I was as green as a Kentucky boy could be. He gave me his help and his advice while we worked. Some of that made a difference, and I managed to hang on. I'll harvest your wheat free of charge, Mrs. Ludgrin, for what he did for me.''

''What else are you wanting?''

''Only that I have the first option to lease the land, if that's what you decide to do. Or buy it, if you're of a mind to sell out.''

''The first option? I don't understand.'' She felt the burdens upon her shoulders weigh more heavily.

''You can trust me.'' It was kindness, nothing more,

as Daniel Lindsay gathered the long reins from the tangle on the sun-baked earth and held them out to her. ''Go home. I'll manage from here.''

''Y-you don't want money? Or the land? Mr. Dayton had asked for it outright.'' Crop's already rotting in the fields, he'd lied to her with the fervor of a traveling salesman. But this neighbor, Mr. Lindsay, had his own lookout. Why was he doing this?

''One good turn deserves another,'' Daniel said as he laid the reins in her bleeding hands.

Chapter Two

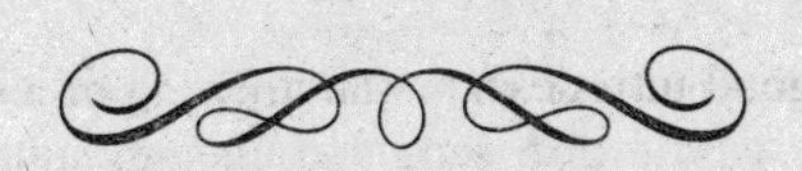

The powerful knock rattled the front door in its frame, echoing through the house and into the scorching kitchen. Startled by the disruption, Rayna set three pans of bread on the stovetop to cool, if such a thing were possible in the stifling heat.

No breeze stirred the lace curtains as she tossed the hot pad on the table and hurried through the rooms. Her youngest was upstairs taking a nap, for his sleep during the last few nights had been interrupted by nightmares and she did not want him startled awake.

She yanked open the door just in time to see old man Dayton with his beefy fist in the air, ready to knock a second time. The man clothed in trousers and sweat-stained muslin spit a stream of tobacco juice across the porch into the dirt at the roots of her favorite rosebush.

Not a benevolent man. He hadn't come for a pleasant visit.

She might as well stand her ground from the start. "Your son was here earlier. I've found someone else to harvest the fields for me."

"I saw that tenderfoot from Kentucky haul his old threshing machine down the road past my place." Another stream shot across her porch. ''He ain't worth dirt when it comes to cutting wheat. He probably offered to do it cheap, and I'm sure money is a concern, so here's what I'm gonna do for you.''

''And what a courteous way to convince me to let you harvest my wheat. For what? Only three-quarters of the profit? Or are you willing to drop down to only half?''

''Now, Rayna, you know the growing of a crop is the easy part. A little dirt, seed and enough sunlight make the wheat grow. But harvesting it, that's backbreaking labor. I've got the newest harvester. It came by railroad last week, and it wasn't cheap.''

''After all that Kol has done for you over the years. He died in your fields. And you would charge me?''

''Friendship is one thing, Rayna. Business is business. A woman can't understand—''

''I understand all too well. I've made a business decision and I won't be changing it. Good afternoon, Mr. Dayton.'' Careful of her bandaged hands, she shut the door with force.

The flat of his hand on the wood and the jam of his boot in the threshold stopped her. ''Be smart. You can't be thinking you will actually keep your land?''

''I would never sell my home.''

''You'll have to. Haven't you figured that out yet?''

Her Kol had built this house with his bare hands, and she'd helped him by holding the floor joists in place, handing him nails and bandaging his scrapes and gashes as they went. She'd been young and in love and expecting her oldest son. How happy they'd been.

Her children had been born in this house.

''Please remove your foot. I'd like you to go.''

''Fine. You'll learn soon enough. It's a hard, brutal

world without a man to provide for you. Who do you think is going to furrow those acres of wheat come spring? This isn't about the harvest, it's about the land. I'll give you a fair price.''

''Before or after you practically steal the wheat from me and my sons?''

''Rayna.'' As if pained, Dayton shook his head as he backed away. ''This is a pity, it sure is, how a pretty woman like you won't face the truth.''

''What truth?''

''There's no shame in it. It ought to be hard to lose your man. But you have to accept it. You can sell now while you can get out with some cash in hand, or you can struggle until you go broke, or you and I can arrange a deal.''

''No deal.''

''Listen to me. The bank's gonna take this place out from under you. I'm the only one around here with enough cash in hand to stop them. The only one who cares.''

The bank? A horrible flitter of fear bore into her midsection. Why would Dayton mention the bank? And why was he looking at her as if she were for sale right along with the land?

There was no mortgage on this property and she knew it. Her dear Kol would have told her if he'd done something like borrow against their hard-earned homestead. They'd had the best harvests three summers in a row, and there was no reason for Kol to have gone into debt.

Dayton was just trying to intimidate her into selling. Make her uncertain so she would practically give him some of the best wheat land in all of Bluebonnet County. That was all.

Fresh anger roared through her. Where was his charity, his neighborliness?

"Ma! I'm back from town." Kirk's awkward gait thudded on the porch as he lumbered to a stop behind Dayton. "Uh, excuse me for interrupting."

He was such a good boy, practically a young man, always remembering his manners. He looked so like Kol with his white-blond hair and jewel-blue eyes, and with the promise of strength in his rangy limbs. Pride surged through her, another raw emotion displacing the sudden anger at Dayton.

First grief, anger and now pride. All in a few minutes' time! What an untidy mess she had become. If Kol were here, he would gently wrap his powerful arms around her and draw her to his barrel chest and tickle her forehead with his beard until she laughed.

"Now, Rayna," she could hear him say as if he were in the room right along with her. "Life is a muddle, we all know that, so take a deep breath and stop all your fussing. There'll always be plenty enough time for worrying later, but not nearly enough time for loving. So, give me a kiss, my love."

Kol, I need you.

Her heart cried out for him, as if her feelings could have enough power to summon him up from the next room or wherever he had gone off to.

That's how it felt, as if her beloved husband were somewhere close, just out of sight. As if any moment he'd be walking through the kitchen door with dirt on his boots and sweat on his brow, calling out for her.

"Rayna?" Dayton seemed alarmed. "Are you all right? I can fetch the doctor."

"I'm fine. Just—" *Missing my husband.* She lifted her chin, tamping down the grief far enough so she could finish her day's work. She didn't want her oldest son to be worried. "I'm just thinking. I'm not interested in your offer. Goodbye. Come in, son. Where's the part?"

Kirk looked uncertain as Dayton filled the space in front of the door, refusing to leave.

Rayna motioned her son inside and closed the door, although the windows were thrown wide-open to catch some hint of a breeze. She could hear Dayton's slow steps as he paced the porch.

Fine, let him pace. He would eventually tire and leave. She would not sell the only home her boys knew.

She led the way to the kitchen, where the Regulator wall clock marked the time—a few minutes more until the final batch of bread was ready.

"Mr. Kline wouldn't give me the part." Only fourteen, Kirk planted his feet like a man, held out his hands the way Kol would have done, a stance of dignity. "He said I couldn't put any more charges on our account. He needed cash."

"How rude of him. Did you try the hardware—"

"I went everywhere. They all said no. I can whittle a piece after I get done working tonight. We'll make do." Kirk fisted his hands, trying to look strong and dependable. "I'd best get out in the fields. I've got wheat to cut."

He was too young to be forced into a man's responsibilities. Still, she was proud of him. "You won't be harvesting alone. Mr. Lindsay was kind enough to bring his harvester."

"For what price?"

"For free. Mr. Lindsay is doing us a fine thing, helping us."

"Pa's friends should have done that. He paid his share

for the new harvester Mr. Dayton bought and he—'' Anger left him searching for words.

It was the grief behind the anger, Rayna knew. It was a hard truth that in this world, people were not often just. Some people *did* rise to the occasion.

''We have a true friend in Mr. Lindsay.'' Careful of her bandages, she sliced off a thick piece of warm bread for Kirk to snack on. ''The butter crock's on the table. Wait, let me cut a few more to take with you. Perhaps Mr. Lindsay is hungry.''

''I'll fill the water jug on the way.'' Kirk dug a knife from the sideboard's top drawer. ''Ma, I heard what Mr. Dayton said. How are we gonna do all the work without Pa? Will the bank take our house?''

''Don't you worry. Your father would never have put us in a bad position. You remember that. He loved us. We will manage just fine. I'll find a way.''

''I can help. I can take care of all the animals and the haying. I can do that by myself without any neighbors helping.''

He took the bread slices she offered, wrapped in a clean cloth, and added them to the lunch pail he'd retrieved along with the butter crock. ''I heard you crying last night, Ma. I know you're sad. But don't you worry. I'm a man. I can take care of you.''

''I know you can.'' Rayna resisted the urge to call him her sweetie and press a kiss to his brow.

Her son was growing up. Emotion ached in her throat as she watched him sprint through the back door. The screen slammed shut in his wake, echoing through the kitchen.

As if nothing had changed, she turned to the stove, mentally listing what she would need to prepare a big supper tonight. Kol would be hungry from working all day in the fields—

The air rushed from her lungs. She leaned against the counter, dizzy. She'd thought of Kol out of habit, from years of cooking for him.

He's gone, Rayna. You have to accept it. You have to stop thinking that he's next door or at town or on his way home. It should be simple, but it wasn't. His chair was tucked in its place at the table. His favorite plaid shirt hung on the peg by the door.

She fought the urge to snap up the garment and hug it tight, to breathe in his scent still clinging to the fabric. As if that could bring back all that she'd lost.

Kol wouldn't want her falling into pieces. He needed her to be strong, as she intended to do. For their boys.

It's what she would do, because she loved him. She'd put aside the sadness and find enough strength to finish up the last of the baking. The loaves were ready, plump and golden. She breathed in the delicious yeasty smell.

The hot pad tumbled from her fingers as she realized what she'd done.

She had baked an even dozen loaves, as if Kol would be here to eat them.

"Whoa, boys." Daniel hauled back on the thick double reins, drawing the lathered teams of Clydesdales to a stumbling stop.

He ignored the thick grit in his mouth and his sandy thirst as he swiped streams of sweat from his face. He bent to unbuckle the horse collars from the traces.

The crash of some wild animal plowing through the field rattled nearby heads of wheat. The forward team shied, turning in the leather bindings.

"Hold on, boys, nothing to be afraid of." He tightened the lead set of reins to bring down the big black's head before he could get the notion to take off in a dead run and lead the other horses into revolting right along with him.

His workhorses were a steady bunch. They ought to be tired enough that nothing short of cannon fire ought to spook them, so what was riling 'em up?

A flash of color emerged from the golden stalks. He spotted a whitish-blond-haired boy, rangy and tall, and out of breath. Fear widened his eyes as he gazed up at the giant black trying to bolt.

"I'm sorry, mister. I didn't mean—"

"Don't worry about it, kid." He laid a hand on the black's shoulder, leaning between the traces to do it, a dangerous place to be.

The mighty Clydesdale calmed, now that the big animal realized it was only a boy.

"He's not used to much company. It's pretty quiet over at my place. Come on over. He won't hurt you."

The older of Kol's boys took a wide berth around the snorting gelding. "I brought water and something to eat."

Daniel took one look at the offered tin pail, battered from years of use, and shook his head. He was too hot to have any appetite. "Maybe when the sun goes down, but I'll take the water jug. Is your name Kirk?"

"Yessir." He offered the heavy crock.

Was it the one Rayna Ludgrin had been using? Daniel wondered as he pulled the cork. It had to be. There was a faint hairline crack at the mouth where it struck the earth when she'd dropped it.

How beautiful she'd looked. How alluring. The sudden image, unbidden and unwanted, shot into his mind. The memory of the water trickling through her honey-blond hair remained. A forbidden thought, but there all the same.

He closed his eyes as he drank. The cool rush of ginger water chased the grit from his tongue but did nothing to dispel her memory. Of her soft woman's curves and her clean, lilac scent.

His gut punched. *Enough of that.* It was wrong to think of her that way. He was a man. He had a man's needs. What he didn't need was a woman of his own. No. He was a man who lived alone by choice. There were times when he regretted the choice and the loneliness.

That's all this was. The lonesomeness of his life affecting him. He couldn't remember the last time he'd been touched by anyone.

Unless it was old Mrs. Johansson down the lane, when he'd stopped to help her corral her runaway milk cow. Was that seven months ago? He'd offered to fix the broken fence line for her. The elderly widow, hampered by rheumatism, had been so grateful, she'd baked him a chocolate cake and delivered it along with a grandmotherly hug the very next day.

Seven months ago. Hell, nothing terrified him more than ties to another human being. Any ties.

"Thanks for the water, kid." He corked the jug and got back to work.

"Uh, 'scuse me, mister." The boy trailed after him, tall for his age, bucking up his shoulders like a man ready to face his duty. "It's downright neighborly of you to lend a hand."

"It's the right thing to do. Your father was a good man. He helped me more than once. I owe him."

"If I help you, then the work will go twice as fast."

"That it will." Daniel tossed over the second set of reins. "You know how to handle draft horses?"

"I feed and brush and exercise ours every day. You still got wheat to cut on your land?"

"That I do." Daniel kept a short lead on the black, turning into the bright, stabbing sunshine. The field fell away to a creek that was more puddle than running water.

"Then I'd best help you with your harvesting, too," young Kirk declared, chest up, chin level, shoulders braced. "That's the way things are done. When someone helped my pa, he helped them right back. That's what I intend to do."

"You're a good man, Kirk Ludgrin." Daniel let the horses drink as he sized up the boy beside him.

You're going to grow up too soon, boy, and there's nothing I can do to help you. Circumstances happened, there was no stopping the bad that changed a life.

It was in the rising up to meet the circumstance that defined the man.

Daniel was glad he'd come. It felt right to repay Kol for an old debt.

"Walk with me to your barn," he told the kid. "We'll use your team for the rest of the afternoon, if you're willing. My horses here have been working since sunup and they're dragging their feet."

"Yes, sir," the boy answered, too young to feel responsible for the land he walked on. Too young to provide for the woman and children who lived in the pretty gray house on the rise, a home surrounded by roses and sunlight and endless sky.

If Daniel squinted, he could see Rayna Ludgrin kneeling in her garden. Such an attractive, slim ribbon of a woman, there was hardly nothing to her. He imagined the wind was ruffling the cotton fabric of her simple calico work dress and batting at the ties of the sunbonnet knotted beneath her chin.

A strange yearning filled him like nothing he'd ever felt before. It was different from need, different from lust, and it hurt like an old wound in the center of his being.

He had no time to give thought to it. There was work to be done. Wheat to cut. He had no leisure to waste on thoughts of a woman.

Or to wonder if her hands were bandaged and if they still bled.

Chapter Three

The low rays of the sun speared through the endless and mighty Rocky Mountains, glared across the miles upon miles of high rolling plains and bore directly beneath her sunbonnet brim. Rayna's eyes watered with the brightness as she trudged down the dirt path paralleling the fence line.

She was running late, darn it! Daniel and Kirk had to be starving.

She hurried, but the world around her took its own time. Larks trilled their merry songs, as they did every evening. Milk cows and beef steers rested in the shade from the orchard, their great jowls working their cuds as she scurried past.

''Nothing for you, sorry,'' she told the animals, who were eyeing her basket hopefully. She shifted the crock against her hip, readjusted her grip on the supper basket and kept going.

A steer bawled after her in complaint.

One thing about hard work, it required all of her concentration. She'd had less time to grieve or to worry about Dayton's comments on the bank as she'd hurried through her necessary household chores.

The path of gold she followed gave way to a sizable clearing. Neat stalks of straw lay seasoning on the ground and at the far edge of the clearing was her Kirk perched on the wagon seat. His hat was pulled low to shade his face and his bare torso shone red-brown from a hard day in the sun. Why, he looked more man than boy as he handled the team.

She was proud of him and the bubble of love that expanded within her every time she saw him, so sweet and pure and unbreakable, remained. Kol would want her to be strong for their sons. She steeled her spine, sure of her course.

"Mr. Lindsay?"

She could see his boots on the other side of the threshing machine.

He didn't answer. Did he know she was here?

"Hold up, Kirk!" Lindsay's bellow rose above the machinery, booming like thunder. "Ease up on the horses. Keep the reins short once they stop."

The man emerged from behind the machine. Rayna saw a flash of bronzed skin and muscled shoulder as he thrust his arms into a blue work shirt. He shrugged the garment into place without bothering to button up, offering glimpses of a strong chest.

Rayna's face heated. She'd never seen another man without his shirt. She didn't know where to look.

"Good. I've been waiting for you." Lindsay hefted up the ten-gallon jug as if it weighed nothing and drank from it with long, deep pulls.

Didn't he intend to button his shirt?

"Ma! Did you see? Daniel let me drive the team! And I handled 'em good, too. Just the way Pa showed me."

"I saw. Your pa would be proud of you."

"Do you think?"

''He's done a fine job.'' Daniel Lindsay handed over the water with a brief nod of approval. ''It looks like your ma has brought your supper. Sit down and eat, boy. You deserve a rest.''

Kirk dug into the basket. He tore into a chicken leg while he unloaded plate after plate of food with his free hand, monopolizing the meal. Daniel Lindsay returned to his machine, as if he planned on working.

''I made food enough for all of us,'' she said. ''Please, come eat.''

He gathered both sets of reins and settled the thick leather straps between his wide fingers. ''I don't stop until dark.''

''But you need to keep your strength up.''

''I need to get as much done as I can. A storm's coming.''

''What storm?'' There was hardly a cloud in the sky. A wisp of white at the rolling edge of the horizon cut through the low sun like a razor blade. ''I don't see any thunderheads.''

''I smell 'em. It may blow over. It may not. Either way, I won't sit on my arse when there's work to be done.''

''I could make you a sandwich—''

''No.'' He snapped the reins, calling out to the horses.

The teams pulled forward, lunging against their heavy leather collars. The machine groaned to a start, blades clacking.

''Then tell me how I can help.''

''You can go in the house where you belong.'' Daniel didn't expect her to understand. ''You'll be happier there.''

''I'm not afraid of a little farm work.''

''Then let me see your hands.'' He slackened the reins

and the horses halted. What was she going to do? Work in the fields like a man? She was a beautiful woman, not rough and made for hard work.

No, Rayna Ludgrin was creamy flawless skin and china-doll fragile. He reckoned he could span her waist with his hands. ''You're wearing gloves, so I can't see the bandages.''

''That's the idea.''

''You need to take care of that.''

''You need to stop and eat, but you're not.'' Pride drew her up straight. She was steel, too. ''I don't see any storm clouds, but I'd rather err on the side of caution. The least I can do is help you. We will get more work done together.''

''You have to be tired.''

''I've been tired before.''

''But it's demanding work—''

''I don't have time to argue with the likes of you, Mr. Lindsay. While I appreciate what you're doing, I won't be more beholden to you than I have to be.''

I'll be darned. He had to admire her gumption. ''Keep the wagon slow and steady. Too fast, and the grain hits the ground.''

She hitched up her skirts to climb aboard the wagon. She looked out of place with the rough leather gloves, which had to have been Kol's, engulfing her hands. She sat daintily on the bench seat, as if taking tea.

She made him feel big and awkward. He was aware of his too large hands and feet. He was a rough man, he knew it. Growing up the way he had, he couldn't be anything else. He wouldn't be ashamed of it.

''Sure you can handle these big boys?''

''I know how to drive.'' She held out her gloved hands, asking for the reins.

He knew plenty of men who couldn't handle draft horses. He'd keep an eye on her while he worked; he wouldn't want her to get hurt, that was all. He held out the reins and her hands gripped the thick straps ahead of his. Her touch tapped like a heartbeat through the lines.

Odd, how he felt a jolt deep inside.

Pay attention to the horses, Daniel. He didn't like the way the big sorrels were testing the bit, rolling it around in their mouths. They were aware of the change in drivers.

"Keep a short rein on them. No, look." He toed up on the foot rail and reached across her arms, catching the sweet scent of spring lilacs on her skin. "Like this. Not like you're used to driving the buggy. Hold the reins two-handed, between your fingers for better control. Tight with no slack. Keep tension in the lines."

She followed his example, moving those gentle hands of hers and leaning forward so the starched brim of her sunbonnet brushed the outside curve of his jaw.

He jerked away, releasing the reins. His chest was pounding. He was nervous about her safety, nothing more.

"More tension," he told her. "You should feel the strain in your forearms."

He caught the nearest gelding's bridle and made sure the animal wasn't nipping the bit. "That's better."

The muscles in her forearms burned, but Rayna held the lines. Her fourteen-year-old son could do this, so could she. She waited for an eternity, or shorter, sweat dampening the band of her sunbonnet. Daniel checked the equipment, readied his team pulling the harvesting machine, and called out.

She shook the reins, but it wasn't enough to urge the animals on.

"Harder! They've got thicker hides. They have to be able to feel it."

He was patient while she tried again. On the third attempt, the thwack of leather against those broad rumps got the horses' attention and the gigantic animals lurched forward.

"Whoa, slow 'em down!"

Rayna hauled back on the reins and the team stopped. She waited, dreading his reaction. He was going to tell her to get in the house where she belonged, and she wouldn't. "Let me try again."

His jaw was tight, but he said nothing more.

She *could* do this. She had to. With all the strength left in her arms, she manhandled the thick reins. The geldings stepped out, moving slow enough to keep pace with the machine.

Hulled grain spit into the wagon bed. Her grain. For her children. This could work, she would make certain of it. She would help bring in this crop.

What if Dayton was right? What if there were bank loans to be paid?

Worry gathered like the clouds on the horizon, black and ominous.

Daniel was right. A storm was coming.

When the last of twilight was wrung from the shadows, Daniel looked up from his work. She was mostly a silhouette, but he could make out the harsh line of her back against the black void of the prairie.

Why was he drawn to her?

He felt sorry for her, he supposed. As sad as she had to be, he tried to imagine the strength of will she had.

After a long day of work, she still perched pole-straight on the unforgiving wagon seat. Her arms visibly trembled from exhaustion.

She was a hard worker; he admired her for it. Her hands had to be bleeding again. Did she complain? Did she find a reason to shirk?

No. Not once. The few times they'd stopped for water, she'd been eager to get right back to work and quick to thank him again for his help.

It was wrong of the neighbors not to lend a helping hand. Where were the Daytons? They were harvesting their crops instead of the Ludgrin's grain, which should have been started on at first light today.

It burned his gut that those men wouldn't help Kol's widow. Not unless there was something to be gained.

He called out—Rayna was so tired she didn't comprehend his words at first. She startled into awareness, looking out in surprise at the few stars twinkling on the eastern horizon. Her shoulders slumped; she saw the fast-moving clouds, too.

By the time she hauled hard on the reins and the wagon creaked to a stop, the coming storm had blotted out the last stars. The black sheen of the night prairie became a fathomless void.

He hated the dark, but he took his time, fighting the fear in his chest. Swallowing against the coppery taste in his mouth, he pulled the match tin from the box beneath the thresher frame. He struck the flint, the flame flared and he hit the wick of the lantern.

"Are you stopping for the night?"

"No. Are you holding up?"

"If you stay, I stay."

She couldn't have gotten much sleep in the past few nights. The effects of it were etched like heartache into the corners of her eyes and around her soft mouth. She looked likely to topple from the seat and get hurt in the process.

"I guess I don't need this anymore." She untied the bow at her chin. Her sunbonnet came away and the glimmering cascade of her hair tumbled over her shoulders like water falling.

He handed her the ceramic jug. "The lady first."

"Thank you."

"Do you have it?" Her arms looked wobbly as she struggled to lift the heavy crock. He reached out to steady it. "Here. Let me help you."

"I can get it."

"Not without spilling."

Her slender hands, lost in her husband's big leather gloves, felt fragile under his. He held the container steady while she drank. Odd, how he could feel her life force like the bite of electricity from a telegraph, zinging from her fingers and into his where they touched.

The shadowed column of her delicate throat worked as she drank, and he tried not to look at the vulnerable hollow at the base between her collarbones, where she'd unbuttoned the lace-edged collar of her work dress to allow in a cooling breeze.

She's a new widow, get a rein on your thoughts, man. Ashamed, he was grateful when he could take the jug from her. Water clung to her lush bottom lip.

He tossed back the jug and drank long and deep, letting the coolish water slide down his throat. What was the matter with him?

He was lonely—he couldn't deny it. He'd sure like a wife as fine as Rayna, but how did a man find a woman he could trust? How could a man who'd grown up the way he had come to trust anyone that deeply?

"The wind is kicking up. Do you suppose we'll get lightning?"

"That isn't my worry."

"Then we should hurry. We need to get as much of this crop harvested as we can." She sat straighter on the bench seat, gathering the reins with renewed purpose.

He'd chosen this time to stop for a reason. He stowed the ceramic jug beneath the seat, behind her slim ankles and the dust-covered black shoes she wore. She wasn't going to like what he had to say.

"The wind's kicking up. My guess is that lightning's gonna start anytime. So why don't you climb down and help me move the team in? Can you hold the second set of reins for me?"

"You want to head in?" Rayna swept from the wagon seat in a blur of fabric and grace. "You're going to quit?"

"No." He watched her study the sky. He knew she was going to argue.

"You're right. The storm's coming in too fast. You can't see it, but I can feel it. We have to save what wheat we can."

As if to prove it, abrupt lightning snaked across the black void of sky to the southwest, giving brief light to a wall of gray skimming across the roll and draw of the plains. Coming fast. Coming right at them.

The tinny crash of thunder made the horses dance in their harnesses, and Daniel calmed them absently, counting. How far away was the oncoming rain?

Five miles. They had time enough, but not by much. He would save this load of wheat, but what about the rest? What about his crop?

All it would take was a gusting wind to ruin his future and Rayna's livelihood.

Worry pinched in the corners of her eyes and it was the last thing he saw as he blew out the lantern. He took it with him, stowing it carefully on the wagon floorboards. The last thing either of them needed was a fire in the fields.

Rain burst overhead as if thrown from a spiteful sky. Big, fat dollops hit the dust in the path ahead of the wagon, leaving inch-wide stains. Could they make it to the shelter of the barn in time?

Rayna gripped the bouncing seat as Daniel laid on the reins. The teams of horses reached out, racing against the wind the rest of the way and into the wide mouth of the barn. The sky opened up and flooded the world with angry rain. Lightning sizzled across the zenith, chased by a rapid beat of thunder.

Daniel leaped off the seat, leaving her behind. Breathless and grateful her wheat was dry, Rayna tugged off Kol's work gloves. The shape of his hands was worn into the seasoned leather.

If Kol were here, he would have done as Daniel did. He, too, would have been helpless to hold back the lightning and rain and stop the fierce gale that tore ripe kernels from the chaff, pushing the sea of gold like waves in the ocean. Rayna closed her eyes against old childhood memories, crossing on the steamer from Sweden to America, lost and alone.

That's how she felt now. She was no longer that child in a strange new world, but she *had* lost her anchor. Kol. Her strong, life's companion who had made her feel safe and protected. No matter what happened, she'd known they would see it through together.

I've lost your crop, Kol. When she most wanted to feel his arm around her, pulling her near, there was only a cool gust of wind at her nape. She shivered and set the gloves aside.

Daniel stood in the wide threshold of the barn, shoulders squared, feet planted, a dark, solitary man outlined by the white flash of lightning and the black void of sky and prairie. He had to be thinking of his fields and of his future.

He could have been harvesting his wheat instead of hers. He would have been better off if he had been. Rayna eased off the wagon seat, ignoring the sting and burn of her overused muscles, moving toward that lone silhouette.

How could she ever return in kind what he'd sacrificed for her family?

She curled her fingers around the wet wood of the door frame and cool rain sluiced down her skin. She shivered. The icy wind drilled into her bones. She felt as if the marrow were bleeding out of her. She didn't know what to say to Daniel.

Lightning split the world of night and storm into pieces, giving a quick glimpse of the wind battering the sea of grain, now only reeds of straw.

"Rayna?" A steely hand clasped her shoulder, a strange grip. "Are you all right? You look ready to faint. Maybe you ought to sit down."

Daniel guided her to a hay bale for her to rest on. He seemed distant and tentative as he ran his hand down the length of her arm, his touch foreign and yet gentle. He cradled her hand in his.

"You're bleeding." He traced the edge of her bandage with his large thumb. "I can't do anything about your wheat. I'm sorry. But I can take care of this."

"You lost your wheat, too. Everyone around here—" Her throat tightened and she fell silent. It was too much to manage. She would think about the effects of the storm tomorrow. "Where's Kirk? I ought to be helping him. I need my gloves, so I can shovel—"

"No." He released her hands and, when he rose, she shivered. He'd been blocking the wind. It hit her full-force, bringing mist from the rain to wet her face like tears.

The next time she saw him, he was carrying her oldest son against his chest like a child. Fast asleep, the boy's white-blond hair was tousled and sweaty, his rangy form slack with exhaustion. Daniel carried him to the house without a word.

Gratitude broke inside her like ice shattering and leaving nothing but emptiness in its wake. She was grateful for the man's kindness. His hard work.

Kirk had worked himself past his endurance today. Is this what lay ahead for him? Being forced to do the work of a man, when what he deserved was the rest of his childhood?

I'll simply have to rent out the land, she realized. Daniel had certainly earned the right to that. With the rental income, would it be enough to cover her living expenses?

She had no idea; Kol had insisted on handling all their finances. He hadn't wanted her to worry, he'd said, and since calculating the profit to be made in planting an extra field of corn instead of wheat was his decision to make, she'd left it to him.

She'd had that much faith in him.

A movement caught her attention. Daniel had returned, ambling through the shadows in the depth of the barn. The hammer strikes of rain on the roof, echoing through the night, hid the sound of his approach. The cloying darkness of the storm hid the bulk of what he gripped in one hand. He knelt before her and the razor's edge of lightning flashed white across his granite features.

"You had a lot depending on this harvest," she guessed.

He said nothing as he reached for her hand. The chilly whisper of metal whisked along her skin.

Raw pain made her eyes tear. The bandage fell away.

There was a clink as Daniel let go of the scissors. "Do you even have any skin left? You need a doctor to look at this."

How much did a house visit cost? She had no notion. Or if she could pay. "It's not bad. Just a little blistering."

"The same way there's just a little breeze outside." Instead of scolding her, he uncapped a tin he'd found on a kitchen shelf. "This may sting a bit."

He bent to his work, ignoring the woman-and-rain scent of her. Ignoring the way soft wisps of her hair danced against his cheek and the satin warmth of her hand in his.

Respect for her expanded inside his chest. Or maybe it was tenderness he felt as he laid a fresh square of clean cotton on her wounds. Tenderness he dared not give thought to as the rain turned to hail, shattering the night.

Chapter Four

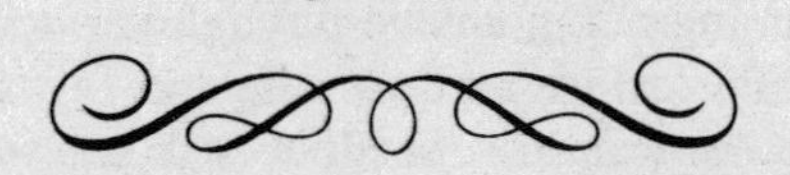

The tick-tick of the wall clock echoed like a ghost in the darkness, marking the minutes and chiming the hours as the void of midnight deepened and with it her despair. The papers she'd dug through every corner of Kol's big rolltop desk to find lay like black moldering leaves on the kitchen table, rustling whenever the wind gusted, bringing with it cold from the north.

Rain came with the first shadows. Icy rain that shot from the black-gray sky to pummel at the siding and strike through the windows and wrestle with the maples in the yard outside. Their limbs scraped the leaves and made it seem as if the trees moaned in anguish.

Her heart made the same sound, locked deep in her chest where no one could hear it. As rain sluiced off the roof to plink in the flower beds at the house footings and smeared the polished floor to puddle at her bare feet, she couldn't move. Like a stick of wood she sat there, the mist from the droplets spilling through the sill. The moisture dampened her face, stained the front of her work dress and crept up the hem of her skirt.

Maybe, if she stayed still enough, the space between one breath and the next could stretch forever. Then maybe time would forget to move forward. The clock's pendulum would freeze. The next hour would not chime. The night would not end. The dawn could not come.

She'd rather remain in this emotionless night where her soul would not have to endure another lethal wound. Another loss so unthinkable she would not survive it.

But her heart beat, her lungs drew in air and the clock's echoing tick pounded through her, loud and unstoppable. The rain turned to mist and fog as the dark became shadow, and the shadow twilight, and the twilight dawn.

A shadow lengthened on the floor, a shade darker than the room.

''Rayna?'' Daniel's voice. His big, awkward hand gripped her shoulder.

That was not the halo of the sun behind the horizon. She would will it back if she had to.

The shadow knelt beside her, warm substance of a man pulling her from her numb cold state as the crest of the sun peered over the rim of the prairie, the distant slate-blue hills topped by gold and peach.

The world seemed to take a breath as the dawn came and tender, newborn light painted the land, illuminating the miles upon miles of downed wheat, sodden and defeated.

Nothing of the harvest could be saved. Not even the stalks could be salvaged for straw.

Her sorrow was reflected in Daniel's eyes. On his face. His hair was a pleasant dark brown, from farther away it had appeared black, and tangled from a night in the wind and rain.

The harsh, square cut of his hard jaw was stubbled with a night's growth. His mouth was a severe line that did not yield as he turned from the endless acres of desolation. His boots squeaked on the wet floorboards as he straightened. His grip remained.

"Even with my losses, I can afford to lease your fields. You should be able to keep your house."

The warm, steady grip of his hand on her shoulder remained, so different from Kol's. Heat radiated through her cold shoulder and into her arm. Into her torso. Dawn's light spilled through the window, too bright after a night of utter darkness and it thawed her, too. The clock marked the hour, chiming in a pleasant dulcet tone five times.

Morning was here and time marched on. She'd not been able to hold it back, of course. Somehow she had to find the steel to face the decisions she must make. Decisions that would break her. She could already feel the cracks, little fissures in her soul, splintering like ice melting on a shallow pond.

She turned to Daniel, but he was gone. She hadn't been aware of his hand leaving her shoulder or his strong masculine presence moving away. Alone, she shivered, only now feeling the coolish air skimming across her damp face. Goose bumps stood out on her forearms.

The iron door of the stove clacked into place. She recognized the rapid crackle and snapping of dry kindling feeding a new flame. Daniel's boots knelled on the floor and the ring of his gait echoing in the still room was all wrong. Too quick, too assertive, not the easygoing thud of Kol's gait.

He's gone, Rayna. She knew that. Logically she accepted she would never again hear Kol's shoes drumming the length of her kitchen floor. The air around her turned to ice, leaving her chilled and aching for the morning routine that had marked the beginning of nearly every day for fifteen years.

How he would come up behind her, wrap his brawny arms around her waist and tickle the crook of her neck with his full beard. She would laugh, spinning in his arms to eagerly accept his kiss and forgetting about the frying eggs—and remembering just in time to save them from charring.

"Rayna?" It was Daniel's voice again, deep with concern. "I've got the coffee on. Are these the milk pails by the pantry door?"

Morning was here, and so the morning chores would need to be done, regardless of what was to come. "While it's good of you and neighborly, the cows are my concern. Not yours. You have chores of your own, I imagine."

"They're already done. You weren't the only one unable to sleep. I'm betting half the ranchers in Bluebonnet County didn't get as much as a wink last night."

The bucket handles clinked and clattered over the punch of Daniel's gait. The screen door hinges squeaked as it was opened and banged shut with a wooden slap. Morning light found him, the golden rays laying a path before him as he cut across the lawn. The carpet of grass, with rain droplets heavy on a thousand delicate blades, gleamed like jewels in the sun.

As if there was hope to be found on this day to come. What hope would that be? Rayna wondered as she rose from the chair, wincing at her stiff knees and hips. Her muscles burned with yesterday's hard labor in the fields, and the raw blisters on her palms had her jaw clenching.

Anger roared through her like hot, greedy flames, burning her up in one bright moment. She was at the stove in a second, not aware she'd crossed the room, huffing with a rage so intense it blurred her vision. Made her feel ten feet tall. How could Kol have done this to her? To their sons? They were nearly *penniless.* And mortgaged to the full value of their land.

She banged the fry pan on the stove, but the ringing bang gave her little satisfaction. She huffed down into the cellar and pounded back up the wooden steps, flinging the hunk of salt pork, the last that they had, onto the worktable. *I trusted you, Kol. I trusted you to provide for us. ''Don't worry,'' you always said. ''I will take care of my precious wife.''*

She wouldn't have believed what he'd done if she hadn't seen the papers for herself. Notes on the livestock and buggy. And of all things, a mortgage on their land. Their homestead. Earned free and clear through their hard work together. And he'd encumbered it without telling her.

I'm so mad at you, Kol Anders Ludgrin. Never once had he mentioned any debt. And to think there was so much of it! She lobbed the basket onto the counter and watched in horror, her anger vanishing, as the eggs inside rolled and knocked together. Fissure cracks raced through the delicate shells. The clear gel inside oozed out, bringing the stain of yellow yolk.

What was she doing, getting worked up into a rage at a dead man? She wished Kol were here so she could give him an earful. She wished for the strong breadth of his chest, the sheltering band of his arms, the way any hardship seemed bearable with the capable strength of his hand tucked against hers.

One thing was for certain. She was not done dealing with Daniel Lindsay. She found him in the barn, hunkered down on her little three-legged milking stool. He was humming the chorus of some song she'd never heard of, but she liked the sound of it, she realized with surprise.

Moll, the gentle-natured Jersey, crunched on a generous helping of corn and molasses, at ease, her weight cocked on three legs as her great jowls worked. The gentle-eyed cow turned to her and mooed a low, sweet welcome.

Daniel fell silent as he became aware of her presence. His wide shoulders tensed as he continued to work, one cheek resting against the cow's soft brown flank. He looked gargantuan, balanced on the tiny stool, and far too accomplished as he stripped long streaks from the cow's full udder.

With the sunlight slatting through the cracks in the weathered board walls and highlighting the capable set of him, the sight took Rayna's breath away. Daniel Lindsay was so different a man than Kol had been. Tall and tough and distant, instead of round and gregarious and jolly.

Daniel seemed like a man who neither smiled nor laughed often.

Yet he was not harsh, she decided, remembering his tenderness last night when he'd bandaged her hands.

She unhooked the gate. "You should not be doing my work, Mr. Lindsay."

"Are you going to warn me off your chores? Too late." He unfolded his big frame, hefting the nearly full pail with ease. "How about we barter my labor for breakfast?"

"Rather forward, aren't you? Helping yourself to my chores and inviting yourself to my table?" She couldn't help the words. They came harder than she meant, but seeing him here reminded her of how her life had changed. And life wasn't done altering on her.

Not by far. "I suppose I could fry up a few eggs for you."

"That'd be fine, Mrs. Ludgrin. I'll be up to the house shortly."

"Give me the milk then, and I'll add some fresh biscuits to our deal. I'm sure we'll have much to discuss." She reached over the wooden gate with her bandaged hands. Dried blood had seeped through the white cloth.

Daniel's stomach clenched. She was too fragile for the hard work this land required.

But Rayna Ludgrin did not complain, she simply took the full bucket he handed over, steaming in the cool air and frothy with foam. The sweet scent of milk was nothing compared to the fragrance of her—a woman's soft, warm smell and lilacs. She smelled like spring. Why that made his eyes burn, he couldn't rightly say.

He seemed to tower over her, the small thing she was, as she handled the heavy pail as if it were light as air. For one span of a breath, only the distance of the wooden gate separated them. He was close enough to see the deep hue of the dark circles bruising her delicate skin, making her blue eyes seem huge in her pale face.

Sympathy hit like an anvil on his chest and he turned away, not sure of the tangle that seemed to coil up behind his breastbone. A tangle of emotions that he wasn't familiar with at all. But they were powerful and he didn't know what to do.

He grabbed the pitchfork and went to work, keeping busy until the dainty pad of her step had disappeared into silence and he was alone with the livestock.

The cow gripped his trouser leg with her teeth and gently tugged. Her grain trough was empty. She waited, her long tail swishing while he took a deep breath to fill his lungs. But the coil in his chest remained.

He snatched a battered dipper and dropped another pile of grain into the wooden tray for the cow who released her hold on his trousers, mooed in gentle appreciation and lipped up the sweet-tasting treat.

The cow in the next stall gave a long, sharp protest. He knew what to do about that—he grained her, milked her, which kept him busy enough that he didn't have to pick apart what was troubling him. He had plenty enough of that as it was. His crop was a total loss that would set him back a year in more than just profit. Wind damage to the fences and outbuildings would cost him in lumber and sweat. He had enough of his own concerns.

He didn't need to add Rayna Ludgrin's problems to his already heavy load.

He wanted her land. It was as simple as that. He was willing to pay her a fair price. Good wheat land was hard to come by on these stubborn plains. It was as if the prairie fought to take back the land it had lost, and it was a constant battle for the average rancher. Montana was a hard enemy, but he was equally tenacious. The wind blew colder through the open barn doors, cutting through his long-sleeved work shirt as if in challenge.

It would be a hard go of it.

Daniel eyed the tight-hewn timbers overhead and the loft brimming with soft hay. The feed room was nearly empty, save for a hundredweight bag of grain that wouldn't see the Ludgrin livestock far into the month. There was enough hay for feeding and straw for bedding to see the animals through the autumn, judging by the size of the stacks he could see out back.

But the winter? No. More feed would have to be bought.

The workhorses were in good shape, young and

strong and healthy. The cattle—he'd have to take a ride out in the fields to get a good look; see if they'd bring a good enough price this late in the year.

He leaned the pitchfork in the corner, out of the way, and took a moment to look around. He'd learned long ago to see beyond the surface of things, so it was no trouble to purge the soggy-brown mess of the ruined crops from the acres of fields.

Yep, that was a mess now, but all a man had to do was to turn the sod before winter set in and these would be good fertile fields to sow come spring. Fields he wanted. A good water supply, even a running creek most of the year. He'd been up half the night working out the numbers on his old school slate and he knew he could just manage it.

It all depended on what those papers on Rayna's table said. Bank notes. He couldn't read, but he knew a mortgage note when he saw it. And judging by the number of pages, more than just the property was encumbered.

But, if Rayna was willing and her asking price was reasonable, this could be his. Sure, it would take hard labor to turn the soil, to plant and harvest one hundred and sixty acres in addition to his own bottom land that kept him busy as it was. He'd be working from dawn until midnight for a good part of the next year. That was a formidable prospect, but the gains would be worth it.

Hell, he'd come this far already. He might as well see if he couldn't improve his circumstances.

Daniel straightened his shoulders as the tepid rays of dawn washed over him, bright but without warmth. His shadow stretched out before him, long and wide, on the ground littered with wheat chaff blown from the fields by last night's heartless wind. Ground that would be his?

I sure hope so.

Determination turned his spine to steel. A little hard work was all it would take. He wasn't afraid of hard work. It was the only kind he knew. What he didn't like was that his future hinged on a woman's decision.

She'd already agreed he'd have first option for the land. But did the bank's mortgage cancel that? Or would she be able to keep her word if a better offer came from one of the other neighbors?

There she was—a blur of dark blue calico and matching sunbonnet—visible through the slats of the chicken pen. She emerged from the coop with a basket on her arm. She was obviously egg gathering. Hens clucked and pecked at the scatter of feed on the dirt and squawked angrily when the snap of her dress startled them.

The wan light teased her blond hair, which she hadn't pinned up yet and fell in a long golden spill from her nape, where a ribbon bound it into a thick ponytail. With it down, she looked young and dainty, her shadow a thin wisp behind her as she swished up the path to the garden gate. She seemed far too young to be a widow and a mother of two boys, one of them fourteen years old.

That tangle of emotions was back, wedged like an ax blade right through his breastbone and bore deep until he couldn't breathe at all. Feeling as though he were suffocating, he watched Rayna Ludgrin with her curving figure and flowing hair and her feminine graceful manner. He was a man. He couldn't help wanting.

But it was more than that. It was admiration he felt at the grit of her spirit. Not many women would have worked like she did without complaint. Even though she trudged heavy with exhaustion and grief, she was graceful and quality. As if she were far too fine for the burden of this land.

We can help one another, he thought, a lone man standing in the threshold of the barn, caught in shadow, the cool, new light falling all around him. Summer was gone, and with it the vibrant warmth. The season had turned, and Daniel felt as if something unnamable were slipping away and just out of his reach, something he didn't even know he'd been missing until now. When it was already gone.

Or maybe it was just that he realized Rayna had disappeared into her house. Seemingly taking the summer with her.

He left the pail of milk on the back porch, in front of the open door. Through the pink mesh of the screen, he could see her at the stove. Her back was to him as she worked, her long hair shifting and moving like liquid gold. Overcome, he turned away, wondering if her hair was as soft as it looked. It wasn't his right to wonder such a thing.

If things went his way, she'd be gone and this land would be his. And he would be alone, as he was meant to be. As he'd always been.

His boots crushed fallen rose leaves and satin pink petals as he retraced his path across the back lawn. Toward the livestock gathering at the empty wooden feed trough. For a long second, it felt as if time had stopped marching forward and the earth had stopped turning between one step and the next. His breath stalled in his lungs. A strange flickering trail skidded along his spine.

What was happening to him?

Awareness moved through him, different from the jerk of instinct that warned him of a predator in the field, but just as strong. It was an awareness that had him turning on his heel to gaze back at the house in time to see Rayna framed in the window. With a batter bowl anchored in the crook of her arm, she returned to her work as if she hadn't been watching him.

He headed to the far side of the trough and kept out of sight of the house while he finished the rest of the morning chores.

At the first tap of his boot on the porch, she straightened. Taking a breath, she wiped the stray wisps from her eyes and dug the hot mitt from the drawer.

You can do this, Rayna. She was a grown woman after all. She had to face the unbearable truth. What was done was done, there was no going back and changing it. Kol hadn't meant to die, of course, and he would never have wanted her to be in this position. Never would have wanted his family broken and his land sold…

It's too much. Too much to manage alone. He never would have wanted that for her. Anger drained out of her and her hand started to tremble. She couldn't get a good grip on the baking sheet through the layers of dense rug yarn that padded the mitt.

The biscuits, golden and fluffy, tipped dangerously and she slid the sheet onto the waiting trivet, the one Kol had sanded and shaped from river rock the long winter when she'd been carrying Hans.

She swallowed hard, somehow managing to flip the eggs without breaking all but one of the yolks. She watched the smear of yellow bubble in the grease and steeled herself for what was to come.

The rap of his knuckles on the door frame was quiet, not bold or demanding, but seemed like the ring of gunfire. She would do this now, while the boys were sleeping in from another rough night, when it was just her and Daniel. So she could spare her boys the heartache.

Daniel Lindsay's step was sure and sturdy as he let

himself in. He was a good man, Kol had said so many a time. And would take better care of her land than Mr. Dayton or whoever won the auction from the bank. Surely that was the wisest decision. Maybe he would give her enough time to settle her affairs and contact her relatives to see if anyone would take her and her boys in.

"Did you sleep at all last night?"

It wasn't what she expected him to say. Surely he'd seen the mortgage papers on the table; they were obvious and hard to miss. "I'll have time to sleep later."

"No, you need to take care of yourself now. Your boys depend on you."

It was the decency in his voice that undid her as he gently removed the spatula from her hand, took her elbow and tugged. Who was this man who'd bandaged her hands, who'd tried to harvest her fields with his machinery and horses, who by rights should have been as happy with her change in fortune as her other neighbors?

When her feet didn't move, he laid his other hand on her back, on the space between her shoulder blades. His touch was unwelcome. He was not her husband, and close contact with her was…well, it was wrong. But the broad pressure of his palm on her spine was comforting, too.

Lord knew how much she needed comfort right now. So she allowed his closeness and let him nudge her to the closest chair. She eased onto the seat, more tired than she'd ever been.

And more defeated.

Daniel Lindsay moved away, leaving her alone in the cool shadows. She shivered. She couldn't get warm, even a few yards from the blazing cookstove. There was a clink and a clatter of stoneware and then a steaming cup of coffee appeared before her on the table, left there by the tall, silent man who'd taken over her duties at the stove.

The coffee was piping hot and stung her tongue. But it steadied her to ask what had to be asked. ''What would you say this land, even with the house, is worth?''

''I'd have to find out all the debt owed. And if a fair deal is possible. If so, then I would make you an honest offer.''

''I know you will.'' She took another bracing swallow of coffee. Felt the heat burn inside her. It was the closest thing to determination she had at the moment. ''I'm afraid any offer you would want to make wouldn't cover all the debt I owe. What happens then?''

''I'll talk to someone at the bank and find out. Likely as not, if you can't make your next payment or if you can't sell for the amount of your mortgage, then the bank will repossess.''

She'd known he was going to say that.

He turned with two full plates in hand and set them on the table, one before her and the other at Kirk's place, where he sat. A solemn man with grim lines cut around his mouth and his eyes. Not the face of a young man, but of a hardworking one. A decent man.

Gratitude warmed her more than the coffee had. When she was down, he'd pulled through for her.

He took a bite of biscuit and chewed, reaching for the loan papers. More creases dug into her brow as he scanned the pages. His granite jaw stilled.

As the clock ticked the seconds away, Rayna watched Daniel's reaction as he appeared to read. The tension cording in his throat. The grim set of his brows drawing together as he leafed through the pages.

Like the hand of destiny laying down the final step in

her path, the silence stretched between the ticks of the clock. Unbearable silence. She saw, as Daniel bowed his head and covered his face with his hands, that it was worse than she'd figured. And that meant—

No, she couldn't face what that meant. With great control, she rose from the table and pulled two plates from the cupboards. Each scrape of the spatula as she began to fill the plates with the rest of the fried eggs, diced potatoes and salt pork gave her something to concentrate on so she could keep the truth from settling in.

If she couldn't sell the land, with the hopes of keeping the house, then she would have no place to go. No way to make a living.

A chair scraped against the wooden floor and Daniel's sure gait tapped on the floor. "I'll talk to the bank. See what I can do. But I don't know how it will turn out."

His silence sounded oddly helpless. "I would truly appreciate any help, Mr. Lindsay."

"Daniel." He seemed to fill the room, his presence was that powerful. As was the shadow that fell across the floor, big hands fisting. "I wish there was more I could do."

"You've done so much already. I can't remember if I've thanked you."

"It's been a difficult time, I know." Daniel swallowed hard, but the tangle in his chest seemed to sharpen and cut like knives at the insides of his ribs. He hated this feeling. Knew, that if he struck a deal to take over the mortgage, that he'd be taking everything from Kol's widow and children. That wasn't what he wanted.

"I have a good relationship with Wright at the bank. I'll see what I can do for you."

She layered salt pork on the two plates she was making, breakfast to be kept warm in the oven for when her children woke, no doubt. What fortunate boys they were, to have a mother like her.

It took only one look around to see the home she'd made for them, clean and comfortable and caring. The sharp feelings sliced into his chest and he turned away to grab his hat. To get as far away from this woman as he could before he remembered too much of his childhood. Or the boy that had never had a kindly woman worrying if he was hungry. Making sure he had a heaping plate of good food to start the day with.

He couldn't spare Rayna Ludgrin one more look as he strode out the door and into the cool morning that warned of a hard winter to come.

It didn't feel as if it were only the weather.

Daniel yanked the ends of the reins loose from the hitching post in the front yard and swung up onto his gelding's back. With the odd feeling that Rayna Ludgrin was watching him go, he rode east and into the rising sun.

Chapter Five

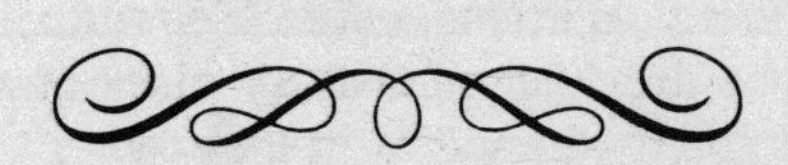

Rayna leaned the four envelopes, ready to post, against her reticule on the stand by the door. She felt brittle and as wrung out as a washrag on cleaning day, but that was one hard chore done and over with.

She'd written to Kol's brother, sister and cousin and asked to move in with her boys. *Please God, may one of them have room for us.* She refused to think what would happen if no one did.

The parlor clock chimed the hour. Nine o'clock. The boys were still asleep. Poor Kirk had worked himself into sheer exhaustion and she hated to wake him, but she would have to if he didn't roust in the next half hour. She had to get those letters on today's train. She dared not risk waiting until tomorrow.

Daniel would be back from the bank with bad news. There was no way it could be anything but. *As long as I can get enough cash to get us settled somewhere else…* Then she would have a roof over her sons' heads.

And as for a job—she wasn't too proud to clean houses or to wash strangers' clothes, as her friend Betsy did for a living. From where she stood on the threshold of so much change, the future looked horribly uncertain.

Somehow, the Good Lord willing, she'd make do. She needed a little tiny bit of providence to come her way. Just a little. And she wasn't asking for herself, but for her boys.

The muffled clop-clop of a team of horses coming up her drive had her opening the door before she realized it couldn't have been Daniel. He'd ridden a dappled mustang rather than driven a vehicle to town. The jangle of the harness drew her gaze to the black buggy bouncing through the mud puddles in the road.

The matching bays, so sleek and fine, pranced to a halt at the post, and there was Betsy, her ringlets springing around her face from beneath the brim of her wide-rimmed sunbonnet.

Dressed for work, in a light calico and matching apron, she hopped to the ground, careful of the puddles that had yet to evaporate, and, arms outstretched, said nothing as she rushed up the steps.

Rayna's vision blurred and suddenly she was enveloped in her friend's arms. Held tight in comfort and friendship. She and Betsy had been best friends since the first day of school when they were both six. They'd shared desks, books, laughter, hard times and grief.

Rayna held on while she could, fighting tears that were nothing but a weakness. When she pulled away, she was glad the tears remained buried deep in her chest where they belonged.

"It's a workday. You shouldn't have taken the time to stop by," she scolded even as she took Betsy's hand, drawing her into the shade of the parlor. "It is good to see you."

"I've thought of you nearly every minute and I had to stop by. Look at you, you haven't been sleeping."

"No. I can't get used to being in the bed alone."

''It's been five years and still I wake up in the middle of the night reaching for Charlie. The bond between a man and wife goes deep. Oh, Rayna, you look as though you haven't been eating. And the storm. I saw the fields when I drove up.''

Bless Betsy for her liveliness. She could chase the shadows from the room with a single word. Rayna squeezed her friend's hand tightly as they made their way to the kitchen. Daniel's plate was still on the table, as was hers. She hadn't gotten to the dishes yet, or the morning housework. The floor needed sweeping, the curtains were wet from the night's rain. Bits of bark and cedar needles were scattered around the wood box.

''Good, there's still coffee and it's good and strong. Just what both of us need.'' Betsy helped herself to the cups from the shelf and poured two steaming mugs full. ''Sit here. Sip this until you feel a bit better. No, don't argue. I seem to remember a certain bossy someone doing the same after my Charlie passed on.''

Yeah, she was grateful for her life and the people in it. For the steaming coffee that had grown bitter on the stove, bitter enough to make her mouth pucker and her eyes smart. For her to remember how this was the way Kol liked it best, when he'd sneak in after taking the boys to school and share one last cup with her.

Her life was gone just like that. It was Tuesday, she realized dully. By rights, the boys ought to be in school, Kol at work in the field and, with the turn of the weather, she would be getting the last of the vegetables up. One more cold night and she would lose every last remaining tomato.

''Mariah told me she'd be over. I'll leave a basket on the counter. I'll just run out and get it. Sit tight.'' Betsy tapped from the room, taking the warmth and sunshine with her.

In the shadows, Rayna drained the hot coffee in one long pull. Tongue scorched, throat burning, she set the cup aside and stood. She was ready. For whatever she had to do. Whatever she had to face.

She wrung the dampness from the lace curtains and, after slipping them from the rod, laid them out on the chair backs to dry. That done, she swept tangled rose leaves and sodden petals from the sill and closed the window securely. Then she found the broom and had the floor swept clean by the time Betsy returned with a heavy bundle in each arm.

"What are you doing with my bed sheets?"

"I wrapped up the laundry I could find in them. Changed the bed, didn't disturb the boys, of course. I'll get these to you by the end of the week at the latest. And no, you have enough on your hands right now, so no arguing. I'll be back on my route home this afternoon to check on you."

"You've done more than enough. You are my friend, Betsy, and that is gift enough."

"We are friends, no matter what." Her eyes shone with emotion. "But we are women, and there is nothing we can't do with a little help from one another."

Yes, she was still so blessed. Even with half her heart gone and her land, too, with the failure of the crop, she had so much to be grateful for. She swallowed past the grief, for it was, after all, only grief.

She was not alone, not really, and even if she was welcomed at Kol's brother's farm in Ohio, she knew distance could not break their friendship.

She had her sons and she had her friends, come what may.

* * *

Daniel took one look at Dayton's polished buggy with the fine-stepping Tennessee Walkers parked in the quiet alley behind the bank, safely away from the mud splatter from the main street. Appropriate, where the man parked. And predictable. Daniel would have bet every last acre of his homestead that Dayton had beaten him to the punch at the chance to buy the Ludgrin land.

Mr. Wright had turned down his offer with true sincerity. There was too much debt, more than the land, the buildings and the livestock were worth, and with a failed crop. All of which totaled more than the value of the property. No, they could not accept a deal for such a grave loss to the bank. They would need collateral. Wright was more than eager to say they'd accept Daniel's homestead to secure the amount on the Ludgrin land.

Daniel could not afford to buy land that cost more than it was worth. It was that simple. But something stuck in his craw as he bought bushel bags for the few loads of wheat he'd managed to get in before the storm.

Maybe what was important was what the banker had failed to say. Maybe they had another buyer who was willing to use his land as collateral to assume the debt. Daniel had no doubt as to whom. There was only one man prosperous enough in these parts. Dayton.

Damn it. Daniel stared at the buggy and drowsing horses and saw red. Boiling hot rage blinded him and he wanted to turn heel and march into that bank and say the land wasn't foreclosed yet. It was good, fertile land, the best wheat land in the county, and to own it was more than a humble man could hope to do in an honest lifetime. Why not see if he could make a better deal with the bank?

No, that would be a poor decision. He couldn't go off half cocked and make a bigger mess of things. He had his land free and clear, good, productive land, horses, his own secondhand thresher and, best of all, no debt.

Debt was a foolish man's solution, and could turn into quicksand fast enough. Dragging down a man until there was no hope left. He'd seen too many farmers lose everything because they'd rather borrow than do without.

No, he wouldn't lose his independence. He refused to risk everything he'd sweated blood for. Lucky for him, he had time. The bank had yet to foreclose. That would take time, and he'd have the chance to think this all through. Take a look at his options.

"Hey, Lindsay." That caustic sneer could belong to only Dayton.

Stomach tight, muscles bunched, Daniel spotted the man he'd come to dislike, breaking through the tangle of a half dozen women gazing at the front window of some dress shop. Typical, how Dayton expected folks to make way for him without so much as a courteous, "Excuse me." Dayton was the kind of man who got Daniel's hackles up.

The kind of man he'd come to despise in his life and with good reason. He'd worked for too many men just like him growing up.

Be civil. As hard as that was going to be, he might as well try jumping to the moon. "Dayton. Tough storm."

"Yep. Wheat's a total loss, but I got investments to fall back on." Dayton hitched up his shoulders, the gesture of a man pleased with his high self-opinion.

An opinion Daniel didn't share. With a low word, he reassured his gelding as he came up to him and loosened his reins from the post.

"Noticed you sniffin' around the Widow Ludgrin's skirts." Dayton sent a stream of tobacco juice into the mud. "She's one fine-looking woman."

"It's not my habit to covet another man's wife."

"She's a widow now, my boy, and you know what that means. A woman without a man to protect her. Or satisfy her. Too bad all that wheat land of hers is mortgaged. Not worth the paper owed on it. Guess you know that."

"Didn't know that was any of your concern."

Dayton didn't have the grace ethic to be ashamed. A cat's grin twisted his features. "I'm just lookin' out for the widow's well fare."

Yeah, he could see what was on the man's greedy mind. Daniel swung into the saddle. "I'm not a betting man, but I'd stake my horse on Mrs. Ludgrin. She strikes me as the type of woman who can take care of herself."

"Rayna? Nah, she's a pampered little thing. She'll be on the lookout for a man to take care of her. And mind you, boy, she won't be wanting to spend her attentions on a Confederate mutt. She's used to being spoilt, and she'll go with the man who can give her what she wants."

Was Dayton talking about himself? He was a married man. Daniel watched in disgust as the older man shot a final stream of brown juice into the street. With a self-righteous wink that looked suspiciously like a leer, Dayton glanced down the boardwalk at something catching his attention—a young and pretty woman.

Yeah, there's another reason I don't trust you. Daniel reined his horse around, anger boiling inside him. What was it the old man had said about Rayna? *That she was a woman without a man to protect her. Or satisfy her.*

What was Dayton thinking—that the new widow

would award her affections to the first man to come along and help her keep her house? Rage blew through him like steam through a whistle, and he sent his gelding into the busy street.

Sure, he didn't really know much about Rayna Ludgrin, but the time spent lately in her presence told him one thing. With the way she'd tried to harvest her crop with a hand scythe, she was a woman not prone to taking the easiest path. She had character and fortitude.

As if his thoughts had conjured her, there she was on the boardwalk in front of the mercantile. Was it his imagination, or did she stand out among the other women hurrying on their errands?

Her wool coat was a plain tan color and finely tailored to show the dainty curves and tiny waist and the flare of her skirts. The pointed toes of her polished brown shoes peeked out from beneath the ruffled hem of a fine black dress. Maybe it was the way she walked, even in mourning, that spoke of dignity.

His heart clutched in his chest with sorrow for her losses, that's what this emotion was. He'd been alone all his life, and he wasn't a man of Dayton's ilk that lusted after a woman, so it *couldn't* be a desire for her that he was feeling. She was newly widowed and vulnerable. He wasn't about to let his thoughts go there.

But he *did* recognize something in her that he struggled with every day—the feeling of being alone in the world, alone to shoulder responsibilities. He knew something about that. In fact, it was all he knew.

But it had to be a new experience for her.

Did he go to her? See if she needed something? Tell her what he'd learned at the bank? Or would that be too forward, here in town, where rumors might spread? It was the way of some people, he thought, remembering how Dayton had suggested any widow's morals were easily compromised.

Speaking of the old devil—there he was. Ambling down the boardwalk as if he owned it. Dressed in his Sunday finest, he raked his fingers through his thinning hair, donned his hat and squared his thin shoulders in what he must have thought was a dashing gesture.

Maybe some folks would be fooled and take him for a moneyed gentleman, but not Daniel. He could taste the dislike souring his tongue as he watched Dayton spot Rayna Ludgrin as she chatted with another woman on the boardwalk. She was obviously receiving condolences from an acquaintance. Her face when she spotted Dayton striding toward her changed from sad to wary.

At least she wasn't fooled by the older man's spit and polish. Daniel leaned back on the reins, nosing his mount out of the way so he could keep an eye on things. He couldn't help feeling protective toward the widow. It was too bad the clatter of wagons and the drum of hooves on the busy street made too much noise for him to hear what Dayton said to Rayna. But there was no missing how tight she set her jaw as she nodded curtly to Dayton and slipped into the nearest store.

Dayton knuckled back his hat, emitted a look of great satisfaction and headed off toward the alley.

What had that lowlife said to her? A bad feeling settled like a lead ball in his gut. He dismounted, wrapped one of the reins around the closest post and hopped onto the boardwalk.

There she was—he could see her through the wide front windows at the postal counter window. Looking composed, she counted out change from her reticule, exchanged a polite nod to the postmaster and headed for the door.

One thing she couldn't hide were the circles beneath her eyes. They were so bruised, she looked as if she'd been hit. The strain showed on her face and in the curled ball of her fists.

She saw him through the glass door, the bell jangling as she walked through it. Frowning at him as he held the door, she said, "Mr. Lindsay. I'd hoped to see you next. Seeing you here saves me a ride out to your place."

"I noticed you on the boardwalk." This was business, nothing more, but that didn't explain the return of the emotions aching like arthritis beneath his ribs. "I spoke to Wright at the bank. What I have to say isn't easy. Maybe you'd want a more private place—"

"The bank is my next stop. It's best to say what's on your mind." Along the side wall of the mercantile she spotted an empty bench washed in the wan sunlight that speared through the gray streaks of the clouds above. "Shall we sit?"

"Sure."

Good. It was a start. She released a breath she didn't realize she was holding. Oh, she was overset with all this worry. She was depending so much on his ability to purchase the ranch. The mountain of debt was staggering.

If he could buy the place, it would be the best solution. He'd certainly earned the right, he would be good to the land and she couldn't think of a more deserving rancher. Anticipating Mr. Lindsay's answer, she settled on the rough wooden bench.

All she had to do was to glance up into his face. His honest face. But he wasn't smiling, and surely that was a poor sign indeed. His dark eyes were troubled, and she knew. While he didn't say a word, the last smidgen of hope died along with the last of the sunlight.

"The banker would not accept my offer."

"I see." A cold gust of wind left her catching her breath. "That's too bad. I think Kol would have approved of you farming the land. He'd always thought well of you."

"And I of him." Towering over her, a long, lean man in a black overcoat, he seemed as bleak as the rain that began to fall. As severe as the days ahead to come. "You haven't heard what I have to say."

"I already know. There are notes on everything. The house, the land, the livestock. The buggy. There is no chance of coming out with cash in hand. It's obvious, but somehow I had been hoping—"

"I was hopeful, too. There is too much debt on the land. I cannot buy it for the total of what is owed. It would be beyond what cash I could fork over."

"Of course, it would be a poor investment for you. What will happen when the bank takes it?"

"Likely there will be an auction. The land will go to the highest bidder."

"You'd do better to try then."

"I'm likely to have stiff competition. Dayton, for one, has his eye on it."

"Yes, and a half dozen others." To think that was to come of the life she and Kol had built. That it could disappear as suddenly as he had vanished from her life. That other people would live in their home. Another man would till and harvest their fields.

And Kol had let it happen.

She tamped down her anger. She couldn't bear grieving him and being furious at him, too. She'd give anything to be able to hold him in her arms, debt or no. And it was impossible, of course, and her arms felt so empty. Her heart wrung dry.

She did her best to clear the lump of emotion from her throat. "I would like to offer you the load of wheat we managed to save."

"I'll sell it for you."

"No. I meant to give it to you. You lost your crop, as well, and of the two of us, it's my hope that at least you can remain on your land."

A muscle twitched in his jaw. "I will take the wheat."

"Oh, thank you." Why that seemed to lift away a part of her burdens, she couldn't say. But it felt right to cancel out the obligation she felt to this man.

No, she wouldn't be beholden to any man. Look at how Dayton had viewed a woman's need. Shivering, forcing the ugliness from her mind, she clutched her reticule, stood and smoothed her skirts.

Daniel Lindsay looked ten times more muscular than her rude neighbor did, and Daniel gave the impression of a good and upright man. Yet it wasn't right to be in his debt. She had enough debt to handle as it was. "Please come and fetch the wheat when you can. Perhaps tomorrow, after a good night's rest. You look as exhausted as I feel."

"I wish I could've done more, ma'am. If you need money—"

"No!" She answered too quickly, startling them both. Seeming so rude. And how wrong that was, when he was only being kind, she was sure of it. "I only mean, I have enough to get by on for now. You have repaid Kol's kindness twofold already."

"It's my opinion I have not."

"There is nothing more to be done, Mr. Lindsay." She gripped her reticule so tightly, her knuckles hurt. "Good day to you, sir."

With all the composure she possessed, she walked carefully away from the tall, somber man watching after her. One foot placed in front of the other until the boardwalk led her to the busy corner.

Over the din from the busy street, she swore she could hear him call her name, but when she turned, he was gone from the corner.

It was just as well. Daniel Lindsay had his life. And her future…why, it lay in an unknown direction. For the first time in fifteen years, she was truly on her own.

Alone, she crossed the street. Marched right up to the front door of the bank and didn't let her terror lead her as she lifted her chin, pushed wide the door and asked for Mr. Wright. She waited, fighting the cold trembles that were taking root in the pit of her stomach.

How long would the process take? Would she be allowed to take the savings from the bank without Kol, for the account was in his name? Wondering what on earth she would do if she couldn't, she saw a familiar pinto passing by the side windows and she twisted in her chair to watch the man riding the mustang.

Daniel astride the horse rode nimbly, straight and strong and dark in the shadows as the rain fell in earnest against the glass panes of the bank's many windows.

In a blink, Daniel was gone, leaving the sight of the street as other riders and horse-drawn wagons scurried by, hurried along by the change in weather.

Chapter Six

There had been no mercy from the bank.

Rayna sidestepped the worst of the puddles and tried to hold no ill will against Mr. Wright, who'd only been doing his job. But with her feet aching in her new shoes that were not meant for a mile and a half of walking, it was plain impossible. He could have waited to repossess the horses and buggy. They had a buyer and in these hard times felt as if they couldn't let the opportunity pass by.

Fine, she understood that, she didn't have the funds to cover the debt, but did it have to be today, when the rain was only getting worse?

The rattle of a harness above the rush of the wind was the only warning she had. She gathered up her skirts and sidestepped the water collecting in the ruts. Her toe caught in a wet tangle of toppled bunch grass and it was too late. She was falling toward the ditch. Her hands shot out, her reticule went flying, oh, Lord no, not in the—

Her knee cracked against a rock, her gloves skidded through the tough thorny vines of dying blackberry bushes and the ditch rose up to meet her. Cold silt slicked her face as she hit the unforgiving ground.

She popped her face out of the trench water, leveling herself up on her stinging hands. She was mud and wet and bleeding and her face—oh, mercy. It was runoff from the Dayton's cow pasture.

Wasn't that the frosting on the cake of her day?

The jangling crescendoed. The muffled thud of horse hooves in the mud stopped and she could feel the great animals towering over her. Every inch of her body protested as she rolled over and recognized Samson and Ash, her matched bays. Her buggy. And Clay Dayton staring down at her, his arms crossed on his knobby knee.

He'd bought her team? He'd been the one to approach the bank? Rage fueled her, streaming into her blood as she climbed to her feet and out of the road. Mud and worse sluicing down her chin and staining her bodice, she hiked her chin higher when she realized Dayton was looking entertained from behind the transparent rain curtains. *Her* rain curtains.

Not anymore, Rayna.

It hit her then, seeing Dayton on her buggy seat, driving her team. All of it was now his. This was the way it was going to go, losing everything in small pieces, bit after bit after bit until nothing remained.

No, that wasn't quite true. She would be left with everything that was more important than any house or any buggy. She would have her sons. Her sons. She loved them with every fiber of her being, and she was deeply lucky to have the boys in her life.

Gratitude washed through her and she found it easier to find the strength she needed to keep going. To wish Mr. Dayton a good day as he passed, the wheels splashing mud droplets on the hem of her coat and dress. She pulled a handkerchief from her pocket that was only slightly wet and washed the sludge off her face the best she could.

Now to get home and get to her housework. She'd go through her closets and dressers. Divide up Kol's things to donate to the church or for things she could cut down for Kirk.

Then she would divvy up her pantry of preserved goods between her best friends and offer her cooking utensils and kettles to Katelyn, the new neighbor down the road she had befriended. As a newlywed, Katelyn would be in need of various household items.

Yes, that would be a help, to start clearing out her house as soon as possible. She'd sell what she couldn't pack—as far as she could tell there were encumbrances on her fine furniture. Then she would be ready to move when Kol's brother replied to her letter with an invitation to come.

Or, rather, she *hoped* Kol's brother would be the family member to offer them shelter.

There was no way around the bankruptcy. Not with the entire crop of wheat destroyed. How was she to tell the boys? Lord knows they had it hard enough. They would be leaving their friends and schoolmates behind to start over in a new town with children who were strangers to them and as guests in a different household—

The splash and plod of what sounded like a double team of draft horses and the clatter of an empty wagon had her checking over her shoulder. She saw a man on the seat, his wide frame obscured by the bulk of a raincoat. His Stetson was pulled low against the rain and hid his face from her view, but she'd know those working man's shoulders anywhere.

Was it just her lucky day or did it have to be Daniel Lindsay coming her way? Her clothes, her face, her *smell.* Oh, she reeked of a cow barn. She wiped a hank of dripping hair out of her eyes and tucked it beneath the brim of her sagging hood. Lord, she was mortified that he'd recognized her and was slowing his team to a stop right beside her.

"Ma'am." He bobbed his head as he set the brake. "It's a bad day to be on foot."

"I'm rather enjoying the rain."

"You could appreciate the weather from up here just as well." He climbed down to offer her a hand up.

She could only stare at his leather-covered palm, wide and broad, as steady and sure as Kol's had been. It was a comfort somehow to know there were men like him in the world. "I would be obliged for a ride. I thought you were on horseback?"

"Doin' some hauling this afternoon."

"To the weigh station?" Her fingertips brushed his glove as she bounced up onto the slick wooden step, and then she was up on the seat and away from him. She slid over to make room for him.

"I took your load of wheat, tarped it down good, what with the downpour, and then mine. I had three trips in all." He rose up on the steps, towering over her so that her breath caught in her throat.

Had he always been that tall? Heavens, every time she saw him he seemed to grow. Maybe men of good character did that, she reasoned as he released the brake and took charge of the thick leather straps. He looked in control, and his tone was firm and low as he murmured to the horses. The double team of giant Clydesdales lunged, jerking the wagon into motion.

She should have been expecting the sudden movement, but she wasn't. Her torso rocked back and then her head rolled forward and Daniel's hand gripped her upper arm, steadying her.

"Are you all right?"

"Yes." The word scraped up her windpipe. The heat from his grip was a shock.

"Rayna, you're like ice. Here." He wound the reins into a twist and wedged the thickness between his knee and the dash, leaving his hands free as he struggled out of his rain slicker.

At once she saw what he was doing. "No, Daniel, you'll only get chilled and there's no sense to having both of us dripping wet."

"Don't you worry about me." He draped the oiled cloth around her shoulders, his movements awkward, as if he'd never done such a thing before. But he was gallant enough to do it anyway, shaking water off the unused hood and bundling her up. "Better?"

She could only nod. Shielded from the bite of the wind and rain, she began to shiver hard. Every inch of her being felt utterly weary. Every corner of her soul drained. Grateful for this chance to relax, she let her eyes drift shut and ignored the slide of the rainwater down her face as Daniel turned west toward home.

Home. She knew the sound of the willows at the corner of her driveway, their vibrant leaves whispering and their supple limbs groaning. Even with her eyes closed, she could feel the change of the land when Daniel guided the horses along the driveway that curved in a lazy circle toward her house.

Peace. She felt it wash over her and breathed it in. There had always been a sense of serenity in this swell of prairie land. She opened her eyes and the beauty of the two-story farm home, with its cheerful windows and wraparound porch, struck her down deep. She had to find a way to leave this home she loved and take all the precious memories made inside that house with her. But how?

"Do you have somewhere to go?"

"That's one of the reasons I was in town. To mail letters to relatives. I hope to hear back before the bank comes for the keys to the front door." She looked up to see Daniel studying her, his brow furrowed, his jaw set.

Unmistakable pity softened his whiskey-rough voice. Pity. How had it come to this? That people she hardly knew would look at her and feel sorry for the poor widow. Sure, he meant to be kind, but it grated on her pride and she had to fight a hot, rising wave of anger.

"Are they good people, these relatives?"

"I don't know. The only one I've met is Kol's brother. He's come out on the train to visit twice. The others are on Kol's side of the family and he's always—" There she went again, talking in the present tense. She had to stop doing that. Her husband was no longer here and yet she ached to reach out to him. To rest against his barrel chest, the safest place in all the world—

Hold on, Rayna. You have to do it. Kol would want her to do her best for their boys. And that thought steadied her. Made it easier to force words past the grief coiled in her chest and to sound almost normal.

"He had always kept in touch with the relatives he was close to growing up. It's my hope they will help me now, for the sake of our sons. Someone is bound to have an extra room we can stay in, until I find work—"

She stopped. She couldn't look beyond that. The future was unthinkable. There was this horrible gaping emptiness in her life to come. An emptiness she had to confront and keep going. For her boys. She would give them a good life, if she had to break her back cleaning houses and toiling in the fields to do it. Kol had wanted his sons to graduate from public school, and they would be the first in his family to be so well educated.

Daniel murmured to the horses, reining the great animals to a gentle stop. Without the pleasant rasping and occasional squeal of the wheels and the bell-like jingle of the harnessing and the creak of the boards of the empty wagon bed, the downpour rumbled like a Mozart concerto across the expanse of the prairie. She shivered, wrapping her arms around herself, but she wasn't only cold. *I will miss this place.*

"Ma!"

The front door blew open and there was Hans, his hair mussed and several strands sticking straight up at his cowlick. His little blue flannel shirt had come untucked from his denims and dark circles marred his sweet face. "Ma!"

Mindless of the wind and wet, he tore down the front steps and she didn't remember leaping to the ground until she was suddenly there, a little boy wrapped around her legs, holding her with all the strength in his small being.

Love as pure as a blessing shone within her and nothing else mattered. Nothing really did. Just this child as she unwound his tenacious grip and knelt to wipe the worry lines from his brow. But they remained deep creases that had never known real anxiety.

I will protect you, little boy. She was alone to do it, and she would. The world was a harsh place, but she was strong. And perhaps Kol would be watching over them from heaven. She wiped the wetness from his cheeks, some rain, some tears. ''Guess what I have in my reticule?''

''P-p-peppermint?''

''You'd better look inside and see.'' She handed him the small cloth bag, sadly sodden, but the candy was well wrapped inside.

His cupid's mouth puckered up in concentration as he plunged his hand into the depths and withdrew a red-and-white striped candy stick.

''See?'' It was a tradition that whenever she returned from town there was candy in her bag. ''Now, hurry inside because you forgot your coat.''

Ignoring her, Hans shot a hard look in Daniel's direction and he clutched her hand so tight, her bones crunched. ''You were g-gone. I waited and waited.''

My poor baby. ''I'm here now. Let's go inside out of the rain.''

He nodded, allowing her to nudge him along. He didn't take his gaze off Daniel until they reached the porch steps. She turned to thank him for the ride and for his compassion, but he was already halfway around the loop of the drive, too far away to call to over the drum of the hard rain.

Oh, well, perhaps there would come another time to thank him for his kindness, as for now she had her hands full enough. Hans's need was as loud as the rainfall, as endless as the sky. As soon as she had her little boy inside the house and out of the weather, she knelt and held him in her arms. Breathed in the sweet, little-boy scent of his hair as he held her right back.

Her heart wrenched. Kol hadn't meant to leave them in such dire circumstances, and she was angry, but not at him. She was furious at fate, that's what, for snatching him away and for the world that was so often without any mercy.

Thank goodness for people like Daniel Lindsay. While no man could have saved her wheat, he'd been a good neighbor and his intentions had given her hope. And that had lent her strength for the tasks to come. She'd start in the kitchen first—

"Rayna, it *is* you." Mariah, in a crisp apron and her long hair tied back for kitchen work, smiled at her from the archway. "It was getting so late, Katelyn and I were wondering if one of us ought to ride into town and check on you. But here you are, safe and sound."

Dismayed, she realized Mariah had probably come to leave off a prepared dinner. It was just the kind of thing she'd been doing since the funeral. But her neighbor Katelyn, too? "You two shouldn't have gone to the trouble."

"What trouble? It's no bother to help you, dear friend. Wait until you see all we've been able to get done this afternoon." Mariah's gaze sparkled with delight, as if she were keeping a big secret.

"What did you do?"

"You'll see." Mariah spun with the snap of her apron and led the way into the kitchen.

Rayna froze in the doorway, not trusting her eyes. She blinked, but the view remained unchanged. Elegant Katelyn at the table ladling stewed green tomatoes into prepared jars. Half a day's work covered the counters, the last of the garden vegetables put up. Her friends had done this. For her.

"Betsy will be along soon. She had deliveries to make and promised to swing by on her way home and lend a hand." Katelyn's sweet smile was sheer generosity. "Kirk is down in the cellar storing all the squash we asked him to bring in. I didn't get a chance to mop the floor yet. Don't look at the mud! It's next on my list.''

''You've done so much already. Too much. Oh.'' Sobs ripped through her and she held them in. Hans's hand was still tight in hers and both Mariah, who'd returned to the stove, and Katelyn, who'd gone back to filling jars, looked happy to be here. Her dear, dear friends.

There would be no more sadness, not on the measured time they had left all together. No, there would be only this handful of days to cherish before she was gone forever.

She guided Hans to his chair, helped him settle in and took the wrapping from him, so he could suck on his candy. Then she set her reticule aside and went to unbutton her coat. Only then did she realize she still wore Daniel's slicker. He was out there, driving home in the rain, wet and cold because of her.

The wind battered the west side of the house, scraping the lilac limbs against the siding. The raindrops turned icy and, as the storm deepened, the ice changed to snow. Unforgiving flakes tumbled from the sky, as if to erase every memory of summer from the world, and drove leaves from the trees.

As if to warn her of harder times to come.

It was a damn shame. Daniel reined in the team in the lee of the barn. On the way home he'd spotted one of the top men from the town bank riding out toward Dayton's place. Wasn't that interesting? It looked like the old man was bargaining for more than Kol's fine-stepping team and fashionable buggy. No doubt Dayton was making an offer on the Ludgrin place. Quiet deals done behind closed doors.

Shoot. Daniel should have known the property would never make it to auction. It was too damn valuable, and men like Dayton too underhanded.

What about Rayna? She lingered in his mind like a pleasant dream. Wasn't that a hell of a thing? He tried but couldn't forget the image of her walking alongside the road, muddy and drenched and miserable in those fancy pinch-toed shoes of hers. Dainty and willowy and elegant. How would she fare on her own?

It wasn't his lookout, but he had to admit it troubled him. He'd come to respect her, that was for sure. She seemed like a good woman, and those were rare, in his opinion.

The lead gelding snorted, drawing his attention. Jeez, what was he doing sitting in the cold? He hopped down, grabbed the O-ring and yanked loose the buckles. The yokes separated and he followed the leather straps unbuckling as he went, and swiping snow out of his eyes when he had to.

Rayna Ludgrin. There he was, thinking of her again. He was sorry for her, sure, but he knew that losing her horses and buggy was a first step of hard losses to come. He'd been inside her house and he'd gotten eyeful enough of her life to see Kol had all but pampered her.

She was a quality lady, sure, but what chance did she have? She'd probably been married young, by the looks of things, and gone straight from her parents' household to her husband's care. She couldn't have any practical experience to make a living with.

How would she survive? He could only wish her the best. Maybe those relations of Kol's were decent folk and would look after her with care. And those boys…

Daniel's gut clenched so hard he tasted bile and the

pain of memories too bleak to bear thinking on. Yeah, he hoped those relatives were good people, or those boys were fated for hard labor and misery. He knew that for a fact. It was a hell of a thing, too, because they seemed to be good children. Kirk with his mature determination and the little one, with his big, innocent blue eyes.

Fact was, it was a hard world. No arguing with that, and he couldn't change it. Didn't know anyone on this earth who could. Yeah, it was too damn bad.

What became of the Ludgrin widow and sons wasn't any of his concern. He had his own concerns—to improve on this claim so it would be his very own, free and clear. For a backwoods orphan, he'd hoed a good row for himself. He lifted the yokes from the horses, led them into the sheltering warmth of the barn, rubbed them down and warmed mash for all four of his gentle giants.

When they were stabled and content, he headed toward the cabin to see to his needs. Rubbed his hands together to keep them from going numb. Even with the gloves, it was cold. Snow come this early could only mean one thing. There was a hard winter ahead. Bitter and long and dark. He wasn't ready for it, but he would be.

What about the widow and her boys? That thought troubled him as he closed the door behind him, knelt to stir the embers and built a fire from the glowing coals.

Hours later, when the little house was warm enough that the potbellied stove glowed red, Daniel couldn't feel the blazing heat. He dreamed that night of his boyhood and woke in an ice-cold sweat.

Beneath the covers, lost in shadow, he could not close his eyes. He lay wide-awake waiting for daybreak so he would not dream again.

Chapter Seven

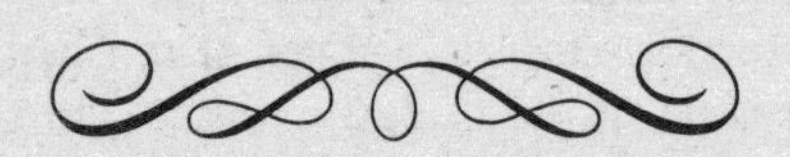

Rayna looked around Betsy's cozy dining room table at the best friends a woman could ever have. Friends who had, for the past week, helped her at every turn. Putting up the last of the garden and turning the soil, so whoever bought this place would have an acre of garden patch ready to tend and plant come spring.

And that wasn't all. Betsy had done her laundry and all the mending. Mariah had finished the last of the preserves, organized the pantry and helped Rayna sort through Kol's clothing and personal items. A task that would have been impossible on her own.

Most important of all, the emotional care they'd given her, sympathetic and encouraging. Betsy had even offered to share her laundry business, so Rayna could support her sons. It was a generous offer, but Rayna knew Betsy was barely scraping by as it was. With crop failures widespread, Betsy had lost many customers. Rayna did agree to do whatever mending Betsy's clients needed. The income, however small, would be welcome until she knew for sure where her and the boys would be going.

Whichever relative took them in, it would be hundreds of miles away. Maybe more. What was she going to do without her friends?

Don't think about that yet. Not yet. Rayna blinked hard against the hot wave of emotion threatening to drown her. "What will I do without the two of you?"

"Rejoice." Mariah measured sugar into her after-lunch coffee. "We have forced our way into your house and refused to leave."

"Especially me," Betsy added, dark curls bouncing as she sliced into the angel food cake she'd brought for dessert. "I haven't seen my house in town for more than a week. Well, it feels that way."

"You can force your way into my house anytime." Rayna accepted the dessert plate Betsy passed to her with an extremely generous slice of sweet fluffy cake. "Of course, you'll have to travel by rail to wherever it is I move to, but you would be most welcome."

"Still no word from Kol's relations?" Mariah's question was light-sounding, but worry dug into her brow.

"Not yet. I'm hopeful that the afternoon train will bring an answer." Rayna refused to feel the endless void in the bottom of her stomach, the void filled with worry and a cold, descending anxiety. Everything—what to sell and what to pack, what to tell the boys, what to expect and when she could leave town—depended on what answer arrived in the mail.

"We've all talked about this, Rayna." Betsy set aside the cake server and even the snap and flutter of the curtains at the open windows stilled. "If the bank removes you before you have your answer from Kol's brother, you will come live with me."

"I can't impose—"

"Nonsense. I rattle around in that big old house all by myself. There is more than enough room for you and the boys.'' Betsy held up her hand to stop the argument before Rayna could make it. ''What do you think we will let you do? Sleep without a roof over your head? What about Kirk and Hans? Let them go hungry?''

''There might be room at the boardinghouse in town—''

''Nonsense. You'll need every penny you can keep for making a new start,'' Mariah broke in, and beneath her gentle tone came something as unyielding as a Montana mountainside. ''You are like family to us.''

''Thank the heavens for you two.'' There was no way she would lean too heavily on these good women, but their words touched her soul.

Family. That's what they had become. Since they were little girls skipping rope at recess. She would never want to ask too much of them, though. She didn't want to risk damaging their bond.

That was why she fashioned a falsehood to tell them. Not a lie, exactly, for she held hopes that it would come to pass. ''I know you mean well, but I will manage just fine from now on. Kol's brother is a good, dependable man. I am certain he will come through.''

''Oh, it's decided then.'' Betsy looked crestfallen. ''I know, I know. You've talked about needing to leave, but I just want you to stay so badly. I have room here. I could share my business with you, until you get on your feet.''

''There isn't enough business in this small town for the two of us, and you know it. It's good of you, Betsy.'' Rayna had guessed, although Betsy had never said, that she was barely getting by as it was.

How could she impose on her friends further? ''No, it looks as though my future lies elsewhere. You two have to promise to write me as often as you can. I know you're busy, but—"

"We promise!" Mariah and Betsy interrupted at the same time.

Their talk turned to happier things. Betsy had more stories of her laundry customers. Mariah told of her children's latest tales. Her friends wanted to know more about all Daniel Lindsay had done for her before the crop was lost. How he'd come to harvest and how he'd bandaged her hands, which were almost healed now, and how he'd given her a ride when she reeked of cow pies and acted as if he hadn't noticed. *That* was a good man.

After dessert was consumed, the three of them gathered in the cozy parlor, drinking in the pleasant autumn sunshine, for the weather had decided to give them an Indian summer after all. And chatting of small things while they sewed gave Rayna a sense of normalcy.

This is one of the things that matters in life. Time spent with friends. Rayna savored the few hours left before she had to hurry to finish her errands and head home. She loved the way Betsy was always making them laugh. And how Mariah could be so much fun.

As Rayna pinned seams together of a flannel shirt of Kol's she was trimming down to Kirk's smaller size, she realized her spirit felt a little stronger. It was amazing how friendship could strengthen a person.

"I swear that man hides in the woods every time I drive out to his cabin." Betsy stopped pinning the hem in her new dress to continue her tale of her most dreaded laundry customer. "I can feel him watching me. And not in a good way, either."

Rayna, remembering the subtle leer in Clay Dayton's manners toward her recently, felt her stomach tighten.

Some of the sun seemed to dim from the room. "Betsy, if he could be a threat to you, you must be careful."

"Oh, I keep Charlie's Winchester right next to me on the seat whenever I head up into the mountains, don't worry."

"I wasn't talking about wild animals. I mean, the human kind. Those who think widows are…are…well, easy women."

"Goodness, I learned to handle that problem a long time ago, don't you worry." Betsy's chuckle was infectious. "A girl doesn't grow up with four older brothers without learning a thing or two about male weaknesses. Anytime I have trouble, I just kick the offending man in the—no, don't laugh, Mariah, I don't get him there first, they always expect that."

Mariah covered her mouth, trying to keep her laughter in as Betsy continued. "I kick 'em in the shin. I'm always careful to wear my brother's old steel-toe riding boots, and, one kick, I'll make a grown man cry. The second blow comes from my reticule right upside the jaw, and you know how heavy my reticule is. It knocks them right over. Then, if they aren't in the middle of apologizing, I *make* sure they apologize real nice, or that's where the next kick goes. Believe me, those men are nothing but polite to me next time I see them."

"Our sweet, little, softhearted Betsy." Rayna threaded her needle. "The lioness who can take down any man in the county but she can't eat her own beef cow."

"That thing's going to die of old age first," Mariah commented as she got up to fetch the coffeepot.

"My neighbor keeps threatening to butcher poor Edgar, if I'm not. But he's my pet. I didn't mean for him to be a pet, you know. I wanted a dog, but the steer simply followed me home. I tried to stop him, but really, how do you reason with a thousand-pound male, even if he does have his, er, oysters missing?''

As Betsy regaled them with that tale, Rayna laughed too hard to baste the interfacing into the collar. She set it down to enjoy Betsy's story. By the time she was done, they were all laughing too hard to speak. As much as Rayna had always treasured this weekly tradition of sewing with her friends, she always took it for granted. The three of them had been gathering to sew and talk and laugh since they'd been girls.

Rayna hated that the minutes were ticking past and the sun was making a slow journey through the room. But there was no holding back time. When Betsy's mantel clock bonged two on the hour, it was with eye-stinging regret that she tucked her needle safely into the seam. She folded up the shirt and placed it into her small sewing basket. As she had many hundreds of times before, she hugged her friends goodbye.

Trying not to think about how hard it was going to be to leave them behind for good soon, Rayna unhitched the placid old gelding Mariah's husband had lent her. Moments later she was riding down the tree-shaded lane to the main street of town, where she hurried about her few errands.

She picked up two pieces of penny candy along with a small bag of flour at the mercantile, for which she paid with the dwindling cash she had on hand. Ever since she'd mentioned Daniel Lindsay this afternoon, he had been at the edge of her thoughts.

She'd left his rain slicker, cleaned and neatly folded, on the top step of his tiny porch. He hadn't been home, and on her way to town she'd spotted him far out in his fields, plowing under the miles of ruined wheat and stalks.

Surely he'd found the coat, but that wasn't what troubled her. The look of him, a solitary figure with his horses and plow small in contrast to the vast expanse of the windblown prairie, got to her. He'd looked…lonely.

Her heart squeezed, remembering, for she knew the bitter taste of that emotion. Of emptiness. In the bed beside her at night. In the chair across the table each morning. The boys kept her busy, and she wasn't alone, of course, but the aloneness when she'd been part of a team, wife to her husband—she could barely stand it.

How did a person live alone, by choice or circumstance, and feel this way year after endless year?

She was about to find out what it was like. Perhaps the real reason she'd done her best to avoid Daniel Lindsay was that image of him alone on the plains hadn't spoken to merely her aloneness. Kol was the great love of her life. She could never replace him. He'd been a part of her soul. She wanted no other, not now, not ever. Loneliness was her only fate.

So when she recognized Daniel's gelding tied to the rail across the street, she whipped her gaze away and hurried directly to the post office.

"'Afternoon, Miz Ludgrin." Walter Svenson looked up from his work behind the counter. "I got a letter come in for you just today. Oof, where did it go?"

Was it from Kol's brother? Nerves buzzed in her stomach through the long minute it took for the postmaster to locate the letter and hand it over.

Yes, it was. Thank goodness. She kept hold of it, rather than slip the envelope into her reticule. She hardly remembered exchanging pleasantries with Mr. Svenson, only that she was outside in the sunshine, tearing at the envelope in her haste.

She squinted at the poorly written and spelled words. "I am agreeved to hear of Kols passing. As I have come on hard times, I wil take one of the boys."

What? Only *one?* Rayna had to read the sentence twice. One of the boys? Did he mean to separate them? But they were brothers, and her sons. There was no way. Surely he did not mean—

Then her eyes followed the rest of his unschooled scrawl. "I wont the stronger boy, to work my feelds."

He wanted a field worker?

She didn't understand. What could he be thinking? She'd very clearly stated in her letter that she needed a place for all three of them. Temporary shelter. But to take Kirk out of school so he could be a common laborer—

No. Absolutely not. She wasn't about to read one more word of such nonsense!

She crumpled the letter into a ball. Angry? No, she wasn't angry. She was *furious.* It was a horrible letter. Kol's brother must indeed have come upon more than hard times. He'd turned into an opportunist, too! Using a child like that for field labor. His own nephew—

"Rayna." A familiar baritone. A dependable hand at her elbow. Holding her up when she would have fallen. "You're as white as could be. Are you feeling well?"

Her head was spinning. The boardwalk tilting dangerously. Yet the steady concern in Daniel Lindsay's honest hazel eyes seemed to be the only thing that wasn't moving. She concentrated on them, but no, she was still falling.

Then she was in his arms, her cheek against the stony hardness of his chest as he carried her.

"No, put me down. Please." The last thing she wanted was to be a spectacle in plain view of the main street, but he didn't listen.

Cradling her against him, he kept on going with his long hard strides, turning down a quieter street and into the shadows of a building.

She breathed in the scent of lye soap on his shirt and recognized the sharp, sweet straw and the warm, comforting scent of animals—he'd brought her to the livery. Quiet and private, he set her down in the bed of a clean stall. Tufts of hay and straw seemed as luxurious as a new feather tick.

Thank heavens. She gladly lay back in the softness and prayed for the dizziness to fade and for her stomach to stop twisting. She wasn't about to be sick—not in front of Daniel. There was a rustling and he placed something soft beneath her head. His jacket.

"Just rest quiet. I'll fetch you some water."

Then he was gone, and she was alone, listening to the muffled sounds of horses shifting in their stalls and then his footsteps returning.

"Here. Just sip slowly." He supported her head as he held the dipper steady for her.

The water was cool and clean, and left a cool trail when she swallowed. Her stomach coiled, but she didn't become sick. She risked another sip.

"I'll get the doctor."

"No—" She couldn't afford it. She didn't want it. "I'm not ill. I just…it was a shock, I guess."

"What was?"

"I was counting my chicks before the eggs hatched. That isn't wise." She didn't know what she'd do now.

"Hmm, did you hear from Kol's relations?" His hand

closed over her fist where the parchment was still balled tight.

She still had the letter? "I was so sure he would offer real help. We don't require much, a corner of his house. The attic, even. Right now I'd settle for a space in his barn."

"You have no other family? What about you? Sisters? Brothers?"

"No siblings. My brothers died long ago, both of scarlet fever. And my parents died many years ago." She couldn't concentrate for the press of his hand on hers offering her comfort and empathy and strength—but only for this moment.

She could shoulder this burden alone, but for an instant, it felt good not to be alone. To feel the hard male warmth of his skin and muscle and bone, and the sense of protection he emanated.

"There's no one else?"

"Back in Sweden. My mother and father came from there."

He fell silent. "Then let me see."

"The letter? No, it's horrible. He needs Kirk to work for him."

"And the younger boy? What are you going to do with him?"

"I'm not going to let either one of them work. They're children. They need to go to school. They need their father." She needed their father.

Right now Kol would know what to do. He always did. Everything he'd done was always right, or it had seemed that way. He'd always been her center, her strength. Now he was gone, and she had to find her own strength. It was in her, and she would find it.

But it wouldn't hurt to confide in Daniel. Would it?

"Let me see." He took the balled-up parchment from her fingers and patiently straightened it out. "Please, read it for me."

"I had hoped to lease the land to you, or to sell it and keep the acre the house sits on. I'd hoped I could find work, enough to get by on. But there is no work in this town. Shops are closing up. We are not the only family losing their farm."

He appeared to scan the lines, and his mouth tightened with frustration. "Tell me. What about your youngest?"

"He's found a place for Hans. The town smithy has room in his home and has offered to teach him his trade, in exchange for his labor. Oh, but he's a *child.*" The image of her sweet baby, his face smudged with ash and smoke from the blacksmith's fires, made her sick.

Fighting the sudden watering of her mouth, she crawled toward the aisle but couldn't make it any farther. She emptied her stomach, wretch after wretch carving up her throat, leaving her shaken and weak. Daniel Lindsay crouched beside her and held back her hair.

When she was through, he withdrew a handkerchief from his pocket, unfolded it and carefully wiped her lips and chin. "It's a common fate for children to get room and board in exchange for long days of farm work."

She shook her head, scattering her soft blond curls that were escaping her hairpins. She looked beautiful—and too young and vulnerable to be a widow. "I've never heard of such a thing."

"I have." Grim, he closed off his memories of that time. "I don't recommend that for your boys, Rayna. No child should grow up little better than a slave."

"No. Not my boys."

There was the iron in her, not glaring or brash, but silent and strong. An unwelcome twist of emotion wadded up in his chest, cutting off his air, opening his heart. He returned the dipper to the pump, taking his time, but it wasn't time enough for the fierce ache that went with that tangle of emotions to fade. It grew until his eyes smarted from the pain of it.

No kid deserved a life like what could await Rayna's boys. Work, work and more work. Hunger and more work. Fear and— *No, don't do it, man. Don't remember.*

He filled the dipper and drank deep. Nothing. He splashed water on his face and the shock of the cold water helped. But there was nothing on this earth that could scratch out the effects of the suffering he'd endured as a boy, and he felt half sick with the thought of Kirk and Hans going through the same thing.

Daniel squeezed his eyes shut against the memories. Kirk was already showing the impressive signs of the good man he was becoming. He didn't deserve to know what it was like to work fourteen hours in a sun-scorched field with open wounds on his bare back stinging from his own sweat.

To work beyond exhaustion just so he wouldn't feel the bite of the foreman's whip—

A distant metallic clatter tore him from his thoughts. From the brief image of cotton fields to the shadowed warmth of the livery stable. Safe, with the dipper at his feet. He didn't remember dropping it.

He went to retrieve it, the bunch and pull of his muscles as he knelt reminding him of the man he was. When he reached for the dipper, his fingertips were whole and not bloodstained. Not the hands of a cotton picker but that of a man in control of his own life. He gave thanks for that every day.

He gave thanks for it now.

"Daniel?" Rayna was in the aisle, her butter-yellow

dress glowing like a gentle spring dawn, hugging her willowy woman's body.

With her hair tumbled down and falling loose around her face and shoulders, cascading over her breasts to curl at her waist, she was a vision. A rare glimpse of goodness and gentility and kindness so powerful he stood in a daze, unable to tear his gaze away.

No wonder Kol had protected her. Kept her safe from the world of cruel, ruthless men. Who would protect her now?

It wasn't his right or his duty. And he couldn't figure that a fine lady like Rayna, with her fancy shoes and reticules to match her numerous dresses, would see much in a man like him. One who had no fancy buggy or fine airs. Just a man with a section of land who felt satisfied with how far he'd come in life. And aspired for nothing more.

''Your coat.'' She held out the worn garment to him.

He took it and didn't know what to say.

She apparently did. ''It seems as if I'm always returning your coat. I'm obliged to you, Daniel. I would have been mortified if I'd become ill on the street in front of everyone. Thank you for sparing me that.''

''Just afraid you'd fall and get hurt. I didn't do much.''

''It was everything to me. I—'' She was strength and fight, despite the tears filling her eyes. Tears that shimmered but did not fall. ''Your kindness matters.''

She gestured again for him to take the coat she'd gathered up, shaken out and folded with care. He couldn't seem to make his feet move forward and he felt awkward, the simple effort of reaching out to take the garment felt strenuous.

Why did being near her make him want to head in the other direction?

When he wanted to run, he forced his fingers to grasp the collar of his winter coat, hardly aware of the sheepskin lining against his skin as sweat broke out on his brow. For a brief moment he inhaled her sweet, warm, woman scent that made him think of lilacs and spring breezes and lark song. Desire stirred in his blood, for he knew she would smell like that all over. Knew her smooth skin and soft curves were made for a man to caress and to cherish.

Unaware of his thoughts, Rayna lifted her right hand, no longer bandaged, to stroke her loose hair away from her eyes.

Although it wasn't a seductive movement, it might as well have been for the blood roaring in his ears.

"I need to finish my errands. Good day to you, Daniel."

She walked away, and it felt to him as if she took all the light with her, leaving him in utter darkness.

"I'm sorry, Mrs. Ludgrin. I can give you a room in exchange for work, but not board. No, I just can't do it." Thora Arneson softened her words with an apologetic shrug. "Not with two growing boys. I can give you a discounted rate on board, but that is the best I can do in these hard times."

Rayna knew the soft-spoken woman was simply being honest. She knew Thora from their school days, though she'd been several grades behind Rayna and they'd never been more than acquaintances. But working for someone as decent as Thora *had* to be better than the alternatives she dare not consider. "I could work more nights a week."

"Three is all I can afford to offer you."

"Then I would be grateful for the work."

"Wonderful." A rare smile touched the pale woman's face, showing a surprising loveliness. "I am so sorry for your circumstances, and I know you will be a good employee. As I said, I don't have a room available right now, but in a few weeks there will probably be space for you and your sons by then."

"I can start work right away?"

"As soon as tonight, but I understand if you'd rather wait—"

"No, tonight is fine." She needed the money. She needed all the security she could give her sons, and a weekly payday was the best place to start. "I can't thank you enough, Thora."

"You're thanking me? Goodness, I've had the hardest time finding good workers. I will see you tonight at eight o'clock?"

It was done. As the somber shadows stretched across the town streets, Rayna gritted her jaw against the burning pain. Her shoes. She had to find something more practical, and yet, how could she afford it?

Mentally she counted the greenbacks tucked safely in her reticule. Between food and sundries she and the boys had needed through the week, the roll of fifties Kol had always kept in the house was quickly thinning.

As shoppers scurried along the boardwalk, hurrying about their late errands before supper, she lingered outside O'Dell's, the finest clothier in all of Bluebonnet County. The front window displayed the fine wool skirts, lightly gathered and beautifully tailored new fashions for the winter to come.

So beautiful, her fingers itched to stroke the rich fabric. But she had no use for a fancy day dress, and the brushed-leather boots on display were no more sensible than the ones she now wore and out of her means.

The general store near the tracks had the best prices in town. She'd never shopped there, but Betsy did, and Betsy was a widow struggling to provide a living for herself. Yes, that was where she would start.

From now on, she would be practical and pennywise. She'd never managed a budget, but it was a matter of mathematics, right? She'd excelled at mathematics in her school days, and she wanted to keep her sons. Protect them.

No child should grow up little better than a slave. Remembering Daniel's words, she fought back horror. There was no way on this earth she would allow her sons to spend the rest of their childhood years in hard labor.

She'd work her fingers to the bone and herself to death first.

Daniel had forgotten the exact reasons why he'd stopped going to taverns long ago. Maybe he'd needed tonight to remember why he preferred the lonely quiet to the smoky noise and easy pleasures for sale in the bad part of town.

Only the whiskey had been any good, but he'd paid a steep price for the two snifters he'd downed and had left smelling of cheap cigars. The card games held no interest for him, nor did the women parading around in their undergarments—he'd satisfied his curiosity over women, booze and gambling when he was young enough to be so foolish as to waste his hard-earned money.

He was no longer a foolish boy. Never wanted to be like those men spending their money and lives in dark places. It'd been thoughts of Rayna that had driven him there. The pleasant fragrance of her skin, the whisper of her hair falling loose over her shoulders, how big and tall he'd felt next to her dainty feminine softness.

On his way out of town, he rode past rows of houses, their small windows dark and quiet. Folks were tucked in for the night, sleeping while they could before dawn came and with it a hard day of work.

Daniel always wondered about houses like these with tended patches of grass where children played during the daylight hours, watched over by their mothers who cleaned and cooked and sewed. Was it as peaceful at it looked? Or was it just as desolate behind those closed windows and locked doors as the families he'd lived with in the country?

He supposed he'd never know. He just got to thinking about it because of his contact with Rayna. The first day he'd come knocking at her front door, he'd gotten a good glimpse inside that fancy house. Spent enough time with Kirk in the field to see a boy full of dreams and grit and innocence.

The boy had no idea what lurked in the hearts of some men. Kirk had grown strong with his life of love and safety. He'd never known hunger and, Daniel wagered, the slice of a bullwhip on his bare back. And never should.

It wasn't his lookout. He'd learned long ago to take care of himself first, for no one else would. But he'd liked Kol, and he liked Kirk and Hans. And Rayna... Why, there was no denying he found a lot to admire in the woman. And it wasn't only admiration he felt.

That troubled him, too. He was glad when the last row of houses gave way to sprawling fields, fallow and silent, blending with the black horizon and blacker sky.

With the town far behind him now, he took a deep breath. He never felt at ease among so many people. Maybe he'd thought he could lose his problems in the noise and smoke of the tavern tonight, but he'd been wrong.

His troubles were still tangled up in his chest. The rocking gait of his gelding, the puff of wind against his face, the faint sound of a coyote calling and another answering far off across the prairie. The night was alive as an owl swooped by on wide, silent wings, hunting in the fields.

Daniel breathed deep and recognized the heavy clean scent of rain. He braced for it, having left his rain slicker at home, but didn't mind it. He liked the rain and the night, almost as much as he liked the freedom of the wide-open space around him and above him.

Freedom. That's what he'd learned to prize more than anything. So he should put aside thoughts of pampered Rayna Ludgrin and her sons.

He had everything he'd ever wanted. It was more than he'd ever believed he'd actually get. So, why didn't that sit right with him? Why did something inside him tug northward, toward her land, and make him wonder what she was doing now?

It was past midnight. She'd be asleep, that incredible fall of gold hair on her pillow. There would be no plain muslin night rail for her. He'd bet every acre of his land on that.

No, she'd be in a pretty nightgown with flowers printed on the soft fabric. Sleeping in a bedroom big enough to live in, with furniture and frills and comfort.

And if he wondered what it would be like to know the warmth found in her bed and the gentle heat of her touch, why, he was just wondering.

Not wanting.

That was one of his first lessons in life. Never want what you can't have.

He followed the road east, away from her and toward home.

Chapter Eight

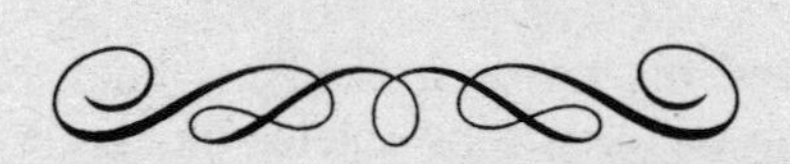

Rayna beat the dawn home. By the time she'd tethered the gelding in the barnyard, the golden rim of the rising sun peered over the eastern edge of the prairie. She raced her shadow to the back steps. Before she could reach for the doorknob, it turned and Hans launched into her skirts.

Without a word, he clung to her, fists full of fabric, shaking with tears.

Her exhaustion vanished. She knelt and pulled him into her arms. Her sweet baby held her tight, his face wet with silent tears. He rocked with soundless sobs.

Kirk closed the stove door on the newly built fire and worry dug harsh lines into his face. "He kept waking up last night, Ma. He wanted you. I tried—"

"I know you did. Thanks, honey." Her Kirk looked as exhausted as she felt. As hurt as Hans, who held her without a sound. His hold so strong it bruised.

She held him more tightly. If he needed holding, then that's what she'd do. Cradling him to her, she straightened, working hard to balance his weight. Her exhausted muscles burned and she panted with the effort it took to cross over to her chair next to the stove.

"You left." Hans sobbed into her neck, his fingers digging into her throat. "You weren't here."

"No, sweet boy. I told you, remember? I had to go into town and work at my new job."

"I don't want you to go. No." Broken, he sobbed harder. His grip intensifying as if he could keep her with him by sheer will, as he hadn't been able to keep his father.

She kissed his brow, stroked his fine, tousled hair. Rocked him until his sobs quieted and he lay calm and spent. His hold on her did not slacken.

Kirk placed a steaming cup of coffee on the table in front of her. "I best get to the morning chores."

Rayna thought to correct him, for now they were her chores to do, but Hans needed her more. She watched with her heart in her throat as Kirk pulled on his barn coat and boots and, just as his father would have done, gathered up the empty milk pails and egg basket and marched out into the morning.

The coffee steamed, and while she watched it cool, she wondered how to make this move easier on her sons. For it wasn't simply a move to a different place, but a change of life, as well. Her cleaning job at the boardinghouse was not enough by far. She would need to find other work to fill her days.

And if she could not get enough cash from the sale of her jewelry, for it was the only thing she had to value that was not encumbered, then Kirk would have to quit school to help earn a living.

Don't think about crossing that bridge yet. She'd keep her attention on the problems she already had. Not go looking for even more worry with problems too far ahead to be able to solve now.

What was she going to do about Hans? He seemed

too young to understand as he clutched her. ''It's going to be all right,'' she whispered in his ear, loving him, just loving him. ''Mama is going to make sure of it.''

''But you went away. And Kirk said that we're gonna have to leave, too.'' Hans gave a final sob, a wavering, vulnerable sound. When he pulled away, pure pain dulled his deep blue eyes. ''How is Pa gonna find us? If we go away, he won't know where to look when he comes back.''

''Oh, baby.'' Her heart shattered all over again. ''Pa isn't coming back. He's going to stay in heaven.''

''No. He's gonna come. I'm gonna be a very, very good boy.''

Determined, as if that would make Kol alive again, Hans climbed off her lap, ignoring her as she tried to catch him. He didn't want to listen. He ran from the room and she didn't know whether to let him go or to bring him back. Which would be better for him?

A movement in the yard drew her attention and kept her from that decision. There, at the back gate, was Clay Dayton on one side of the fence and Kirk at the other. Her oldest seemed to be holding his boot against the gate, effectively keeping it shut as Dayton gestured angrily. What the—?

''Mr. Dayton?'' Rayna hurried down the steps. ''What is the matter?''

''I've come for my cows.'' A stream of tobacco shot through the gaps in the fence to splat on the sodden grass at her feet.

The brown juice mixed with the remnants of last night's rain, darkening the mud on the ground. ''I paid Tom Wright for them last night. Said I'd come over to save him a trip and git 'em myself.''

''Then let Mr. Wright come take them first, like he

did with the horses.'' Kirk's knuckles turned white as he gripped the gate's top board, holding it forcibly closed. ''Ma, I don't trust him.''

''Now ain't that cute?'' Dayton's harsh chuckle was meant to cut deep. ''A boy protecting his mama. Well, step aside, son. I've come to take what's mine.''

Kirk blushed with anger, his jaw snapping tight.

He was still a boy and no match for Dayton's sly ways. Rayna stepped forward, gently nudged her son aside and asked him to go into the house, check on the fire and on his brother. Kirk, looking furious enough to fight, stalked off with enough temper to melt the early snow on the mountain peaks.

Rayna waited until the slam of the screen told her he was safely inside the house before she leveled her neighbor with, what Kol had always called, The Eye. ''I'll thank you to be courteous as long as you are standing on my property. Is that understood?''

''Sweetheart, the land your pretty little feet are standing on will be mine in a matter of days. Then we'll see if you're whistlin' a different tune. Now, I want my cows.''

''Fine, then stay here.'' Rayna whirled away, her exhaustion forgotten. Of course Dayton was striking a deal to buy this land from the bank—before it went to auction. He was the only landowner for miles around that probably had the means to acquire more property after this year's disastrous storm. Why did that make her so mad?

Kol wouldn't have minded. He and Dayton had gotten on well enough as neighbors, but she'd never liked the man. And now...now, it could be her imagination but she felt—she didn't know how she felt alone in his presence. She couldn't remember a time when she'd spoken to Dayton alone. Kol or the boys had always been with her.

She was simply tired. Imagining things, that was all. She'd get a few hours of sleep and then get started with her day. The barn echoed around her as she tugged open the heavy doors.

Sunlight sifted through the cracks in the boards, lighting the way through the hay-strewn path to the stalls. Empty stall after stall, gates open. Just get the halters and give Dayton the animals.

The sooner she handed them over, the easier it would be. And then—

A footfall whispered on the dirt floor behind her. Her neck prickled as she turned. Clay Dayton's long, lanky form made a grotesque shadow at her feet. Then the shadow disappeared entirely as the barn door drew shut.

Blocking her way out.

"I said to wait by the gate." Her voice sounded thin and small, echoing in the rafters overhead. Not at all the way she meant to sound.

Dayton looked amused as he took off his hat. "I don't take no orders from a little woman. Now, it's time you listened to me. And listened good."

"The cows are here." She felt exposed despite the bulk of wool and flannel and muslin that shielded her body. Exposed and alone and...small.

Dayton stalked closer. "You can't do this alone. Look at this place. All your horses are gone. Next it'll be the beef cows in the field. I heard about your job in town—"

"How did you—"

"I've got my ways. I hear things." He spat again, juice puddling on the hard-packed earth between them.

"It's a shame, it is. You're a fine woman, Rayna. Too fine to wear yourself out working the day and night through."

The way Dayton said it, it didn't sound as if he were truly concerned. It sounded as if—

Warning fluttered in her midsection and she grabbed the halters from the nails in the wall. Briskly, she crossed in front of him, focusing hard on the cows watching her silently.

"I'm worried about you." His fingers bit into her upper arm, stopping her.

The flutters in her stomach turned to ice. "I didn't know that it was any of your concern."

"You and your husband have been my neighbors for, what? Over a decade? Kol would want me to keep an eye out for you."

"I'm sure Kol, wherever he is, is grateful." She shook off his grip, surprised he let go, and hurried to the nearest stall.

The ice in her middle began to break apart into sharp, jittery shards. She dropped the halters on the closest stall rail and took off toward the front door.

"They're your animals now," she said over her shoulder. "Take them and please go."

"Whoa, hang on, Rayna." His hurried step slammed after her. "Don't go thinkin' I'm about to take orders from a woman. Just because you had Kol wrapped around your little finger, doesn't mean that you can do that with me."

The jitters turned to fear. She needed away from him and she needed it now. Skidding to a stop, she seized the heavy double door latch and struggled with the two-by-four rod.

Dayton's hand slammed down next to hers, stopping the door. ''Although I might be willin' to help you out—you know what I mean—''

His hot breath shivered against her bare nape. Bile rose in her throat. ''I know what you mean. The answer is no.''

''Now don't be hasty. I know you're upset, what with losin' your man and all. What woman wouldn't be?''

She broke away.

He followed her, stalking her back down the center aisle. The slow grin on his face tugged downward, into a frightening grimace. One that said he intended to get what he wanted. ''You've got to be practical. A woman can't provide for two growing boys. You need a horse. I have an extra team. You need things. I can get them for you. For a price. Let's say, a barter of services.''

''Stay away from me, Mr. Dayton.'' She walked faster. The end doors were locked up as tight as the others had been. There was no way out. Not unless Dayton let her go.

''That's no way to talk to a man with an extra milk cow. A man who's in a position to help you out, if only you'd just be—'' He caught up to her at the other end doors. Laid a possessive hand on her nape and squeezed. ''Friendly. That's all I'm askin', Rayna. That you and I get to be real good *friends.*''

She fought his hold, determined to face him so he could see the mettle of her and that she refused to be afraid. Her morals would not be compromised. She lifted her chin as his hand closed on her throat.

''There's no way out, Rayna. You can't outrun me anyway. You're a weak little woman, and a widow in need of a man. You're such a pretty thing, all sweet and enticing. I bet you know just how to please a man, don't you? With a mouth like yours so plump and seductive—''

She opened her mouth, but she couldn't draw in enough air to answer him. His thumb dug into the base of her throat as she stared at him, unable to believe what he was saying. And yet his tobacco-stained lips descended toward hers, his knee jabbed between hers.

''N-no—''

The heel of his free hand slammed against the side of her jaw. Pain exploded through her teeth and cheekbone and ratcheted through her head. She couldn't drag in air, she couldn't think, all she could see was his darkly glittering eyes and the triumph in them.

He outweighed her by a good hundred pounds. She tried to launch off the door and he laughed, hauling her along the wall, the bumps of her spine colliding with the wood as he dragged her to the corner where she was trapped.

Trapped. She could smell his excitement. Feel the trembling rise and fall of his quick breathing. This couldn't be happening, she couldn't let this happen. She had to stop him, she had to.

But he was too strong. Her head reeled from his blow and blood trickled from inside her mouth. She couldn't swallow, couldn't breathe, her chest swelling up, her vision was swimming, she was vaguely aware of the jangle of a belt buckle loosening—

No! The single word tore through her entire being from the bottom of her soul. Think! She needed a weapon. If she could just reach a little farther along the wall—

Aware of a cool draft on her knees and thighs and the thick taste of panic on her tongue, she tried to think. Betsy's story flashed into her thoughts, but she was off balance. She couldn't shift her weight to get in a good kick to his shin. But she could inch her fingertips along the wall as far as she could reach.

Please, let there be something within my reach. Wait— The smoothness of a leather driving glove collided with her searching fingers. A glove? No good.

She kept searching, stretching nearly as far as her arm could go as she heard the pop of a trouser button ping off the wall and roll along the hard-packed ground.

Please, let there be a hoof pick. Or a currycomb— Her middle finger jammed into something cold. Metal slid beneath her fingernail. She bit her lip, moaning at the pain shooting beneath the quick. She reached again—

"You and I can strike a deal, Rayna." Dayton caught her hand and his grip bruised deep as he twisted her wrist, torquing her arm back against the door. "But if you hit me with that currycomb, then you'll have to pay for it. I'm not going to force you. No, just give you a taste of what's waiting for you out there in the world."

"Stop it, Clay. I want you to leave."

"When I'm good and ready. When you and I come to an understanding. I'll let you keep your house and your pretty things. If you are willing to pay me in rent and in *other* things." He ground closer until she could feel that part of him hard against her hip. "A widow gets lonely in her bed without a man to satisfy her. I'd be helping you out. Your needs satisfied and a roof over your pretty head. Think about it. I'd be real good to you."

Bile bubbled upward. What she would give to have gotten hold of that currycomb. She'd like to whack him where he was most vulnerable and watch him writhe, but with the pain bursting through the ball of her shoulder joint and streaking down her arm, she didn't dare move.

If he broke her arm, then she'd never be able to work for a living. Then she couldn't keep her boys and they'd be made to work for strangers.

"Let me go, Clay."

"We have an arrangement?" He crooked one bushy brow, his gaze raking down her throat to stare at her bosom. His eyes went black. "Say it, Rayna. I'd be good to you."

"This is no way to convince me. You're hurting me."

"Fine." He released her arm, freeing his hand to help himself to the buttons at her collar. His sour breath wheezed in and out of his open mouth, his wad of tobacco visible, as he freed the carved button from the loophole and saw a bit of frothy French lace. "Woowee, you're one fine woman, Rayna—"

"Yeah, that's what Kol always said." She lunged against him and it was enough—just enough—for her fingers to grab a wooden handle. Not the currycomb, but a pitchfork. She swung it with all her might.

"What the hell?" Dayton looked up from working the top tie of her corset.

Just in time to see the wooden handle smack him in the forehead. The impact knocked him off balance. It was enough—just enough—for her to slide out from his weight.

Okay, she was free. But it wasn't enough. The doors were still closed. There was no quick way out.

At least I have a weapon. She adjusted her grip, lower toward the sharp spines, and held it like a sword, ready for a duel. He was a strong man, and she was only a woman, but she was going to make him bleed before he won.

"You're only making it better for me. I appreciate that." Dayton's upper lip curled. He spat out the wad of tobacco. "Let's have fun, Rayna. C'mon. Try it again."

His move was sudden and she swung.

Missed. His hand clamped on the handle and yanked the pitchfork. The wood scraped over her scabs and broke open the healing blisters. She was only distantly aware of the warm stream of blood and the sharp pain. She hung on with everything she had, shifted her weight and kicked as hard as she could.

"Ow! Damn it!" Clay tumbled back, off balance for a second, but it was enough.

She swung the wooden handle, but Clay was quick. He caught the neck of the pitchfork and jerked hard.

Her arm popped and pain blinded her.

Or maybe it was the sun breaking through the opening doors and around the figure of a man like a myth, striding closer. The Stetson shaded his face, but she knew him anyway.

Daniel Lindsay's whiskey-rough baritone boomed with the authority of a hanging judge. "Dayton, leave the woman alone."

The click and roll of a bullet turning in the cylinder of a pistol made Dayton release his hold on the pitchfork. Only then did she see the knife, the blade sharp and serrated, in the older man's hand. He slipped it soundlessly into a sheath at his belt.

Rayna started to shake. She never would have had a fighting chance. He would have… Lord, she couldn't let herself follow that thought. Fear squeezed like a vise and she set down the pitchfork.

"One day you're gonna see what a good thing you turned down." Dayton snarled low, so only she could hear. ‘‘One day you’re gonna be hurtin’, and you’ll come to me. You beware, Lindsay, because it won’t take much to bring you down—’’

‘‘I’m not afraid of you, Dayton.’’ Daniel was there, hauling the man out by the scruff of his neck. Or, more rightly, the back of his collar.

Hefting Dayton off the ground with the strength in one hand. ‘‘Now get goin’ while I’m still in a generous mood.’’

‘‘Those are my milk cows. I paid for ’em last night fair and square. Wright and I shook on it.’’

‘‘Man, you ought to be more concerned about how blue you’re turning.’’ Daniel sounded incredulous as he gave Dayton a toss. The man landed on his knees. ‘‘Get the cows and go. My patience is on a short fuse. I don’t think you want to see my temper blow.’’

‘‘I wasn’t doin’ nuthin’ that she didn’t want.’’ Dayton knew damn well there was little the law could do.

Daniel had learned more about the ineptitude of the law while he’d been growing up than he’d ever wanted to. To his own heartbreak. Rayna wasn’t the first woman he’d seen on her knees, bleeding in front of a threatening man. He knew just how it would pan out with the sheriff.

He blazed with anger, feeling as if it were consuming him while he stood guard over Rayna, his trigger finger ready as Dayton took his sweet time haltering up the nervous cows and leading them, udders full, toward the sun-filled doorway.

‘‘This isn’t over, Lindsay. I don’t reckon you want me for an enemy.’’

Unbowed, the old man had enough cockiness to try to threaten him.

The bastard. ‘‘I’m not scared of you, old man.’’

"You oughta be." Hate filled those words as the man left, but the dank ugliness of what he'd done remained. The barn felt heavy with it.

Or maybe, Daniel figured, that was his emotions. Shards of rage spiked through him as he lowered the Colt, eased the hammer down and holstered the weapon. He stood over her; she was so small at his feet. She crawled to her knees, her hair tangled, breathing as broken as if she were sobbing. But no tears fell.

He hated that she saw the rough behavior he was capable of. Would she look at him with that same revulsion in her eyes as she'd given the old man? Daniel choked on his shame. He supposed a fine lady like Rayna didn't approve of violence, for the good of others or not.

He couldn't look at her as he held out his hands, ready to help her up.

She didn't touch him as she struggled to stand. Her face went white with the effort, and muscles stood out beneath the creamy skin of her jaw and throat. She'd been hurt, and he broke apart inside.

If he hadn't gotten the notion to bring over a pail of milk, figuring her cows were already gone, then he couldn't have saved her. But had he made things better? He'd protected her, but at what cost?

He'd lived with a family for a while, a fine family, and he knew how cultured women felt about rough and base men. He'd been about Kirk's age at the time, too loud, too fierce, too…everything.

There was no way to repair the damage. There was no way she'd trust him now. He still felt like tearing Dayton into pieces and leaving the remains for the vultures to feast on. A man who forced a woman deserved no less.

But the law didn't always see things that way, and neither would genteel Rayna Ludgrin who was as silent as could be as her knees gave out and she sank to the ground.

He didn't know what else to do, but that tangle of emotion was back and it confused everything. He knelt beside her, the little thing that she was, and knew she'd pull away when he set his hand on her elbow.

She didn't. She gazed up at him with big eyes brimming with anger. "Did you hear? He...he thought I *wanted* this. As if it were all a fun game to him."

"I heard."

Grim, he studied her. Blood stained her mouth and red thumbprints marked her throat. At the sight of peeping lace and womanly undergarments from the V of her unbuttoned dress, fierce and blinding violence coursed through him, overtaking him like a river at high flood.

Yeah, he could punch Dayton into the next county and keep on going.

"He never would have dared behave like that when Kol was here." Rayna put her dress to rights, her cheeks flaming. "Is this how it's going to be from now on? Men thinking that I'm missing that particular closeness?"

"Probably."

For the second time since he'd known her, he took the clean, folded handkerchief from his pocket and dabbed her soft lips. Lush and made for kissing, not drawing blood. What was wrong with men like Dayton?

When he was done dabbing at her wound, she gingerly felt her lips, winced when she hit the cut from her front teeth.

Rage squirted anew into his veins and he had to take a deep breath. Be calm. He was a big and rough man, and he didn't ever want to scare her. Make her look up at him with fear.

"You were doing a fine job of defending yourself. You swing a mean pitchfork."

"I only wish I'd been able to hit him harder. I wish—" She looked so tense, as if she were holding herself up from sheer will. Her porcelain complexion was so pale, her skin was nearly gray. She seemed tired and beaten and as if she hadn't got a lick of sleep all night.

There was that tenderness again, drawing up like a fist right in the center of his chest. "Let's get you inside. Get some coffee in you. I'll ride into town and fetch the sheriff. I don't know what good he can do, but it's worth a try."

Rayna nodded, as if in agreement—about the sheriff coming or his ability to do anything, Daniel didn't know. He cradled her elbow and she winced.

"Hurt my arm, I guess."

She didn't look too happy, and he didn't know where to hold her, so he slipped an arm across her slender back and gripped her by the waist. He was big for a man and he knew it, and Rayna felt so delicate as he helped her stand.

There was that tenderness again and that hard punch of heat in his loins. He stepped away before that single urge could go any further. She wasn't his to have and never would be. But for some reason he couldn't figure, he was in her life.

Maybe he could make a difference, he didn't know. "Want me to take a look at that arm?"

"What are you, a rancher, protector and a doctor, too?"

There were sparkles in her eyes, as blue as pictures

of the ocean he'd once seen in a book, and so he knew she wasn't scared of him.

Either that, or she was too fine of a woman to let him know his display of violence had frightened her. "I've done a lot of things in my life."

"Then come inside, have some coffee and I'll let you take a look. And you can tell me why you're here at this time of morning. You didn't come over just to send old man Dayton on his way."

There was hurt when she mentioned that old man's name, and he knew she'd been scared. What happened was no small thing. This is what happened to the weak, without a strong man's protection. Daniel didn't know how to say it. This was the first of many injustices in store for a pretty widow and her boys. He'd lived through most of them. Remembering made him hold her again, supporting her at the waist, although it was her arm that had been hurt and not her leg.

The sound of harnessed workhorses and the rattle of an empty wagon stopped them from stepping into the kitchen. Rayna swung away from him, cradling her arm, hurrying along the wraparound porch to the front.

Daniel drew his Colt. If it was Dayton bringing more trouble, then he was ready.

"Oh, it's Mr. Wright." The only sign of emotion was the slight tremble of Rayna's chin. "He's here already. Come for the furniture. And my piano."

Her heartbreak lifted on the morning winds, an intangible emotion. No outward display of tears or drama. Daniel watched in amazement as she greeted the banker and his hired men, come to move the heavy wooden pieces, and offered them coffee and breakfast first.

Maybe he'd imagined her sadness, he thought. Until she touched his shoulder, drawing his attention.

''Come and eat with us,'' she said.

And he saw it then, the grief in her heart. Like the shadows stretching over the land, long and silent, and it touched him. Not that he was wanting or wishing, but Kol Ludgrin, dead and buried, had to have been the luckiest man in the world.

''I'll ride into town,'' he said, because the last thing he wanted to do was to sit in her kitchen and look at her across the table. ''You'll be all right?''

''I have no other choice.'' She closed off her heart, just like that.

Leaving him to wonder if he'd really seen what he had, and if it was possible to look inside another person like that.

Chapter Nine

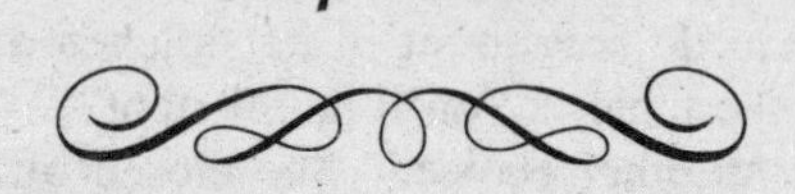

Hans squeezed her hand so tight, her finger bones felt as though they were fusing together. ''How are we gonna know when to leave for school?''

''We will use the kitchen clock to tell the time.''

Rayna turned her back on the movers carefully hauling the beautiful cherrywood and etched-glass grandfather clock out the front door. It was only a bauble and didn't matter in the slightest.

She knelt before her son, who truly mattered, and brushed the huge tears from his cheeks. ''You're not to worry, baby. When you're ready to go back to school, we'll get you there before the first bell.''

''But where are we gonna sit?'' Hans gazed around the empty parlor, his bottom lip trembling.

Her poor little boy. If she could protect him from this change in their circumstances, she would have gladly traded her life for Kol's. He would have known what to do. He would have made sure to have kept the boys' lives as normal as possible by marrying for convenience, providing them with a mother, and, if he had to, would have found work in town or on the railroad for the winter. Other men in this area had done the same.

It was why dear Mariah had married—her husband had been widowed with small children and a big ranch to run and he'd had to have a new wife. It was a cold, practical fact that it took two adults both willing to work hard to survive on the wild Montana prairie.

But it was different for men who'd been widowed. They had the chance to work for good wages. As for her—

She could teach, but she didn't have certification and that would take time she couldn't spare. Kol's brother's solution was simply not an option. She was not about to put her sons to work. She had one job cleaning the boardinghouse, but it wasn't nearly enough. There were no other jobs to be had.

The movers returned. They were courteous as could be. Grateful for the meal she fried up for them. Good thing she still had her chickens. There were plenty enough fresh eggs for everyone. But Mr. Wright had warned her he would be needing her out of the house very soon. She'd move in with Betsy until a room at the boardinghouse came open. And then she didn't know what she'd do.

The kitchen table whisked by her. The men stopped at the door to tip it to get it through the door.

Hans was silent. He said no more as the movers paraded back through the house, their boots echoing loudly in the empty rooms. The chairs were next. Then the bedroom pieces. Hans had grown so pale, she led him outside and sat with him on the back porch. He said nothing as larks darted up to the rose vines to sing. The barn cat came wandering over, looking for company.

She was almost out of good options. Sure, she'd hold out hope that the other letters she'd sent would be answered and a perfect solution would present itself in the form of an able relative willing to take them in. But she wasn't going to count on it.

If you're out there watching over us, Kol. Help us. Show me what I should do.

The leaves overhead rustled, but it was only a gusting of the wind and no answer from heaven. Yet she swore she could almost feel him, just beyond reach and sight, a whisper in her soul that said everything would be all right.

Against all hope, she clung to that thought.

The image of Rayna on the barn floor stuck with him all the way to town—the blood trickling from the corner of her mouth, her throat marked from a man's hand, her bodice torn.

It troubled him when the sheriff said sure, he'd go out and talk to her, but he'd seen this before, widows tempting a man for their own benefit. Even if she was telling the truth, what could be done? It was her word against his, and a man's word carried more weight.

Daniel had called it. He knew nothing would be done to the old man who'd fooled enough folks into thinking him so respectable. It sickened him as he mounted up, the morning air cool with the promise of rain by nightfall. The melody of the school bell tolled from several streets over.

A few schoolboys, big enough to be in the fields, gave a shout and started running, their lunch pails clanging as they charged out of sight.

"Mr. Lindsay?"

He spun his horse around to see Kirk Ludgrin, his books neatly stacked on his slate. "You'd best hurry up or you'll be late."

"I don't care none about bein' tardy. Sir, I was hopin'

you might have need of a field hand. I know you've got a big spread to furrow. You know I work hard, Mr. Lindsay. I could start right now. This morning, if you want."

"Is that so?" Daniel took his time studying the boy. No, a man in all the ways that counted. "Does your ma know you're looking for work?"

"No, sir. I told her I was headin' to school. They took our furniture today. All of it. Next it'll be the house. I can't let that happen to my family."

So straight and honorable. Yeah, he liked this kid. "Go to school, Kirk. You and I will talk later."

"After school gets out?"

"Come over to my place. I'll be in the fields."

"Thanks, sir!" Kirk's relief was as tangible as the dust he made taking off toward the schoolhouse.

Smiling to himself, Daniel reined his mount to a stop at the side street where the schoolyard was in plain view. Children bundled against the cool morning streamed in while the teacher watched from the covered porch, calling in stragglers.

He nosed his gelding around and headed down the street.

At least Hans was finally asleep, tucked beneath his quilt on his mattress on the floor and lost in dreams. Good ones, she hoped as she drew his door closed and avoided the squeaky board in the middle of the hallway on her way down the hall.

It was baking day, they were almost out of bread. But she'd gotten such a late start, there was no point in it now. Not when she had pressing matters in town to see to and her job tonight. Maybe she'd buy a loaf of bread, enough to see them through until tomorrow, for surely tomorrow would be a less turbulent day.

In the parlor, she tapped out the loose rock with her good hand and reached into the space behind it, found the tin and opened it. The noise as loud as thunder in the empty, echoing rooms. It broke her heart to look, so she turned her back to the space of polished wood floors and wide, comfortable window seats and peered into the tin.

One, two tens left. Twenty dollars. That wouldn't get her family far. She stole one of the bills and tucked the tin and rock back into place.

Somehow she'd make this last through the rest of the month. If she was careful and nothing unexpected came up—

Horses? Who would be coming to see her at this hour? She followed the sound of steel-shod hooves and ringing harnesses to the window where she recognized Daniel on horseback trotting up the rutted drive. Behind him was a small black horse and buggy—the doc's buggy.

No, there had to be a mistake. She blinked, but the horse and buggy were still in her driveway, stopped now. Doctor Haskins, his shiny medical bag in hand, climbed down to shake hands with Daniel.

How could he be so presumptuous? She tucked the ten into her skirt pocket, so angry she didn't know where all her rage came from. At Dayton, at Kol, at Daniel.

Men. That's who she was angry with. Men who did what they wanted regardless of how it impacted others. Like her. She wasn't at all sorry she'd thwacked Clay upside the head and she wished she had some weapon of merit—too bad the broom was in the kitchen—because Daniel was way out of line just stepping in as if he had the right to make decisions for her.

She yanked the door open, the wrenching pain in her wrist reminding her she'd have to be gentler with it. But all she saw was Daniel accompanying Doc Haskins up the walkway between her prized rose shrubs, talking like a man who owned the place.

Maybe she was wrong, but it irked the heck out of her.

''Rayna.'' Daniel stood tall and mighty and didn't crack so much as a smile. His hard features were too rugged to be handsome, but when his gaze softened as he studied the arm she was cradling, the fight went out of her.

He didn't have the right to bring the doc here, but he'd meant well by it.

''Daniel. Doc Haskins. Come in.'' She unlatched the screen and stepped back.

''Let me take a look at that arm.'' The doc was a kind man, but she couldn't imagine what this would cost.

Too late now, she gestured to the cushions of the window seat. It was the only place to sit. Every breath, every rustle, every footstep magnified and echoed as the three of them crossed the room. Daniel stood, watching, his hat in his hands, as the doc examined her wrist.

''You might have yourself a bad sprain if you're lucky. Move your fingers for me.'' The doc frowned as he waited for her to comply.

Her fingers didn't move right away. She fought hard to make a fist. Shooting pain screamed through her wrist and radiated out from the palm of her hand, but she didn't make a sound. A sprain was better than a break. She could keep her job with a sprain, but with a broken wrist…

No, her boys were depending on her.

She gritted her teeth, ignored the pain and her fingers obeyed.

''A sprain, then, but you've got to keep this bandaged, Rayna.'' The doc reached into his bag to pull out a thick roll of bandages. ''I don't want you to use this hand for anything but light work. It needs rest to heal.''

''Of course.'' Rayna looked sincere.

Daniel knew she wasn't. He'd seen the wince of pain in her brow and swore he could feel how much she was hurting. But she hadn't said a thing, and chances were she'd be using that wrist as if it hadn't been hurt at all.

A woman who'd lost her husband, her livestock and her furniture and knowing her house was next didn't have time to coddle an injury.

The coffeepot was still on the stove. He lifted the lid—it was still steaming and smelled burned and bitter. Just right.

He searched for a cup in the cupboards and filled it. Sipped long and deep. Stood at the window and studied the best wheat land in Bluebonnet County. Kol had always bragged of it, and Dayton had always commented on it with jealousy.

But it was easy to see—rich fertile land, not a rock in it. Plentiful water come spring, judging by the lay of dry creek beds and the faint glint of a small pond far to the north.

Twice his acreage and the wheat yield from it, hell, he'd seen the thick, tall, healthy crop with his own eyes.

If he'd been able to harvest that wheat, then Rayna would have been able to keep her furniture and her house, and feed her boys for an entire year. Think of what profit Kol had been making every harvest?

This was one fine house, with the best and newest

everything. It had to have been easy accumulating so much debt, knowing full well that a good season would pay it off entirely.

Daniel drained the last of the coffee, grimacing with pleasure at the acrid bitterness. It was a harebrained notion he was considering. He'd been resigned to Dayton snapping up this property, but not after this morning. Dayton didn't deserve this place. He wouldn't appreciate it. He'd wear it down with his carelessness, the way he'd done his own land, and in time, it would produce less wheat.

And he'd wear down Rayna the same way.

She didn't accept it yet, but a woman couldn't support her family. It just wasn't possible. Wages for a woman's work weren't high enough. He could hear her telling the doc how she had a job now, cleaning at a boardinghouse in town.

Sure, she could juggle two jobs for a spell, but Daniel had grown up with plenty of children whose mothers had thought the same thing. Then worked themselves to death or close enough.

It took one injury, one sickness, one lost job, and she and her sons would be out on the street. The boys would be free labor for whoever agreed to take them on, and Rayna, she'd be alone and dead inside without her sons.

Yeah, he'd seen that, too. Mothers who worked even harder after losing their children and never being able to get them back. Life was hard and it was unfair.

He poured the last of the coffee into his cup, waiting while Rayna exchanged pleasantries with the doctor, brushing off his concern and seeing him to the door. He started sweating a little when he heard the tap of her gentle gait ring closer until it stopped behind him. He was aware of the swish of her skirts, the cadence of her movements, the way she sighed, sounding frustrated, when he didn't turn right away to face her.

"You paid the doctor." It came as an accusation, not shrewish and harsh, but more powerful for the mild way she said it. "I'm sure you meant well, but you've done enough for Kol. Consider your favors paid in full. He's gone and not concerned with whatever you feel you owe him for helping you long ago. And I'm perfectly capable of taking care of myself."

"Doesn't look that way to me."

"I don't care how it looks. I'm just fine on my own."

Spoken like a woman who had never seen the life he'd been forced to live. Dark, cruel images he shoved from his mind. She was like those fancy roses in her yard, ordered from England or wherever something so delicate and expensive would come from. Not suited at all for this harsh land.

Just looking at her made that tangle in his chest hurt as though he'd broke every rib. No wonder Kol had accumulated such debt.

A good man would do anything, risk anything, for her happiness. It even got him to thinking…

No, she'd say no if he said anything. Judging by the way she was looking at him, she didn't think too much of him right now.

"I heard you tell the doc you've got a job. Will you be able to work with that wrist?"

"I don't see how it's any of your business." She held her head up high, as if the bandage thick on her wrist and hand didn't exist.

Pride, he guessed. And it had to be all that was holding her up. "You might have fooled Haskins, but not me. You broke that wrist, didn't you?"

"You're wrong."

It was the way she flurried about, anxious to straighten up the counter that was wiped clean and had only the empty egg basket to be put away. That told him he was right and that he might have a chance after all.

More sweat dampened his palms as he waited for her to return from the pantry, where she took her sweet time dispensing of the egg basket. Giving him the chance to calm down, gaze outside and look at all that good land.

Hell, he might as well go ahead and tell her. "I talked to the bank this morning. Went over Wright's head. Talked to his boss, one of the owners of the bank."

Her movements in the pantry froze. "Did they happen to tell you for sure how long I have to move the rest of our things?"

"No, ma'am. But I did explain how well I've been doing on my own land. I might have lost this year's crop, but I've been wise with my money. Banking it instead of buying a fancy harvester and newfangled sewing machine for my wife."

That did it. She marched into the kitchen. "Kol may not have been the best at handling money, but he was a wonderful husband. You'll not insult his memory in front of me."

Daniel's brow drew into deep frown lines as he pivoted from the window to study her, as if seeing her for the first time. "I didn't mean to sound disrespectful. I only meant to say I'm getting by all right, even losing this year's harvest."

"Oh." She didn't know what she was going to do with all these emotions running wild inside her.

What she needed was sleep and peace from worry, and she knew that wasn't going to happen any time soon.

Either way, Daniel Lindsay didn't belong in her

kitchen or think he would get away with paying for the doc's visit. She yanked the ten from her pocket and slapped it on the windowsill beside him.

There. "Consider that a down payment. I still owe you another five. I'll get that to you before day's end."

"I'm not expecting you to reimburse me."

"Then what do you want?"

"I don't want Dayton to get this land. I don't want him being in any position to hurt you like that again." He straightened his shoulders, the movement making him look even bigger. Infinitely dependable.

But he fumbled as he rolled his hat around in his fingers, a nervous gesture. "Dayton isn't willing to pay more than this land is worth. You know with the failed crop, ranchland in the county has fallen. This property isn't worth what it was, but if I put my homestead up for collateral against this loan, then the bank will let me take over the payments."

"What?" She couldn't have heard him right. She sank into the window seat's soft cushions, her mind spinning. "But I thought you said they wouldn't. I mean—"

What if by some miracle the bank had had a change of heart? If Daniel could take over this place, then maybe she had a chance to stay here, with the boys. She could rent from Daniel and the boys wouldn't have to move. She'd still have to work two jobs, but they could keep their lives as normal as possible. Maybe in time she could think about finding a father for them. Maybe even Daniel—

No, not Daniel, she thought, remembering his stinging words, watching his deliberate movements as he took his time laying aside his hat.

"The bank said the account has to be made current

by the next payment or they'll repossess, and there's a catch.'' He knelt in front of her. He looked so grim that she knew it couldn't be good news. ''We have to marry.''

''No. It's too soon, and I know I can do this. I already have a job and—''

''Rayna.'' His broad hand covered hers and engulfed it. There was pain in his eyes. ''You have to admit it. You have a broken wrist. How can you work scrubbing floors for a living? That injury is only going to get worse.''

''It's a sprain.''

''The other relatives didn't answer you, did they? And they aren't going to. No one wants to take on the burden of providing for a woman and boys who aren't their own. I've seen it. Women who work themselves into ill health, or death, desperate to keep their families together. I've seen it, and I don't want that to happen to you.''

He didn't know where the tenderness came from, but it was there, oddly taking root in his heart. She was going to be his woman, his wife, and what in tarnation did he know about taking care of a woman like her?

Not one thing, but he brushed the hair out of her eyes. Lord, it was the softest thing he'd ever felt, and caught a single teardrop on the pad of his thumb.

''You know I'm right.'' He said the words kindly, because he meant them that way, and he hated seeing her so defeated. ''This is our one chance. For me to buy more land and for you to give your boys a good life. They can stay here and go to school and grow up with their mother home to take care of them.''

She shook her head, more tears falling. ''I even thought about marrying again. That's what Nick Gray down the road did. He married my dear friend Mariah not three weeks after his first wife's death. He had little children and—''

''It's an arrangement, that's all.'' What else could it be? Daniel wished he knew what to do with a woman in tears, but he didn't. Still, he had a strange urge to pull her to his chest, to hold her so she felt safe.

Because that was how he would keep her: safe from this world. ''You'll think about it?''

''I don't see how I can.'' She moved away, and it was too late to pull her close, too late to protect her as she made up her mind. ''Marriage is so important. It ought to be about love. Real love. The kind that you can hold on to even when you feel like you're losing everything else.''

She didn't want him. That stung, but he ought to have expected it. Deep down, he had to admit he never thought she'd accept.

But it *was* too bad she hadn't. It would have been nice to live in a dream like this. A fine house, good boys as his stepsons, and Rayna with that smile of hers that was like the only light in a dark place.

It wasn't meant to be, I guess. He grabbed his hat and there was nothing left to say to the woman standing in the threshold, gazing through the pink mesh screen to the acres of ruined fields.

''Your boys are lucky to have you for a mother. One who loves them so much.''

He saw himself out. His gelding was waiting for him, as if sensing how anxious he was to get the hell away from here. So he wasted no time mounting up.

The squeak of the door stopped him and made him pull the horse around. There Rayna was, coming after him. She went as far as the porch would allow.

When her good hand gripped the railing, her knuckles were white with strain.

''I'll marry you,'' she said as if it were the saddest thing that had happened to her yet.

Chapter Ten

The week had passed quickly and Rayna was grateful her wrist was improving—slow, but sure. She pulled the pot of beans from the oven, wincing when pain streaked through her bandaged wrist, but it took two hands to balance the heavy clay pot. It took two hands to heft the roaster brimming with a quarter of beef from the rack.

Hot grease popped and sizzled on the browned roast as she eased the heavy pan to rest on a trivet.

Her left fingers felt numb and swollen. That couldn't be a good sign, and she still had a night of work ahead of her. For she intended to work. There was little money, and Daniel's finances would be stretched taking over the payments on the land and house.

The boys needed winter things, they needed furniture, they just *needed.*

With a sigh she drained the kettle of potatoes. Daniel had brought the roast over with him when he'd brought Kirk by after school, waited for the boy to change into his work clothes and disappeared with him as they'd been doing all week.

Daniel hadn't said much as he handed over the wrapped meat. Only that he'd spoken to the town minister, who could marry them tomorrow at ten. She only nodded because she couldn't bring herself to say anything else. This stranger was to be her husband.

No, that didn't feel possible. Kol was her husband still, in her heart.

She rubbed her wedding ring as the potatoes steamed in their pot. She so loved the beautiful gold band crowned with rubies and pearls that had to have cost Kol a fortune. But he'd said on the day he'd slipped the ring on her finger that she was of more value. As he was to her.

The potatoes, Rayna.

Remembering where she was, she startled into action. Found the masher and the butter. Measured out some of the milk Daniel had brought over this morning and went to work. Pummeling the potatoes at least gave her an outlet for her emotions.

Sadder than she knew how to measure, she dumped the whipped potatoes into a serving bowl, stuck it in the warmer and went to work on the gravy.

There was a clatter out front. Hans, sitting quiet on the window seat, launched onto his feet and stomped through the house. She measured flour and stirred, scraping the droppings from the bottom of the roaster as she went. Careful to keep the flour from lumping, she listened, expecting Kirk to come through the door.

Instead there was a *thunk* as the doorknob smacked into the wall and Hans's excited shout. Muffled male voices resounded in the parlor and then suddenly there was Daniel backing through the door, shouldering something heavy.

"Tip it a little more. Are you okay, Kirk?"

"Yep," came the energetic answer.

There was a scrape and a simple pine table appeared,

followed by Kirk holding up the other end. ''Look, Ma! Mr. Lindsay said he'd give us his table.''

''It's not like ours.'' Hans rubbed the flat of his hand along the wooden top. So serious.

''It's a thoughtful gesture. Thank you, Daniel.'' Rayna was surprised her voice could sound so normal when that was the last thing she felt. Having a different man in this house was going to take a lot of getting used to. ''Hans, run over to the linen drawer, would you, sweetie? And get a cloth for the table.''

''It's not round.'' Deeply troubled by this change, Hans sidled off, watching as the table was lowered into position in front of the window.

Dusk was coming, leaching light from the sky. It felt as if it were draining from inside her, too. *This is the best decision for my boys.* She repeated that thought as Daniel and Kirk left the room and kept repeating it until the gravy was thick and fragrant in the pan.

By the time she'd poured it into a bowl and dug a ladle from the drawer, she was ready to take the cloth from Hans and spread it over the smaller square tabletop.

''See? I told ya.'' Hans shook his head, his hands planted on his hips, the way Kol always did when he had to give something serious thought. ''It's not right.''

''No, but we'll make do.'' She folded the cloth in the middle, pleating it so the circle of fabric draped all four corners and nothing was left to touch the floor or get caught up in little boy shoes. ''Oh, the chairs.''

Kirk turned sideways, carrying a sturdy ladder-back chair in either hand, and slid them into place at the table. ''Mr. Lindsay made these. Can you believe it?''

''It doesn't surprise me.'' She ran her fingertips over

the top rung of the chair back. The pine was smooth as glass.

What skill. Daniel did seem like the kind of man who could do anything well. The furniture looked very fine indeed in her kitchen. Her woods were a little darker, but that didn't matter.

Already, look at the change he'd made.

"Ma, can I ask you something?" Kirk lowered his voice, leaning close to keep his voice from carrying. Like the young man of good character he was, he made sure his brother, who was climbing up on a chair, couldn't hear. "Are you and Mr. Lindsay gonna get married?"

Hearing the words was like a punch to her middle. It was one thing to know what was to come, but hearing it out loud made it seem real. Tangible.

Irrevocable.

"He was gracious enough to propose, as a way to help us out."

"I figure that's up to me, Ma." He squared his wide but still coltish shoulders. "It's my job to take care of you and Hans. I know what you said about school, but that's before Pa died. It's time for me to buck up."

"No. You need to finish school."

"But Mr. Lindsay's paying me to help in his fields on the way home from school! And I talked to Mr. Halloway at the station and he said—"

"The railroad? No. Absolutely not. Over my dead body will you work laying track and blasting up mountains for a train tunnel—"

"Ma. It pays a lot of money! We could stay right here, we wouldn't have to move. And you wouldn't have to work with your hurt arm scrubbing floors for some business in town—"

"I said no." A sprained wrist or a broken one didn't matter. Keeping her sons in school and Kirk away from dangerous work was everything. "We'll discuss this after supper."

"But, Ma—"

"You heard me." She used her firmest voice, and Kirk hung his head, mouth compressed, as if he were muttering to himself but knew better than to say it.

He was a good boy, ready to take on adult responsibility for her and Hans, but he didn't know what backbreaking work was, fourteen-hour days swinging a pickax. And he would never know. Thanks to Daniel.

Daniel. Who would be her husband by this time tomorrow, and she couldn't begin to let that truth into her heart.

He stopped by her side, holding two chairs as if they weighed nothing, and to him they probably did.

He gathered his breath, as if figuring out what he had to say first, before he spoke. "Kirk had a lot of questions, but I didn't tell him what happened in the barn this morning. Or what we agreed to do, you and I. I'll do it if you want, but it's your call."

She couldn't speak. Some men would have seen it as their right to act already as if they owned the place and had the right to make decisions for her. But not Daniel. He was a mighty, authoritative man, anyone could see it. It was in the way he moved, straight and noble as a soldier facing battle even in small things, setting the last chairs up to the table.

He'd make a fine husband, she was sure, for there was kindness in him.

"That roast sure smells good." He meant to compliment her.

He couldn't know that's what Kol always did, too.

Kol had always loved her cooking too much and had had the extra inches around his belly to show for it. Struggling to keep the grief from reopening like a wound, she grabbed up the carving knife and meat fork before he could slice the roast, as Kol had always insisted.

With relief she sank the sharp blade through the steaming hank of beef and sawed one slice after another. Feeling Daniel behind her watching. He stood there for what seemed a great while before the pad of his boots told her he'd retreated to the table. His low voice was a mumble as he tried speaking with Hans, who didn't answer him.

Then came the familiar clink of plates and silverware. Kirk, she guessed, helping out. What a fine son she had in him, always responsible and helpful. After supper was over and Daniel left, she'd have to sit down and talk with her oldest. Tell him of the plans to marry and how he would not be working on the railroad north.

When she'd cut plenty of meat for the males in the house, she hefted the platter with both hands, ignoring the stab of pain in her wrist, and nearly dropped the meat. Daniel, not Kirk, was the one setting the table. The plates were down, the cups to match, and the flatware on the wrong sides of the place setting.

As he distributed the folded napkins like a poker dealer, he caught her looking at him. His smile wasn't wide and infectious, or brash and jaunty. His came slowly, quietly, with only an upturning at the corners of his mouth. It was his eyes that changed, that glowed with a brightness she'd never seen in him. A single glint in his shadowed gaze that made her stumble.

With unsteady hands she set the platter beside him on the table.

* * *

''Sleep tight, baby.'' She kissed Hans's brow, his soft hair tickling her nose. He looked so sweet, sleepiness making his eyelids heavy.

Those long, curled lashes, which any girl would envy, framed his big blue eyes. Kol's eyes. Although she was in danger of running late, she tucked the covers under his chin, savoring this last moment with him.

''Daniel stayed for supper. I don't want him to do it again.'' His bow-shaped mouth broke wide with a gigantic yawn. ''I want Papa.''

''I know you do.'' She brushed his head with her hand, stroking tenderly, for it was the only comfort she could offer him. ''Close your eyes.''

Those lashes flickered as he struggled to stay awake.

''That's it.'' Soothing, she began humming her favorite lullaby, the one her mother had always sung to her.

She waited until his eyelashes drifted shut and his breathing fell into a peaceful rhythm before she eased from his bed, careful not to disturb him.

At the doorway, she paused, making sure that he still slept. He seemed to be, so she pulled the door closed and turned the knob slowly so there would be no click.

Kirk was across the hall in his room, lamplight shining on his slate and open mathematics book. He sat with his hands folded, studiously calculating a problem.

She didn't want to disturb him, but there was no choice. ''I'll be leaving for town now.''

''Oh, Ma.'' Startled out of his concentration, Kirk put down the stylus and pushed away from his slate. ''You can't go tonight. Your arm—''

''It's almost healed, so don't you worry. I will be fine.'' She loved her oldest boy all the more for his concern. Pride glowed inside her, brighter than any lamp, bigger than the sun. "I have many things I need to tell you, but I keep putting it off, and now there's no time."

"I think Daniel's still here. He said he was going out to the barn. Why? Is he gonna rent the place from us or some such? Does that mean we get to stay?"

"We're staying." She was out of time, running late, and there was no other way than to just say it baldly. "Daniel has agreed to marry me."

Kirk recoiled as if she'd reached out and slapped him. "You just can't up and get married. What about Pa?"

She couldn't find the words to answer him. He was too young to understand what depth of love she felt for Kol, how it was still alive in her heart, just as her need for him was.

How did she explain that she could remarry as if Kol were so easy to replace? That she had to do what was best for him and Hans no matter what it cost her. Even if it was to marry in name only. To bind herself to a man she did not love. Never would love.

Never could.

But she didn't know what to say. Daniel deserved her respect and Kirk's. "You have to realize what a good opportunity Mr. Lindsay is offering us."

"You should have let me go to work." Anger ground in Kirk's jaw and he turned his back on her. "There's no way Pa would want some other guy to come in like he never even existed."

"This is exactly what your father would have done, if I had died. He would have found a dependable woman to marry, so you boys would be taken care of."

"I'm man enough to take care of this family."

She'd broken Kirk's heart, and there was no way to

fix it. ''I know you can, but I want more for you. We can talk more tomorrow.''

''When is this going to happen?''

''Tomorrow.''

Kirk said nothing. He held himself stone-still, his back to her, his bitterness like a ghost in the air.

A bitterness that wrapped around her soul and stayed there, like a bitter frost, as she hurried down the stairs, glanced at the clock—twenty-eight minutes to eight—and grabbed her warmest coat.

The night air had enough bite in it to make her eyes tear as she dashed down the stone path, slick with the start of frost. She'd have to ride bareback; she didn't have time to saddle up. A single glow of light from the cavern of the barn told her that Kirk had been right.

Daniel was still here and probably making plans to move his things into the barn tomorrow. They hadn't even discussed the most basic aspect of this arrangement. Where would he sleep? Or would he want one of the boy's rooms and Hans and Kirk would need to share?

There was a lot left to be settled between them. She wished she could tell herself it would work out, but she didn't know. Daniel was more of a stranger than a husband should be. Thinking about what tomorrow would bring… No, she couldn't do it.

One step at a time. That would be the best way to go about this. And pray she wasn't making the worst mistake possible. Not all marriages turned out well. She'd seen that sad fact with her own eyes. Every time she saw Blanche Dayton, for example. The woman's haunting sadness had made Rayna grateful for her life and her husband.

It's just the worries that came hand in hand with a

hasty marriage. That's all. The moment Daniel came into sight, from where he'd been busy in the tack room, she could plainly see the man he was. The man who'd bandaged her hands when her palms were nothing but open blisters. The man who'd pulled his revolver and protected her. The man who'd given her his table so her sons would have a comfortable place to eat.

"Are you heading off to work?"

"I'm going to be late as it is." It was the only apology she could offer him. He may be taking over her property, but she had her own responsibilities. "I don't have any time to hear you tell me not to go."

"Then I won't." He held out his hand, his palm up. "Come. I have my wagon hitched to take you to town."

"I'm going to ride on my own."

"No. Not with how Dayton treated you today. He won't be the only one. I'm not your husband yet. I can't tell you what to do. But, Rayna, I don't ever want anyone to hurt you. I'd like to make sure of it, starting now."

Kindness. It wasn't what she was expecting. She laid her hand on his. His touch was firm, almost fierce. He was not what she was used to. Nor was his silence as he helped her into his wagon and followed her up.

He didn't seem to be a man of many words. That would be a change in her life, for Kol was one to talk and talk and talk. As the horses gained speed on the road to town, Daniel's silence remained. There were so many things she had to say to him, but beneath a starless sky, she lost her courage.

It didn't really matter whether he would sleep in the barn or the house. If he was the kind of man who believed he would make all the decisions and handle all the money.

Or, as he'd said in the barn, the type of husband who would tell her what to do.

Daniel was kind and he was honest and he was hard-working. She didn't believe she could find a better solution for her boys or a greater man to watch over them.

As twilight gave way to the endless shadows of night, the world seemed capable of such cruelty, or, more accurately, the men in this world. What if Daniel was right? What if Dayton wasn't the only one of her neighbors who thought she was a widow in need of "comforting"?

She felt safe beside Daniel on the seat. His words came back to her, in regards to his proposal. *It's an arrangement, that's all.* It wasn't as if it would be a real marriage. It wasn't as if Daniel Lindsay could ever replace Kol. Not in any of the ways that mattered.

Daniel halted his team in front of Thora's boardinghouse. The gentleman he was, he climbed out first and helped her down with one easy lift, as if she hadn't weighed more than the chairs he'd brought into her kitchen.

"What time will you be through?"

"Around three this morning, Thora said."

"I'll be waiting right here." His single nod emphasized his promise. "You take care with that wrist."

"I will."

"I don't know how to say this, so here it goes." He swept off his hat, looking oddly vulnerable in the darkest of the night's shadows. "It's not an easy thing, risking my hard-earned land. But just so you know. I think you're worth it. That if I can keep you and your sons from the kind of hardship I've known, then I guess that makes my life mean something."

She watched him go, in her view, taller than ever.

Watched as he gathered the reins and clucked to his horses. Waited until the straight shadow of him on the wagon seat disappeared into the night and distance.

Only then did her heart start beating again.

When Daniel pulled up to the Ludgrin house, he saw only one light on. He figured it must be the older boy. He'd been left in charge, no doubt, while Rayna worked in town. It was getting late, past ten, for a school night. Maybe Kirk stayed up past this hour all the time. What did Daniel know about this sort of white-picket-fence life?

Work. That's what he knew. And that's what had kept him busy and there was more ahead of him before he would lie down to sleep.

The heavy wagon groaned as it bounced and jostled down the rutted lane to the barn. Daniel's skin itched. He glanced around, wondering who was watching him. The light from the second-story window remained unchanged, and the curtain covering the glass still. It could be Kirk, but Daniel doubted it.

Either way, he made sure his Colt was ready to draw.

The barn seemed filled with loneliness. A gray striped cat came to study him with eyes that flashed in the dark. Daniel said howdy to the creature and began unloading the wagon bed. It was too late to bring over the cow, already bedded down for the night. Or to move the feed and stacks of hay. That could be done when the more pressing work was finished.

It was with contentment he took his time putting up the saddles and the extra yokes and harnesses. It sure was a nice setup in the tack room. Easy to use, easy to store, a big open place for him to clean and repair the rigging come winter.

It was hard to believe that come tomorrow morning, this would all be his. He'd be giving up too much of his freedom, that didn't make him comfortable. But if he worked hard—and he would—he should be fine.

"Mr. Lindsay?" It was Kirk's voice sounding uncertain in the shadows by the open door.

"Come on back." He hefted down the first of the furniture he'd brought and leaned the headboard against the inside wall. "I suppose your ma told you what we plan to do."

"Yes, sir." The boy lingered in the aisle, safely out of reach of the lantern light.

He must have something on his mind, and that was an important thing. Daniel left the wagon bed half full to join the boy in the shadows. Although it was cold, near to freezing outside, he was overwarm from work.

He took advantage of the pump, which was nearby, and splashed cold water over his face. Then filled the dipper and drank deep. That gave him time to think of what he'd say, but it was Kirk who spoke first.

"I appreciate what you've agreed to take on an' all. But this is my family. Not your lookout." Kirk cleared his throat, for his voice was wavering although he stood unbowed in the dark. "You don't need to marry my ma. I can take care of my ma and my brother. I'm man enough to do it."

The boy's message was clear. He didn't want his father replaced so soon.

There was no way around that. Or, was there?

Chapter Eleven

Daniel took his time answering. He might know near to nothing about reading and ciphering, but he knew what it was like to be a man too young, as Kirk was forced to be now. And the remembering hurt like an old wound. Daniel dropped the dipper into the bucket, the pump spout was dripping—he'd fix that as soon as he could—and took his spot near Kirk.

He leaned up against the wall, considering what to say. "I know you're man enough to look after your brother and your ma. You're a hard worker. I've seen it myself. You could do fine going off to—what was it you were fixing on doing?"

"The north line of the railroad's hiring."

"Right." Daniel considered that. "You're strong enough and responsible enough to hold down that job, and that's a tough job. Long, hard days sweatin' in the sun without a break or freezin' in the winter without a fire nearby. Sleeping in a tent. Every Sunday off, but there's no point in coming home for a day. Not when you start at five sharp Monday morning."

Kirk swallowed. "They pay well."

"That they do. I can't argue with you about that. I admire what you want to take on, Kirk."

"Then you don't gotta marry Ma. We can find a place in town, and not a room neither, but a house. We'll do all right."

"Yep. But consider this. Who's here to take care of your ma? What if she should run into some trouble? You won't be here to help her out. You're old enough to know what happened to her in the barn this morning."

"She had an argument with Mr. Dayton. I was to keep my little brother from seeing the cows being taken, but I should have been—" He made a choked, angry sound. "If I'd been there, he wouldn't have pushed her down."

"Is that what she told you?"

Kirk grew silent. "No, sir. She said she hurt it using the pitchfork, but I don't think that's the truth."

Was Kirk so untouched by the ugliness of this world he couldn't imagine what had happened to his mother? "No. You're a man now, Kirk. You've got to know there are plenty of men who take what advantage they can. They don't have to be evil men, or bad men, sometimes just desperate or in a bad pinch. They need money or the feeling of power that comes from hurting someone weaker.

"If you take that job, then there'll be no one to keep your ma safe. She's a widow. Folks have their opinions about women without a man to protect them. There are some who will take advantage."

In the shadows, Kirk's head bowed forward. He had to be thinking this through. He had to come to his own conclusions; Daniel wasn't going to try to be a father to the boy. There was no way he could—one good thing he learned in his growing-up years.

"Have you considered that if I marry your ma, then

she doesn't have to work so hard? She can keep her house, the one that's got to mean a lot to her. I intend to get a job through the winter, so there will be money enough to keep your ma and your brother warm and fed and healthy."

"You sure have this all thought out. Begging your pardon, but we all loved Pa."

"I can't give you all the fine things your father did, but I promise you this. I'll work hard. I'll be fair. I'll treat your ma right. That will be a far sight better for her, I think. But your opinion matters to me. Tell me what you think."

Kirk dragged a hand through his hair. He was troubled. But he'd listened. He had to be at least considering the larger view.

"Ma wrote to my uncle, Pa's brother. He'll help us. I know he will."

So Rayna hadn't told him? Daniel wasn't sure it was his place, but the boy had to know how lucky he was to have had the parents he did. "Do you know what I was doing when I was fourteen?"

No answer.

"I worked every day in the cotton fields."

"Your pa was a cotton farmer?"

"Nope. I was an orphan. I was hired out to whoever would take me, and that year it was a man by the name of Nolan. He owned a lot of land, and he took on boys like me to work his fields, to plant and tend and harvest his crop. My hands were blistered from handling a hoe from dawn until night, and then they were torn raw from picking cotton. Did you know it grows on shrubs, sorta like rosebushes, with thorns that are sharp. Whew. I still have the scars."

"What happened to your folks?"

"I don't know. They fell sick, I guess. I was just a baby and no one cared, to tell the truth. Mr. Nolan wasn't a good man, and that's a year and a half of my life I try every day to forget. You don't want to go work in your uncle's fields just to earn enough bread to eat by the end of the day. I'm not saying your uncle is like some of the men I've worked for, but you might want to give this pause. There isn't a better place out there, Kirk, than what you have right here."

"My uncle wanted me to work in his fields?"

"He did. I saw the letter. He'd found work for Hans, too."

"Oh." As if shocked, the boy fell quiet again for a spell. "Pa always said that a good man treats a woman real fine. He wouldn't want Ma working day and night. He wouldn't want me leaving her and Hans alone, if I got that job."

Daniel waited for the rest to come. He was comfortable with silence while Kirk mulled things over. He was a patient man. He breathed in the dark night. Scented the coming frost and the promise of rain by morning. Heard the hush of an owl's wings glide past the open doors. The rustle of hay as the horses bedded down.

Finally, Kirk had his own answer. "If you marry Ma, then you have to treat her good. You can't ever h-hurt her."

"I've never hurt a woman in my life and I don't plan to. Besides, I happen to share your pa's opinion. A woman deserves a man's respect, especially his wife. Think we can take good care of her, between the two of us?"

"I s'pose so. You need help unloading that wagon?"

"I'm almost done. It's late. You've got school tomorrow?"

"And a mathematics exam." As if that were a terrible fate, the boy headed off, stopping to pet the cat that slinked out of a stall. A few minutes later, the whap of a screen door told him Kirk was safely inside the house.

Wasn't that something, a mathematics exam? Daniel didn't know what all that might involve, but it was good for a man to have education. He'd signed papers he couldn't read at the bank today. There would be more papers tomorrow before this land would be officially his. And every penny of the mortgage.

Hell, he hated debt. Still, it was worth it.

He worked late into the night. Until fog gathered in the cool air and settled into his joints. The prairie was soundless as he headed home. The endless draws and knolls of the high prairie were hidden by mist and darkness. Not unlike a man's future. Or a past he'd rather not think about.

As they always did in this weather, his arm and wrist began to ache like a bad tooth. Dampness settled into his bones as he rode one of the Clydesdales bareback home.

He'd brought up the past tonight, and he felt numb from the experience. Numb, deep inside, where a man's true feelings hid. Like the fog cloaking the prairie, that's the way he wanted those memories. It hadn't been easy to talk about them tonight. Lord knew he never wanted to remember them again.

As if by luck, the fog thickened and hid the road ahead of him.

Grateful for the obscurity, he rode on.

"Ma?" Kirk's whisper in the dark hallway was rusty with sleepiness. "Is that you? You're home safe?"

Rayna hated that sound of worry in her son's voice.

"Of course I am. Daniel made sure of that. Why aren't you sound asleep?"

"I guess I was just sorta listening for you."

She could make out the shadow of her son, leaning against the doorjamb. Too grown up to want to accept the hug of comfort she wanted to give him. Kirk had been terribly close to his father. Was he having bad dreams, too?

Not that he'd tell her if he did. "Did Hans wake up at all?"

"No. He didn't even have one nightmare that I could tell."

Thank goodness for that. It was her hope that things would be easier for Hans from here on out. "Good night, then."

"Ma?" His voice squeaked with emotion and he cleared his throat, his voice still in the process of changing. When he spoke, he sounded so very like his father. "Daniel told me about what our uncle did. Saying he'd found work for Hans and me."

"Oh. I thought that you were better off not knowing that."

"Nah. Daniel said that's how he grew up. Workin' for his keep. He was an orphan."

So it's true, that's how he knew. She remembered the afternoon she'd received the brother's letter. *It's a common fate,* he'd said. And how he wanted to spare her and her boys the hardship he'd known.

Oh, Daniel. She'd wondered what hardships he'd endured as a boy, while she'd soaped and scrubbed sheets on a washboard. And couldn't bear to think that he might have known about children working like servants long hours for their evening food because he'd been one of those children. It was unthinkable. And yet, she could see how easily it could happen.

How her children had come close to a similar fate.

Kirk yawned, apparently having said what he'd needed to. "I've got an exam in the morning. G'night."

"Night." Rayna listened to her son's door click shut. So, Kirk had had second thoughts about working on the railroad.

Good. Grateful for that small miracle, she eased Hans's door open, saw his motionless form cuddled beneath his covers. His breath came with the slow, relaxed cadence of a deep sleep.

Another good thing to be grateful for.

She eased the door closed, tiptoed the few steps down the hall. Now it was her turn to sleep, for however few hours she could manage it. You'd think with how tired she was, she'd be able to drift right off.

But no. She could feel the tension coiled so tight within her, she could barely move her neck enough to see to light the crystal lamp.

That done, the small pool of light spilled across the bed she'd made up on the floor. At least the feather tick felt almost as comfortable as it had on a bed frame. Her weary bones seemed to sigh when she eased onto the side of the mattress.

Sitting up, her knees bent, she could just reach her shoes. She unbuttoned and loosened the lacing, pulled them off and rubbed her aching arches. That felt good.

With a sigh, she glanced about the room. There was no moon to shimmer through the curtains, and it was just as well, for it would only shine into emptiness, save for her feather tick and personal items on the floor.

Already her life had changed dramatically and Kol had hardly been gone from their lives at all.

If she closed her eyes, she could still feel him in memory. Imagine the way he filled up a room with his hearty, jovial presence. The scent of his tobacco—

She'd always been after him not to smoke that blasted pipe in the house. The warm love that had simply filled the air between them and shone like a light in the deepest places of her heart.

Kol, wherever you are, I miss you.

There was no answer of course. Just the stillness of the house. The rustle as she changed into her flannel nightgown and climbed beneath the covers. She tucked the edges of the sheets and blankets over the top edge of the quilt.

She'd made the double wedding ring while Kol had been courting her.

Oh, what good memories those were. She'd been so young then, what a funny girl she'd been, worrying about pin curling her hair so it would fall in ringlets around her face and working Saturdays sewing for the tailor in town to earn material for new dresses.

She recalled how she and her mama had spent endless hours of an evening sewing and crocheting and embroidering pretty things for her hope chest. How she'd light up with excitement and sheer adoration whenever she saw Kol.

They'd been young and in love and, oh, how wonderful that time had been. This quilt was the last thing she'd made for her hope chest, with Mama's help. They'd sewed and pieced and pinned the entire thing so it would be ready for her wedding night.

Drops tapped on her pillow, one after another. Just thinking of him made her relax. Of how he'd take her home from school each night, for he'd graduated the year before. How he would buy her butterscotch, her favorite, and serenade her with that horrible singing voice of his until they were both laughing and in each other's arms.

Could he forgive her for what she was about to do?

Troubled, she lay awake until shadows came into the room, letting her know that dawn was on its way.

Daniel was well awake before dawn broke on the eastern sky. Long streaks of rain clouds gathered overhead, their brooding underbellies painted purple and orange by the light. If he hustled, then he'd be able to get the livestock moved before it was time to take Rayna to town.

To get married. Now there was something he didn't figure he'd ever do. Not at this time in his life.

When he'd been younger, sure. He'd always thought to meet a nice lady, maybe he'd like the look of her or the way she talked or just something that would let him know she'd be a fine wife.

But that had proved damn near impossible, seeing as how young women weren't nearly as plentiful as men looking to be married in this rugged territory. Not that he'd know how to go about courtin' anyhow.

Since he'd been content enough by himself, it hadn't mattered so much. After sixteen years of overcrowded orphanages in the winters and boiling hot attics packed full of other boys, who were field workers, too, and not enough beds, of chaos and heartbreak and violence best not remembered, he rather liked the quiet.

It was a luxury, having all this space to himself. The cabin wasn't big, but it was roomy in his opinion. And with acres of his very own land spread out around him, why, he was grateful for that. Grateful every day.

It would be a change, living with other people after

so much time by himself. Two boys and a woman. Hell, he knew next to nothing about women, let alone a pampered, dainty beauty like Rayna. Theirs wasn't to be a marriage based on love, but then he'd seen enough marriages growing up, in the households where he'd stayed, to know a bad marriage was its own brand of hell.

He figured he and Rayna wouldn't have problems like that. They'd get along all right. He had Kirk on his side. As for the little one, why, there was time enough to make friends with him.

The back of his neck was itchy again. Uncomfortable, he glanced around. The fields were newly plowed, all but the back acreage, and a fresh footprint would have given him warning enough. But there were no footprints he could see save his own.

No, whoever was keeping watch on him wasn't anywhere close. In rifle range? Folks were hurting in this part of the country. The past few growing seasons had been busts for most of the ranchers. That brought out all kinds of behavior, including those who'd steal to feed their young ones.

He unsnapped the Colt, leaving it holstered for now. He went about his work but stayed vigilant—just in case. The feeling dogged him through the hour it took to toss feed bags into the back of the wagon and to hitch up his workhorses. He wasn't imagining it, for the big black was unsettled, too, ears pricked as he nervously scented the cool wind.

By the time he'd finished milking his cow and led her out of the barn, the black's flanks were twitching.

Trouble. And it was getting closer. Daniel took his time knotting up the cow's lead rope to the tailgate. Looking for something, anything, out of ordinary.

He secured the top of the pail and stored the milk

beneath the seat, listening to the stretching stillness. Not a single lark was singing.

A predator, maybe? That was usually the first problem, for it seemed man could try to settle and tame this wild rolling prairie, but this was a stubborn land. Too spirited to give in docilely to fences and crops and claim shanties. And that meant wolves, bears and big cats, but this time of year?

Probably not, but he took his extra rifle from above the barn door, just in case. A Winchester repeater could stop a cougar better than a .45.

He could feel whatever it was out there—predator or human—watching. Waiting.

Let 'em, Daniel thought as he leaned the cold metal barrel against his shoulder, the butt cradled in his palm for fast action. He was ready if trouble came his way. He might be a target on the wagon seat, but he had a good view.

Taking the reins in one hand, his rifle against his shoulder, hand on the stock, he scanned the frost-crusted furrows where he'd been turning sod and the fields beyond.

Nothing. The back of his neck went back to normal. The big black calmed, although his ears remained up and alert. As the road rolled to the bridge over the creek and beyond, Daniel watched as his land crept out of sight and with it the sense of danger.

A coyote, startled by the clap of steeled hooves on the wood bridge, darted out of the undergrowth. A brown streak that had Daniel taking aim, but that scavenger wasn't the problem. A predator was. And human, most likely. That brought a whole other nest of problems.

He laid the Winchester on the floorboards at his feet, where he could grab it if he needed to.

The road curved and he followed the fork left, where the first corner post marked the border of the Ludgrin property—*his* property. He had to get used to that. When he'd brought his old harvester over that first day to cut Rayna's wheat, he'd wanted the chance to work this land so bad, it had made the meat in his bones ache.

It sure was a dream to think that a man who'd started with nothing but the clothes on his back and the willingness to work hard could own all this. He had Rayna to thank for that. By agreeing to marry him. He was more grateful than there were words to say.

This good turn she'd given him was something he was committed to repaying for the rest of his life.

A weak sun speared through the clouds when he drove up the last rise, crowning the gray two-story house, one of the finest in the county. The windows winked and it struck him hard. That was about to be his home. The real thing. Not a claim shanty he'd built, no fancier than any of the thousands cast about the vast Montana prairie.

A real home. With a porch made for sitting on come a fine summer evening.

He'd never had one of those before.

After he settled the cow in a stall and unloaded the feed sacks and supplies, it was a good feeling that filled him as he brought the bucket up the path through the back lawn. Smoke from the stovepipe and the glow of a lamp in the kitchen window told him Rayna was up. She couldn't have gotten much sleep, and already she was at work.

His boots sounded loud on the board steps, and she must have heard him because there she was in the window. Her hair down, falling over her bosom to her waist, long golden ribbons of it, so soft it made his fingers twitch. He knew how soft her hair was, for he'd brushed soft wisps out of her eyes. His heart twisted hard in his chest.

"Morning." He swept off his hat and lifted the bucket for her to see at the same time.

As dark as those circles were beneath her eyes, her smile came as bright as he'd ever seen it. "You are a wonder, Daniel. I saw you from the window earlier. You brought us your cow."

"She'll be yours, too, in a few more hours."

Tension pinched the corners of her eyes. "Come in and warm up at the stove. I've got coffee ready."

"That would be mighty fine."

The words seemed to stick in his throat and come out ragged, but Rayna didn't seem to notice. She returned to the stove as he closed the door behind him, hung his hat and his coat on the handy wall pegs.

Making himself at home, maybe too much so, for the way Rayna looked at him with sorrow in her gaze.

Briskly, she went back to work flipping salt pork that sizzled and popped in a hot pan. He swore he could feel Kol's memory like a ghost in the corner and wondered if Kol had been in the habit of hanging his things in the same place. Probably. Daniel made a vow to try something different next time.

"Here." She tugged a chair from the table, the one closest to the stove.

Before he could take a step to get a cup of coffee, she was already pouring one. She set it on the table, as if doing so was of little concern.

He could only stare at the cup of coffee. It steamed in the cooler air, and he gripped the back of the chair.

Out of the corner of his eye he could see Rayna stop to wipe her hand on her apron and then crack an egg on the side of the big black fry pan.

Wasn't that something? He sat, hardly feeling the heat from the stove at his back as he took a sip of that coffee.

"How many can you eat?"

"Uh." He'd never been treated like this in his life. "Is four too many?"

"As long as you can eat them." Her soft words were an attempt at kindness.

He couldn't think it was easy for her to go from cooking up breakfast for her husband one morning and practically the next day frying up eggs for a second one.

It didn't strike him until that moment, sipping good coffee and chasing out the early morning chill from his bones, what he was getting into.

It was more than the land he wanted. More than the responsibility he was willing to take on and shoulder. It was having a life in this kitchen with a pretty, good-hearted woman.

"More coffee?" she asked, setting an extra cup on the table for herself and filling his first.

She'd been this kind when he'd eaten supper here, as a guest. But this morning he was no guest. And during supper, she hadn't served him.

I'm going to be so good to you, Rayna. Daniel's soul strengthened with that vow. Nothing on this earth would make him break it.

"Thank you," he said to her.

"You're welcome."

She stirred sugar into her coffee and, as if it were nothing remarkable at all, returned to the stove to flip his eggs.

But it was special to him.

Chapter Twelve

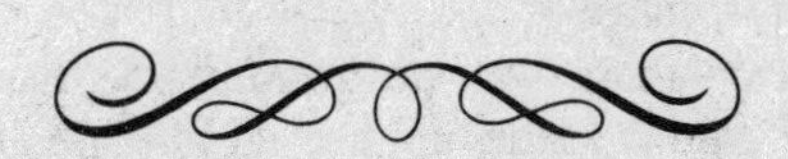

It was hard to know what to wear. Rayna went through her closet again. So many pretty dresses for spring, any one of them would be nice. Hopeful. But she kept drifting back to the black worsted. Black was a color more suited to her mood. This wedding felt like a loss.

She chose her navy-blue wool, for it was tailored so beautifully. The mother-of-pearl buttons glowed like hope against the dark fabric, so there was a chance it would lighten her mood. As she slipped into the fabric and fit her arms into the narrow sleeves, she saw for a brief flash of memory another wedding day.

When she, Mariah and Betsy, so young and giggly, were bouncing with excitement. She'd been the first of them to marry, with secret oaths sworn the night before when her friends had stayed over, to tell them in great detail what the wedding night was really like.

And when she told them, two days later in the tiny kitchen at the tiny table of the little house Kol had rented in town, none of them could believe her that *that* could really be wonderful. How embarrassed she'd been and how hard they had laughed when she'd drawn detailed pictures on her school slate to demonstrate what happened between a man and wife. How hard they'd laughed!

Oh, goodness, the wedding night. She hadn't given any thought to the practical aspect of this marriage to Daniel. There was the bed, made up neat and cozy on the floor. Her double wedding ring quilt looking so light and cheerful. Would he expect to join her there tonight? To sleep? Or, more?

Either way, there was no going back. Daniel was a good man. She'd made up her mind. She intended to marry him in less than forty minutes. This time, there would be no excited preparations.

She could almost hear the past, the memory was so vivid and cherished of the three of them so lighthearted and gay as only the young can be. Fussing over shoes and petticoats and getting the last details just right. Something old, new, borrowed and blue.

The breathless gasp when she fit into the gown Mama had sewn for her, stitched with a mother's love and hope for her daughter's life to come.

What would Mama think of this loveless marriage? Rayna's fingers stilled at her throat. She remembered Mama's words to her as they were climbing out of the buggy at the church. *Remember my words to you, my daughter. From this day on, this man is your life. Love him above yourself always. Honor him in all you do. Never take for granted the great gift of a good man's love.*

Rayna fastened the top button and tucked the lace collar smooth over it. If Mama were alive, she'd never understand this. Or would she? Mama had died when Kirk was small. She'd said how lucky Rayna was at the time, a precious child, a doting husband, and a happy and cozy home. Mama would have understood a mother's duty. There was a lot to admire in Daniel Lindsay.

Her wrist ached as she used both hands to secure the string of pearls at her throat. Her grandmother's pearls, grown richly hued and radiant with time. Something old. Her dress was blue. She'd wear her poke bonnet, that was new. As for something borrowed...she went across the hall to Hans's room and fingered through his wooden bowl of stones and things. She chose his favorite rock, a small multicolored pebble with a fragment of fool's gold in it.

Fool's gold or not, it was one of Hans's most prized possessions. She slipped it into her pocket for safekeeping. There. She was ready, and a few minutes early, too. She made a quick trip into her closet to grab her bonnet.

As she was tying it on, careful to pin it just right, which was hard to tell in the small hand mirror, she noticed the glint of gold on her hand.

Her wedding ring. It was still on her finger. A circle of gold without end, as love should be.

"Rayna?" Daniel's baritone called from downstairs.

She hadn't heard him pull up. Hadn't heard him come in. "One moment. I'll be right down."

"I'm a few minutes late myself, so we need to get goin'."

"All right." She twisted the ring up over her knuckle. Tucked it into the small jewel box. It felt as if she were leaving her heart behind her, as if she'd somehow been able to rip it out of her body along with the ring.

Empty, she hurried down the hall, took the stairs at a brisk pace and rushed into the parlor where she heard Daniel's boots echoing in the large room.

The man who was to be her husband was gazing out the front window, broad hands fisted at his hips, emphasizing the long line of his shoulders. This was the man who had protected her from Dayton's unspeakable behavior and who would protect her sons from a merciless world when she could not.

He turned and slow appreciation softened his stony features. "You look mighty fine."

"So do you. I've only seen you in your work clothes."

"I don't figure I'll get married but this once. I might as well wear my Sunday best for the event." He looked self-conscious, but he didn't need to be. He was a fine-looking man, but it was him she was grateful for as he opened the door to hold it for her. "Ready?"

She nodded, because she didn't trust her voice. There was no excited anticipation, only simple politeness as he helped her up into the wagon and settled beside her on the seat.

It was a cruel wind blowing as the horses headed toward town. With any luck the rain would hold off until after the ceremony.

A fine mist wept from the sky as Daniel helped Rayna from the wagon. "Looks like we beat the storm."

"The question is, would you still be willing to marry me if I was dripping like a wet dog?"

"Even then, I'd reckon you would still be lovely." He'd said too much. Clamping his jaw tight, he held the door for her. It was hard to believe a woman like her was going to be his wife. An arrangement, sure, but his wife all the same. "You're shaking."

"It's the cold." The lie was in her eyes, and the apology, too.

He wondered how much sleep she'd been able to get. Not much by the look of those rings even darker beneath her eyes. Her heart-shaped face was devoid of all coloring. She glanced toward the empty pulpit and the long row of empty pews, and whatever was on her mind, she didn't share with him.

"This is it. Your last chance to change your mind."

She had the kindest eyes he'd ever seen. They looked at him now as if she were seeing him for the first time, taking his measure. Maybe, finding him wanting? He sure hoped not.

"No, I'm certain." Her fingers tightened around his.

Even though all he held was her hand, it felt as if he were holding more. Her heart, her future, her sons' happiness. It weighed on him mightily. "You didn't ask your friends to come?"

"No. When I married Kol, this church was crowded. Folks were standing in the back. It was a joyful time, for he and I were celebrating our love. Vowing our hearts to one another. I was young, not yet seventeen. I was a girl."

"I know this wedding is not about joy."

"No, but it is about something important. It's about a greater joy. My sons." A brilliance, more lustrous than the string of pearls at her collar, lit her up. "You said that if you can save me and my boys from knowing the hardship you have, that your life will mean something."

"That's what I said."

"I can't begin to imagine the hardship you've known. But I'll do my best for you every day. So whatever hardship is ahead, you're not alone with it. A load is never as heavy when two people share it."

That tangle in his chest shattered, leaving only sharp, cutting pieces. He couldn't speak. There was no way he could trust his voice. As rain tapped in a lazy cadence on the roof, it felt like pieces of his heart. It was something, having a woman at his side. This woman.

The minister peered into the sanctuary. He didn't know the man, but the Reverend Phillips seemed to know Rayna. His eyes lit up with what could only be concern.

"Dear Rayna, I've been meaning to get out your way since the funeral, but I've been busy with all the trouble that comes in these hard times. How are you faring? I suppose your ranch was hard hit, as well?"

"The entire crop was lost."

"Sad, it is. Families losing their land all across the county. I am pleased that you'll be staying." The reverend cast his gaze on Daniel and nodded slowly. "Mr. Lindsay, you couldn't be gaining a better wife."

A better wife? Rayna felt the minister's words like burning arrows to her soul. In her heart, she could not be a wife to Daniel, not the way she'd been to Kol. "I would say I'm getting the better bargain gaining Daniel for my husband."

She felt Daniel's gaze like a question in the air. She never wanted him to know what this was costing her. How with each breath she took, it felt like a part of her died a little more. The wind lashed as if in protest at the eaves, spattering rain against the dulled hue of the stained-glass windows.

Reverend Phillips, who'd been ever so good friends with Kol, cleared his throat. There was apology in his kind brown eyes as he laid his Bible on the plain wooden pulpit. "Shall I begin?"

At her side, Daniel nodded. He'd never let go of her hand, and because the sanctuary was so chilled, they were still in their coats. The vacancy of the long rows of empty benches felt as if it were the innermost part of her. Void of any life as the good man at her side vowed to love and honor her, his voice rough and ragged, until death parted them.

"Rayna Amelia Ludgrin." Reverend Phillips's words were spoken with compassion, as if he were sad, too. "Do you take this man..."

Her left hand felt curiously light. The place where Kol's ring used to be tingled. It was not a betrayal, but it felt that way, to turn her back on the love still alive in her heart, to close it up like a box and store it away in a dark place. She had new vows to make. "I do."

And she would. She'd honor and cherish the man at her side with everything she had. Including her broken heart.

To her surprise, Daniel produced a ring from his shirt pocket. A slim band of gold. Simple and plain. The right ring for this practical wedding.

Her hand was stone-steady as she watched him slide the band on her finger. The faint echoes of memory, from so long ago, when she'd stood in this exact place bursting with love and joy and hope, made her eyes burn.

Not for loss, she realized. But with gratitude.

Heaven had granted her a beautiful life with Kol. One she'd always suspected that was rare in this world. The chance to love and to live with her soul mate. Give birth to his sons and to live day and night in the soft luxury of his love.

She saw now, as Daniel brushed the tears from her cheeks, how lucky she'd been. Few had the chance to love as she'd been loved. And now, for whatever reasons, providence had put this man in her life. A man who'd never known his family. Who, she guessed, had always been alone. It was not sadness she felt or sorrow at the memories that echoed in her mind. It was understanding.

This man at her side was her husband now. As he leaned close and brushed a soft kiss on her cheek, she swore she could feel Kol, wherever he was, approving.

It was pride that glowed hot in Daniel's chest as he helped her down from the wagon. The gold ring caught his attention. His wife. That hard tangle of emotions that hurt in his chest had only become worse. He didn't know why, but he suspected it had to do with how he felt about her. And not just pride.

Tenderness tugged inside him as he held the door of the bank for her. That tenderness grew as she swept past him, sweet smelling, like spring flowers, and so female. Her dress was pretty on her, a modest dark blue, but it hugged her in all the right places. He wasn't particularly pleased with the hot lick of desire that was troubling him.

"Mr. Lindsay. Rayna." Wright came out from behind a messy desk, obviously busy at work. "I have your papers ready here. I assume you two have married?"

"Just came from the church." He laid a protective hand on Rayna's shoulder. Or, if he was honest with himself, possessive.

The banker got the hint. He stopped in midstride and nodded. "Then, please, come sit. We'll get right to work."

"I appreciate it." It was a lot he was about to take on, but as he held out a chair for Rayna, waiting for her to sit before he settled into the chair at her side, he was dead sure. He'd work twice as hard, that was all.

"Please read and sign these." Mr. Wright pushed a pile of pages across his polished desk.

He couldn't read. There was no shame he felt in it. He'd never had the chance to go to school. He nudged the papers toward Rayna. "Would you?"

Her somber gaze met his. She nodded once. If a small part of him feared she might think less of him for his ignorance, it didn't show. And that part of him relaxed as she bent to the task of reading the words, the soft golden locks of her hair curling against her cheek.

The tenderness inside him bloomed in full.

Finally she reached the last page and nodded. "There's nothing out of the ordinary."

Good. He took the ink-dipped pen Wright handed him and scratched his X on the line Rayna had pointed out to him. It was done. He handed the pen back. If he felt a little shaky over signing over his freedom to the bank, one look at Rayna calmed him.

Her words in the church came back to him. *Whatever hardship is ahead, you're not alone with it.*

It was the first time in his life he wasn't alone. He reached out to take her hand, and the gentle pressure of her palm to his reassured him. She was no dream. He was more awake than he'd ever been.

He held the door for her. Walked on the street side of the boardwalk to protect her from the cold, blowing rain. Gave her his slicker to keep her dry as they drove home.

Home. There was a word with a new meaning. He'd first thought his cabin so fine. It was all his. Four walls and a tight roof. No drafty boardinghouse rooms, where he'd lived while he'd worked in the fields, following the crops, to earn enough money to homestead. He'd been mighty grateful for the humble dwelling that was clean and safe and dry. The first place he'd called home.

But as the lightning flashed, leading him around the

last bend of the road, home took on a whole new meaning. While he was no fool, he knew Rayna didn't love him. But they had respect and a mutual goal. That was enough in his mind. And what she'd said to him made all the difference.

He stopped the horses as close to the porch as he could before climbing down to help Rayna out. The ring he'd placed on her finger caught his eye. No small amount of feeling filled him. He had a *family.*

His wife led the way through the cool house, her gait tired as she slipped out of his slicker and handed it back to him. "You'll need this, I imagine."

He took it. "I noticed the wood boxes are low. I'll fill 'em before I go."

"That would be a boon. I've got to get baking done today. I didn't want to stop at the bakery and pay for what I could do myself. Want me to put on a pot of coffee before you head out?"

"That would be mighty fine," he answered on his way to the back door.

Politeness. It seemed a strange way for a newly married couple to act. Rayna supposed it would always be this way. For what warmth could a loveless marriage have?

She stoked the embers in the cookstove, adding kindling and the last of the cut wood in the box, and leaving it to burn while she hurried upstairs. As she unbuttoned her dress, she heard the back door open. The clatter of wood tumbling into the box rang through the floorboards.

Although she wore her undergarments and petticoats, she felt exposed. How was she going to face tonight, if this was how she felt in broad daylight with Daniel at the other end of the house? She tried to imagine what it would be like to have him in this room while she wore nothing but a nightgown. She hurried into a calico work dress as the door closed downstairs and she was once more alone.

She pulled back the curtains. There he was, leading the horses to the barn. He handled them well, and the animals seemed to trust him. The big black Clydesdale rubbing his poll against Daniel's shoulder in affection.

She had work to do, and no time to dwell on regrets and losses. The ring on her hand felt uncomfortable, only because she wasn't used to that band. Or maybe it was her heart refusing to accept this new man in Kol's place. But duty was duty, and so she went downstairs to boil a fresh pot of coffee for the man who'd put his ring on her finger.

When she went to check the fire, she was surprised to see Daniel had added enough wood so that she wouldn't have to. The fire blazed merrily, but the heat couldn't chase the chill from her bones.

Careful of her wrist, she spooned coffee beans into the hand mill and ground them up fine. A knock at the back door startled her, and she was half expecting Betsy or Mariah, but it was Daniel, hefting the head- and footboards of a bedstead.

She opened the door, since his hands were full.

"I thought it was best to get my things moved," he said on his way through the kitchen. "I mean to rent my cabin. Might as well. It'll help make ends meet."

That answered her unspoken question. He would be sleeping here tonight. In her room. With her.

She returned to her putting the coffee on, hardly aware of what she was doing. Her entire awareness was focused on the sounds from overhead. Daniel's progress down the hall. The thud of the pieces of the bed being lowered to the floor. Daniel's progress back down the stairs.

Rayna set the pot on the stove to boil and put away the mill. She was carrying the flour canister from the pantry when he strode into the kitchen, filling it with his presence. He said nothing on his way out the door. In truth, what was there to say?

She got to work, setting out the pans, the cooling racks, the rolling pin and batter bowls. Daniel returned, this time able to open the door himself, with a hank of rope and side rails made of rough wood.

By the time she'd greased and floured all six pans, Daniel had returned and she poured him a cup of coffee.

"I'll take this with me," he said on his way to the door. The final click seemed to echo through the warm, yeasty-smelling room, and in the empty places in her heart.

Was this how it was to be? Endless silences and polite exchanges. Work and duty and that was all?

She didn't know what she expected. In truth, she hadn't thought too much about what followed the wedding. *Daniel is a fine man, you're lucky to have him.*

Lucky, yes, but her heart just kept dying a little more.

The knock on the back door wasn't Daniel's this time. She recognized that happy rap even before she spotted Betsy's smiling face in the window and opened the door.

"I have your laundry!" Her dear friend burst into the room like a tornado, arms full of stuffed pillowcases, which she dropped on the window seat. "You were on my afternoon schedule, but I was driving the other way at the turn in the road and I thought, it's silly, I've been thinking about you and missing you. Oh! I've caught you in the middle of baking."

"If you have time to stay, the coffee's fresh. As long as you don't mind me mixing dough while we talk."

"Me? I'd take any chance I can to sit and visit with you. I'll get my own cup, you just go about with your baking."

Like sunshine on this rainy day, Betsy seemed to light up the kitchen as she hung her coat on the back of a chair on her way to the pantry. "I saw a grandfather clock just like yours in Horner's front window and I had this horrible feeling it was yours. Tell me, whose wagon is out front?"

"You're not going to believe what I've done." Rayna leveled a cup of flour and shook it into the bowl.

"Your wedding ring. It's gone. It's different." Betsy stood slack-jawed with the china sugar dish clutched in both hands. "Rayna, what did you do?"

"It's best for the boys." She took a steadying breath and set down the cup measure. "Daniel Lindsay and I were married this morning."

"*Married? Why didn't you tell me before this?* I could have stood up with you. I could have planned a party. Does Mariah know? Of course she doesn't, or she would have told me when I stopped by this morning. What do you think you're doing, getting married without telling us?"

"It's an arrangement, that's all. It's so soon, I'm still walking into a room and part of me is expecting Kol to still be here. And now there's another man in his place."

"Good. I can't tell you how worried I have been for you, my dear friend. Daniel Lindsay. I can't say I know him well at all, but my impressions of him are nice." She rolled her eyes in womanly appreciation. "That's his table?"

"And his bedstead upstairs."

"Oh. I have a bright side to this. Believe me, I know what grief is. I know what it takes to get over a man you love. But, Rayna, you will not have to go through this very lonely period of being unmarried and, well, there are certain benefits to having a husband in your bed."

"Betsy Louise Hunter! I can't believe you said that!" Mortified, Rayna blushed and quickly went back to measuring cups of flour.

"What? You always laughed and joked with me about that."

"I didn't have a stranger as a husband then. Mercy, what am I going to do? There's no way, I mean—"

"Daniel is your rightful husband. I know it has to be a burden being married to that fine specimen of a man, but one day you'll be comfortable enough with him to want, well, *you know.*" She waggled her brows suggestively. No one could be both serious and humorous quite the way that Betsy could.

"I'm *so* glad you came by." Abandoning her work, Rayna wrapped her oldest friend in a hug. "How about you? Do you have your eye on any possible candidates?"

"For husband material? Well, there's the blacksmith, Zeke, but I don't know. He's nice, but he just doesn't make my blood warm. And since the storm, half the eligible men in town have gone bankrupt. Signed over their property to the bank or the land office and are packing up. Pickings are getting slim. Besides that, I've lost half my clients."

"You were having a hard enough time as it was."

"It's going to be a long winter, but I'm determined to remain optimistic. You can never tell when good fortune is right around the corner. For both of us.'' Betsy's look was one of empathy.

Just then the door flew open and there was Daniel, manhandling a chest currently missing the drawers. His mumbled, "'Scuse me,'' was aimed in their general direction. He hauled the piece of furniture on past them and his labored gait knelled as he progressed upstairs.

''He's just darn handsome. I don't think I've ever gotten a good look at him.'' Whispering as she went, Betsy closed the door against the wind-driven rain. ''Those shoulders. I just love a man with wide, dependable shoulders.''

''Betsy, stop trying to cheer me up.''

''Honestly, look at this wonderful silver lining! Open your eyes. Gosh. Wait until I tell Mariah how bashful you've suddenly become!''

''Betsy!'' It was a warning, for Daniel's steps were returning.

''He's that strong, silent type of man. I don't know, but I think it's the quiet ones that make the best lovers.''

''Betsy!'' Rayna felt her cheeks flame as Daniel lumbered through the doorway, the tips of his ears pink. If he'd heard what Betsy said, then she'd make Betsy pay.

''You might want to go upstairs and see if that chest of drawers is where you want it.'' He kept his gaze on the floor ahead of him as he went back out into the cold and rain.

''Yep, I stand by my assessment.'' Looking far too pleased with herself, Betsy poured a cup of coffee. ''And don't look so mortified. Goodness, if he did hear me, so what? I just gave him something to really think about.''

''Daniel and I don't need that kind of help.'' Trying to stop blushing, Rayna wiped her floury hands on a dish towel. ‘‘Come upstairs with me, if you can behave yourself. I think you’re right. You’ve gone too long without a husband.’’

‘‘It’s bad for a woman. It’s like starvation. The longer you go, the better food looks.’’

‘‘I feel better now, you can stop trying to make me laugh.’’ In truth, she didn’t think she could handle any more thoughts about the night to come.

Daniel hadn’t told her what he expected from her, and she felt more as if she were walking in the dark, just feeling her way along.

Chapter Thirteen

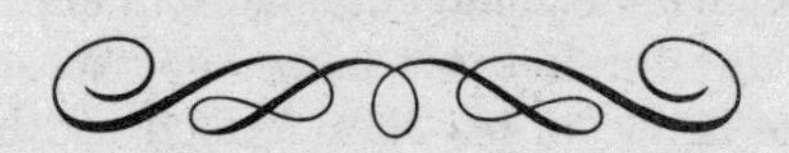

Daniel braced his feet, planted his fists on his hips and studied the drawers stacked on the barn floor. He wanted to get this furniture moved so he could bring over a load of hay and get it stacked before he ran out of daylight. He'd gotten a job in town shoveling coal at the depot.

He should be thinking about all he had yet to do to get squared away before starting work, but that woman in Rayna's kitchen had derailed him. He'd heard what she'd said about him. *He's that strong, silent type of man. I don't know, but I think it's the quiet ones that make the best lovers.*

The worst part was that Rayna hadn't agreed. Otherwise, he might have liked being thought of as strong and silent. But it was the thought of being intimate that had made his wife scandalized.

There's my answer. He figured a lady like Rayna would need time. He was no fool. He knew the only reason she married him had nothing at all to do with him. She didn't love him. Hell, she might not even like him. She would have married any decent man who had made her the same offer.

Since there was no point in standing around debating

about it, he grabbed the stacked drawers, pinching his thumb in the process, and carried them up to the house. As he started up the pathway across the back lawn, he could just make out Rayna in the bedroom window. The lustrous cloud of her hair piled up on her head. The graceful line of her profile, her perfect nose and dainty chin. The willowy way she moved.

That's my wife. Daniel still couldn't believe it. As he made his way through his home, up the stairs to his woman, the tangle in his chest, which had been coiled and knotted up every time he looked at her, unraveled. Like a spool of fishing line with a fighting salmon hooked and playing out. He felt the tug on his heart like a hook sinking deep.

A practical marriage or not, she was his wife. His family.

This time when he came within hearing range, the women's talk was about some ladies' meeting in town. They fell silent as he entered the room, and he felt Rayna's steady presence the way the earth felt sunlight.

"Daniel, do you know Betsy Hunter?" Rayna asked as he lowered the stack of drawers to the floor.

"Howdy." He began sliding the drawers in place.

"This is lovely wood." Even though her friend was there, Rayna's attention turned to him. She stroked the pad of her forefinger along the beveled cover of the chest. "Thank you."

The emotions in his chest kept on unraveling. It was her. She was making him feel this way.

Behind her was the bedstead he'd set up in the same place her other bed had been. He'd roped up the stays and set up the mattress. The dainty quilt on top, colorfully stitched circles interlocked looked strange. He was used to the army blanket on top, not something so frilly.

But it was something he could get used to.

He paused at the threshold. "I'll bring over a few more pieces tomorrow. I only use one of the drawers, so I guess that makes the rest of them yours."

"And I have enough things to fill them, too."

"Good." With a brusque nod in Betsy's direction, he left without another word.

"He's not much of a talker, is he?" Betsy said after the downstairs door rattled shut.

"No. He's certainly a change around here." Rayna's throat closed up. Why did the past feel so far away? The room was the same, the curtains and quilt the same, but she…she was different now, too.

She ran her fingers over the pink calico wedding ring, sewn so long ago. All her dreams for her life had been stitched along with the thread. Dreams that had come true.

She folded the quilt carefully in two. Then halved it again, until it was a small neat rectangle that she gathered up in her arms and held to her heart.

"Oh, Rayna." Understanding broke in Betsy's voice. Her hand settled on Rayna's shoulder and stayed. "I have an extra quilt at home. I could lend it to you."

"No, thanks. Maybe I'll piece another quilt. I've been wanting to start a new one."

The bed looked better without the marriage quilt on it. A simple bed, made of white muslin sheets and a dark brown wool blanket. To match the plain headboard. Yes, that's what she'd do with the long winter evenings ahead. She'd piece a new covering for this marriage bed.

On the way down the hall, she stopped at the linen closet and hid the quilt away on the top shelf. It felt as if she were stowing what remained of her heart there, too.

* * *

The street that led past the feed store to the school was jammed full of wagons, buggies and surreys, and moving like molasses. Parents come to take their kids home. Cold rain splashed down by the buckets, and he shivered inside his rain slicker. He didn't like the feel of the wind. There'd be snow by morning. He had a lot of work to do before then.

The front doors of the two-story schoolhouse flew open. Hell, he was late. He'd spent more time at the sheriff's office than he figured. It had been his third visit, since Dayton's attack on Rayna, but the sheriff was new to Montana Territory and to the West. He wasn't bothered by a distraught widow's accusations. It didn't seem to count that Daniel had seen him trying to hurt Rayna.

Hell, it probably made it worse. The lawman only saw two men fighting over a beautiful widow with valuable land—and both men wanting the property *and* the woman. Rage licked at his soul as he took a deep breath to calm himself.

That was why Rayna wasn't fetching her sons from school. He didn't want her alone by herself. When he was hitching up and pulling over the cover, Nick Gray's wife, Mariah, had shown up with her little boy on her hip. It gave him some comfort that Rayna wasn't alone. He'd have to teach her how to protect herself, because he couldn't always be with her. And he suspected Dayton was plenty ticked off about missing the chance to get his hands on Rayna's piece of land. Mine now, he thought, with no small bit of satisfaction.

Well, it truly belonged to the bank, but he'd sit down with Rayna and have her cipher for him. They'd figure out a way to get that debt whittled down.

"Daniel!" It was Kirk who spotted him, with his

books slung over his shoulder, and leading his little brother by the hand.

Daniel could see that the stream of children rolling out the front door and down the steps was fanning out. Those that lived in town headed off in groups, walking home. The country kids climbed into their family wagons or carts or buggies. This was the side of life he'd never known when he was school age, and didn't really want to look at when he was grown, for it made the long span of years behind him feel desolate.

But that wasn't his future. He sure liked the feel of sitting here in line, the rain tapping off his hat brim. He would have hopped down to help the little one, but Hans was already climbing up on his own. He peered up at Daniel with those huge blue eyes.

"My Pa used to come get us." His chin trembled and then he was gone, scrambling over the seat back and into the covered bed.

Kirk threw their books and slates in back. The empty lunch tin rattled as it rolled to a stop. "Don't mind him. Did you and Ma—?"

Daniel nodded as he took up the reins, but there was no going forward or back. Too many other horses and vehicles were in the way. Little kids were everywhere, and he made sure his wheels were clear before he followed the buggy ahead of him.

Kirk knocked water off the hood of his slicker. "I've been thinkin'. I know Pa left us in a lot of debt. He never could say no to Ma. Fact was, he couldn't say no to himself. He treated her real good."

"Is that what you're worried about? That I won't?"

"Some. She's an awful nice ma. Some of my friends, well, they don't have a mother like mine."

"I know she's nice. You don't have to worry."

He thought of the lunch she'd brought him. Noon, on the dot, there she was, as pretty as any sunrise he'd ever seen, appearing out of the rain with a lunch pail and a steaming jug of coffee.

Inside the food tin he'd found two sandwiches thick with meat and good sourdough bread. Steaming baked beans, enough to warm him right up, and a couple cinnamon rolls, iced and topped with walnuts. The like of which he'd seen in bakery windows but had never tasted. There was no possibility that he'd ever do anything less than cherish this woman.

It was hard to form it into words so that Kirk could understand it. So he didn't even try. But to a man who'd known little kindness at all, who'd been useful for his blood, sweat and free labor, to have her treat him so fine…why, dedication melded hard in his soul. He was glad he'd married her. Glad he'd put up his land to secure Rayna's future. As she honored him, he intended to honor her in return. And more.

"Now that you're my stepfather, I don't figure you'll pay me for helpin' out in the afternoons. But I think I ought to get a job, maybe in town? To help out with taking care of everyone."

"You're a good man, Kirk Ludgrin. It's a good idea, but the truth is that I need your help, if we're going to keep hold of both ranches. It's too much work for one man to do alone."

"Then I'm your man." Kirk straightened up a bit with his determination.

It was a strange feeling, this tug of warmth in his chest. His stepson. He'd always wondered what that would be like, if he ever had a son of his own. It must feel something like this, this softer, purer affection. Kirk was his to protect, too. And so was the little guy tucked out of the rain in back, even if he was so quiet.

It was like being whole, as if his life had some worth, as he turned the horses toward home.

"My marriage began as a necessary thing," Mariah said with assurance as she slipped on her coat in the small foyer. "For the sake of Nick's children. But love can grow in time. True love. The real thing."

"That's what I had with Kol." Rayna scooped toddling Jeremy up before he could help himself to the fireplace poker. "I know you mean well, but there is a time for everything in this life. I had the beautiful gift of Kol's love, and now that time is over."

"You need to mourn him. He's part of your soul."

"Exactly." So, Mariah knew the depth of that real love, too. "It's a rare thing."

"Yes. And deserves to always be honored. But that doesn't mean you are doomed to a life trapped in a cold marriage." Looking troubled, Mariah stole her son and settled him on her hip. He cried out, still wanting the fireplace poker. Mariah kissed his brow and kept talking over his protests. "I don't want that sadness for you."

"I've had my time to love. I am glad to say that I treasured every moment, and still do." Rayna grabbed the umbrella from the stand in the corner and unwrapped it, concentrating on the task instead of the void in her soul. "Daniel is my life now. We don't have love, but we have respect. That is a great deal more than any marriages I've seen."

"Respect isn't love. And I worry. He's a big man. A strong man. Betsy noticed, too, when she rushed over to tell me of your sudden wedding, that you conveniently never answered her question. You've done the same with me. So, I'll ask it again and I want an honest answer. Please, my friend. How did you hurt your wrist?''

It was the look in Mariah's gaze, of concern, of protectiveness, that startled her. The umbrella slipped from her fingers and clattered on the floor, the sound was like cannon fire in the vacant room. ''You think that Daniel did this? No, Mariah. No. I had a disagreement with old man Dayton.''

''What kind of disagreement?''

''The kind where he thought I was a widow with, um, *needs.* He never would have dared such a thing when Kol was alive. If Daniel hadn't come when he had...'' She shook as she remembered. Ice settled in her veins.

''What about the sheriff? You did report it, right?''

''It's my word against a man's. This is not a fair world.''

''Then I'm grateful to your Daniel. If he kept you from harm, well, and because of him, you get to stay. Betsy and I didn't know what we'd do without you. We've known each other since we were six.''

She retrieved her umbrella instead of trusting her voice to answer. She'd always taken her life for granted. While she cherished her life and the people in it, she'd never stopped to realize how truly precious they were to her. Mariah's steadfast friendship, Betsy's sunny cheer—how they could talk about anything and often did.

And now, when she felt as if every part of her was eroding away, no one understood like her friends.

The season of her life was changing, but the hug Mariah gave her and the squeeze of her hand, said everything. It gave her strength to gather up the pieces of herself and to take a step forward. Then another.

The echo of the room behind her whispered of times

past. Of Kol reading by the fire, his newspaper crackling, the chair squeaking as he stood to steal a smoke on the porch. Kirk at his homework, the scratch of his stylus as he unraveled the mysteries of algebra. Hans's railroad cars clacking on the real steel tracks. The click of her knitting needles a background rhythm to the evening.

Like autumn, with all the leaves fallen from the trees, that's what the room reminded her of. But spring always eventually followed, right? Perhaps, in time, she could have some manner of happiness with Daniel.

"Keep the rag bag as long as you need to," Mariah said on her way out the door. "Betsy said she'd drop hers by. So you can start on your new quilt."

"Don't forget your rolls!" Rayna remembered at the last minute to grab the wrapped bundle on her way out the door, protecting Mariah and little Jeremy from the rain as they hopped into their covered buggy.

Once they were snug and settled behind the rain curtains and Mariah was gathering up the reins, Rayna hurried back to the porch. She waved off her friend, while shaking the wet from the umbrella. Mariah pulled her horses to a stop for Daniel's wagon to pass by.

Daniel. Sitting so straight and substantial on the seat, despite the rain falling with a winter's cold. His hat brim hid his face. Betsy was right. He was a fine-looking man. Would love grow between them in time?

She didn't know how it could. Maybe her life would stay like this cold, wet season, barren and grim.

"Ma! You won't believe it!" Kirk hollered from the front seat, hopping down before the wagon was fully halted. "I got one hundred on my exam! The best in my class."

"I knew you could do it."

She longed for the days when she could pull Kirk close, but those days were gone, too. Her baby, her first-born, was almost a man now. He walked with a wide stand, talked with a deeper voice, but there was enough of a boy that he forgot to stomp the wetness off his shoes.

He charged into the house shouting, ''I smell cinnamon rolls!''

Daniel held up a hand for Hans, but the boy ignored him and hopped the last step to the ground. Big eyes wary as he gazed up at the man in his father's place.

''Ma.'' Somber, her littlest came to her side and filled his fist with her apron. ''That man is still here.''

''That's Daniel.'' Not at all sure how to begin to explain things, Rayna knelt, taking her apron ruffle from her son's tight grip. ''Did you have a good day at school?''

''No. Can I have a cimma-non roll, too?''

''Yes. Go on in.''

With one backward glance at the man securing the horses, Hans took off for the front door and slammed it hard behind him.

It was just the two of them, her and Daniel, with the cold rain falling between them. ''Would you like to come in? I have plenty of cinnamon rolls.''

''I want to get one more haystack moved before supper.'' Daniel knocked the rain from his brim. ''But I wouldn't mind another of those rolls. They sure are tasty, Rayna.''

''I'm glad you like them. Did you want me to wrap them for you?''

''That'd be best. I'll just drip all over your floor, and your little one isn't too sure about me.'' Daniel moseyed up the steps. He seemed to accept Hans's reticence handily enough. "Is there anything I can do for you before I go?"

"I'm planning dinner early tonight, if you don't mind. If you'd rather, I can leave a plate for you in the warmer, if you don't want to interrupt your hauling. But I need to get to town early."

"For?"

"My job. Three nights a week, remember? Tonight I'm doing laundry, and I need a head start so I can finish up before dawn."

Daniel swept off his hat and the cool wind ruffled his hair. Maybe that could startle his brain into thinking. He couldn't have heard her right. "You're keeping that job?"

"If you don't mind. I'm as much to blame for the debts, because they're everywhere. The feed store, the mercantile, the grocery, the butcher. Even the dress shop. I want to do my part."

"I'm surprised, is all. Like you said, two working together makes a load lighter."

"Good. Then I'll go fetch those rolls for you." She hurried off, closing the door, leaving him alone as hail started to fall. Hard, icy bits that felt like his old life breaking apart and falling way.

Some of the ice inside him, too. Maybe that's what came of living like this, caring about people. Wanting them to care about you. He liked the way Rayna looked at him when she returned a few moments later with a small pail, lid on tight to keep out the weather.

She looked up at him, as if he was something to her. He didn't feel the bite of the wind or the ice of the hail as he rode off, knowing she was watching.

And feeling glad that she'd be waiting for him to return.

* * *

''Ma.'' Hans tugged once at her apron. ''That man is here again.''

''You can call him Daniel.'' She checked the corn boiling in the kettle. A few more minutes. After peeking in at the potatoes roasting in their skins, she saw the stew was bubbling and fragrant. Everything was on schedule.

She whirled toward the sideboard, looking to sidestep her son, but he was climbing onto the window seat, staring out at the cloaked figures in the barnyard. Kirk and Daniel, working fast to get the last of the hay stacked and shaped so it would shield the weather.

''How come he's doin' that?''

''So the horses have something to eat for breakfast. His horses are our horses now.''

''No. We oughta go get our horses from town.''

''Can't do that, baby.'' She gathered flatware from the drawer. ''Daniel is going to stay with us and share his horses with us. Like the table.''

''No.'' Hans said nothing more, his little shoulders tensed tight, his hands white-knuckled fists on the sill.

She didn't push him. Lord knew he'd been through enough already. He would understand in time. Perhaps when he was ready. She set the table, popped a fresh pan of rolls into the warmer to heat, and poured fresh milk into the glasses. She'd never felt so grateful for the necessities in her life. Milk for her sons. A table to eat at. This kitchen full of sweet memories.

She had supper on the table when Kirk came to the door. He said to dish up a plate for Daniel and leave it. After she did so, they all sat down to eat. The space at his table—the same spot where Kol sat—remained empty.

Daniel was a hardworking man, the hardest worker she'd ever seen. Hours later, while she soaped sheet after sheet on a worn washboard in the lonely corner of the boardinghouse kitchen, she would bet that Daniel had brought over a third haystack after he'd driven her to work. He was probably in the damp night air, fog shrouding him as he pitched forkload after forkload of hay.

As the hours passed, she wondered if he was asleep yet in the modest upstairs bed. Sleeping beneath the old spare blanket she'd used as a cover. She didn't know how to ask him if he planned to ask more of her than to sleep.

She still didn't know hours later when the sheets were clipped up to dry in the boiler room and she'd mopped up the wash tubs, stored them and scrubbed the floor where she'd worked. That he was on time didn't surprise her. She knew he was out there in the fog before he came into sight abruptly, the mist breaking apart.

A day's growth blackened his jaw and his hair was tousled, what she could see of it beneath his hat brim. He said nothing on the eerie drive home, the fog as thick as the stew she'd prepared for supper. The prairie slept, obscured by fog and dark. Not even an owl hooted. She noticed the rifle against the seat, held in place by Daniel's knee, but didn't ask about it.

He let her off by the back gate. The walk to the kitchen wasn't far, although she was freezing by the time she arrived. Cold from the inside out. Heat welcomed her. Daniel had made the fire before he'd left. He was a thoughtful man. She held her hands out, letting them warm. Did she wait for him? Or would it be better to go up and be first in bed?

The door was opening, stopping her debate, and there

was Daniel, shrugging out of his overcoat. He wore his long johns, the dark gray fabric clinging to him everywhere. She could not look away. He was mesmerizing. The hard planes of his chest and abdomen, the lean strength of his long legs and in between, a sizable bulge that hinted he was no small man in any sense of the word.

Betsy's prediction haunted her and she looked away blushing. *He's that strong, silent type of man. It's the quiet ones that make the best lovers.* It was wrong to even think of another man in that way. Or was it? The man stalking toward her was her husband. The brush of his hand against her cheek, pushing the hair from her eyes, was rough and awkward and tender all at the same time. It was the tenderness in his touch that made the void in her chest, where her heart used to be, bleed.

She could take anything but Daniel's tenderness.

"You're tired, pretty lady." Affection, naked and honest, made his baritone rough. "Come, let me put you to bed."

"To sleep?"

If he was disappointed, he didn't show it. Stoic, as yielding as granite, he led her upstairs, his hand at her elbow, and opened the door to her room. Their room.

He stopped at the doorway. "Sleep well. I'll get the boys ready for school if you need to sleep late."

"That's my responsibility."

"You look as though you haven't slept much at all since the funeral. Sleep. I'm here. You're not alone." His kiss to her brow was chaste. Gentlemanly.

Why, then, did her pulse thud wildly in her ears? Why did she long to lean against his chest? His words had touched her, found her weakest spot. She was alone. She would always be desperately alone. This was not a marriage. It was an arrangement. And it could never be much more.

Love happened in time, Mariah said, but Rayna didn't believe it. Her time for that had passed, turning like a season from the bright summer to the cold shroud of fall, a season of despair.

She sat at the window a long while, watching the last of the leaves fall before climbing into her bed. Sleep did not come.

Chapter Fourteen

"Ma. That man's here." Hans hopped down from the window seat. "It's been days and days and he's *still* here."

"I know. Remember I told you? Daniel is going to be staying with us from now on."

"No he isn't."

Rayna covered the warm muffins with a cloth and set the basket on the breakfast table and considered her son. He'd woken before dawn from terrible nightmares each night since the wedding. She could hear his voice in memory calling out in fear for her and for his papa.

Wishing she could take the pain from him, she knelt to draw him into her arms. Exhausted and heartbroken, he pushed away to stare hard at the back door.

He needed to handle his father's loss in his own way. She felt so helpless. She didn't know how to help him.

In the meanwhile, the eggs were sizzling, the sausage patties needed turning, and the coffee was ready to burn. She turned to the immediate needs of preparing their morning meal. Cooking breakfast was something she could take care of without a problem. But Hans…she was too exhausted to see any easy explanation.

Boots rang on the porch and snow blew in with Daniel. He handed over the pail of fresh milk and she set it aside, to be strained later. The meal was ready. She poured Daniel a cup of coffee first, for he looked as if he'd gotten little sleep, too. Snowflakes clung to his dark hair as he folded his big frame into the chair by the fire.

"That's just what I need. Thank you, Rayna."

"You're welcome." The sausages were getting a little too brown—she snatched up her spatula and rescued them from the popping grease.

"That's where my papa sits." Hans's voice, low with anger.

Rayna moved, but not fast enough. The little boy had launched toward Daniel's chest and was hitting him with all the fury of his little fists. "Get out! Out. I want my papa!"

The look on Daniel's face— Rayna scooped her little boy, grown so big and heavy, into her arms. Held him as he kicked and punched at the air.

Sobs racked him from head to toe and she sank into the closest chair, the one Daniel had vacated. It was his hands guiding her down, his movements at the stove saving their breakfast from crisping.

He set a cup of coffee beside her, filled two plates and left the room.

Hans's cries had changed to sobs. Her poor baby boy. She held him tight, humming the melodies she'd sung him to sleep with long ago, waiting for him to quiet.

Kirk came to grab his muffler from the wall pegs by the back door. He looked exhausted, too.

"Daniel's going to let me ride his gelding to school, if that's all right, since he's not going." Misery settled on Kirk's face. He laid a hand on Hans's back.

Rayna understood, for it was the same misery she felt. "I have your lunch ready on the counter."

Kirk nodded, ruffled his little brother's fine hair with affection and left, only to return to grab his lunch. Then he was gone, the door slamming shut.

Rayna couldn't get warm. Daniel came in to stoke the fire. Hans stiffened, tension coiling in his muscles, and he buried his face against her throat and held on with all his might.

"Is there anything I can do?" Daniel knelt. What a steady, good man he was. His touch to her arm was welcome.

She didn't know what he was thinking. She couldn't guess what he would do next. Would she ever? But his goodness surprised her as he brushed the palm of his big hand against Hans's head.

The tenderness etched into his face was genuine.

Of all the men who could have made this same offer to her, there couldn't have been a better one. Not just to work the ranch and to step into a man's duties around this place.

But who better to know a child's worth than one who'd never been valued.

She could see that, too, in his dark eyes, shadowed with a strange longing. The man who'd kept himself separate from others, a true loner, so much so that his neighbors hardly knew him by name, had dreams, too.

"Do you need me to stay?" he asked, his gaze searching hers, and she swore she could feel the impact deep within her.

"No, he's calming. I just need to hold him."

Daniel rose, greater for his kindness as he rubbed something from her cheek. A teardrop marked the pad of his thumb. "Let me know if you ever need someone to hold you."

She didn't ask and the seconds beat between them before he turned. His boots thudded on the floor and the hinges squeaked. Then he was gone for town with a click of the door, taking a part of her broken heart.

There it was again. The itch at the back of his neck that had Daniel's senses on alert and had been troubling him on and off. When he looked up to wipe the sweat from his eyes, he saw why.

Clay Dayton's fine team—Rayna's former driving horses—were tied up in the far corner of the yard, near to the office door.

That lowlife. Hatred for the man churned in his guts and if it weren't for the job he had to keep, he would hunt Dayton down and make it clear. Rayna was his. The land was his. The old man needed to stay far away or he'd be sorry.

In Daniel's view, a man did what he had to in order to protect his family. Last time, he'd dragged the man out of the barn and thrown him on his horse. He'd had to hold himself back from doing more.

He wouldn't next time. One thing he intended to do was to keep his wife safe. He went back to work, but the back of his neck kept feeling itchy. It was as if Dayton was keeping an eye on him from inside the building. The windows made it impossible to see in, but Daniel kept vigilant.

He didn't know much about Clay Dayton. Only that he had a wife and a large, extended family. And that it was rumored he owned more land than anyone else in the county. How he got that land, by hook or by crook, was up to debate. Either way, Daniel figured that Dayton was none too happy losing out on getting his hands on the Ludgrin property. And on the Ludgrin widow.

Yeah, he pretty much despised the man. He knew the exact moment when the office door opened and Dayton strolled into sight. He wore a fine black suit as if it was Sunday, acting so fine when he'd have violated Rayna if he hadn't come along.

Daniel sunk his shovel deep into the coal pile and from the top of the rail car sized up his enemy. Dayton glowered at him across the distance and there was no mistaking the look of hatred in the man's eyes. And something else. A glitter of warning that had Daniel wishing he could take care of Dayton here and now.

Later. Daniel vowed to choose the place and the time. He glared right back at the man who climbed into the fine buggy as if there were no better man in the county.

All Daniel could think about was his lovely wife, her precious children and how he would give his life to keep them safe.

Rayna turned the gelding off Main Street, slipping a little because she just couldn't get used to the blasted sidesaddle. She steadied herself, nearly dropping the bundle of mending she'd done for Betsy, when she saw him. Clay Dayton watching her from the benches near the bank building.

She set her chin and met his glare before he disappeared from her sight. But not from her mind. She'd worried about meeting up with him on the road alone. Daniel, if he knew she'd come to town by herself, would not be pleased. But this was business—she had promised Betsy she'd bring the clothes by before she left on her afternoon deliveries.

So she was stunned when Mariah opened Betsy's kitchen door. Her eyes were shining. "Surprise!"

"What are you doing here?" Rayna stepped through the threshold to see Betsy and their new neighbor Katelyn Hennessey at the kitchen table, slicing up some very delicious-looking desserts. "I smell apple pie!"

"Guilty!" Katelyn admitted with the pie cutter gripped firmly. "Congratulations on your marriage, Rayna. There's nothing as nice as being a new bride. A doting husband, everything is so exciting and, oh, just lovely."

"It sounds as if Katelyn has found the secret to a good marriage." Betsy winked as she passed silverware around the table. "The trick is to never let the honey-moon be over."

"Life gets in the way," Mariah argued, glancing over to check on her little boy toddling around the kitchen, hand outstretched after their gray house cat, who kept one step ahead of that grasping hand. "But an enter-prising wife can find a way to make time for what's important."

"And that is important." Katelyn blushed again. "Es-pecially to a marriage made for convenience's sake. It's a…well…a way of bonding."

"Well said!" Mariah didn't seem the least bit bashful about the subject of marital relations as she shut the door and led the way to the table. "My marriage was for convenience, so Nick and I were friends first, before we became lovers. I imagine that's what Rayna is struggling to do. Just to get to know this man she married. He's a stranger to all of us."

"He certainly keeps to himself," Katelyn agreed as she began filling dessert plates with the rich cinnamony apple treat. ''Dillon knows him, though, and speaks of him highly. He says it's a fine man you married, Rayna.''

''He certainly is that.'' His patience, his hard work, his care. She could still picture him kneeling before her as she'd held Hans and offering to hold her if she needed it. If she needed comfort from her pain.

''Daniel is a good husband, but we are still getting to know one another.''

''Still?'' Betsy looked crestfallen.

''Give her and Daniel time to come to know one another first.'' Mariah pretended to scold. ''So, you and Daniel are getting to know one another, right?''

''We have a companionable arrangement.''

''What does that mean?'' Katelyn looked confused as she put the pie cutter in the wash basin.

''It means—'' Betsy waved her fork in midair ''—that they are not quite consummated. Right, Rayna?''

''I'm not going to dignify that with an answer.''

''See? She's blushing. It's true. I bet by this time next week, she'll be humming a different tune.''

Rayna took a bite of pie, hoping to distract Betsy. ''Katelyn, this is excellent. I would love your rule.''

''I'll be happy to write it down.'' Katelyn's eyes twinkled. ''I bet your Daniel looks at you like you were a piece of this pie and he was the hungriest man in the world.''

''I give up!'' Rayna tossed down her fork and covered her face with her hands. These women were apparently having a lot of fun at her expense. ''I'm not in love with Daniel. This is a practical arrangement.''

''You know what's *practical?*'' Mariah rose to top off the coffee cups. ''Sharing body heat to keep warm through the night. It's a good idea. You should invite him to your room."

"And if any snuggling is involved, then that's just another way to keep from getting frostbite," Katelyn said, stirring sugar into her cup as if she hadn't said anything outrageous. "True love deepens with time. It certainly did for me. I'm just very hopeful that Rayna and Daniel will have a happy marriage."

"We've all been married." Betsy turned serious and reached for Rayna's hand. "We know how important that is."

Mariah had slipped into the pantry and quietly returned with a ribbon wrapped around the folded square of a wooden frame. A quilt frame.

"We knew you needed a new one." Betsy's grip squeezed, conveying all the love and friendship of a lifetime. "This way you can work on your new quilt at home, instead of having to borrow Mariah's."

"Oh." It was too expensive. It was too lavish. It was…just right.

"This is from all of us, to wish you a happy marriage," Mariah explained as she set the gift into the seat of an empty chair. "In time, I hope you will find great love with your Daniel."

In time? She doubted she could love again if she had her entire life to recover from her loss. She thought of the past nights, coming home from the boardinghouse in the freezing cold. How Daniel was there waiting for her at three o'clock sharp in town. How tired and cold he must be, but he never seemed to mind. Not when he would drop her off at the door and head off to the barn to put up the team.

Not when he made up his bed on the sofa, shivering with cold, to crawl beneath the pile of blankets alone.

Marital relations. She couldn't deny she longed to have said yes this morning. To lean against his chest and to let his comfort sift over her like powdered snow.

He was her husband. She wore his ring. But what if her heart remained lost? As frozen as the Montana prairie in midwinter?

Daniel saw her coming through the stubborn snowfall, the lunch hamper hung over her good arm. It heartened him to see her bundled well against the cold. He had to keep his attention on the plow. Every time he glanced up to check her progress across the acres of upturned earth, crowned with snow, the plow went off course and he had a crooked row to show for it.

There she was, wearing a hooded woolen cloak that draped around her face and gold curls and made her so dang beautiful it made his chest hurt just to look at her.

He halted the horses, lathered and panting. ''How's your little fella?''

''Finally asleep.'' She looked tortured as she bit her bottom lip, as if thinking. Or debating what to share with him. She must have come to a decision because she kept on talking. ''Maybe it was too much for him to have returned to school yesterday, but he wanted to go. He seemed to be doing better, and there was no reason not to send him.''

''You did right. It'll take a long time. A papa is a lot to lose for a little boy.''

''It was everything.''

For her, too. He could see it. He didn't know much about what bonded a man and a woman together, but spending time with her, he had some notion.

''I can't leave the team standing for long.'' He snapped the reins and the Clydesdales dug in, pulling the heavy plow like a spear through the thick, rich earth. "Walk with me."

"Okay." She stepped over the raised furrows of raw earth. "Can you stop long enough to eat lunch?"

"I'll eat and work. I used to always wait until after I was done working, but I've learned my lesson. You're a damn fine cook. I'm not about to let whatever you got in that hamper sit. My mouth is watering and I don't even know what's in there."

"You're making it impossible for me not to like you."

"You were determined not to like me? Or do you mean you just didn't like me first off?"

"When I first met you? I thought you were out to try to steal our crop. But you proved me wrong. You keep doing that." She didn't look at him.

She didn't have to. He felt the change. She was walking a little closer to him. Not much, but she was more at ease. Didn't look at him as if he were a stranger. His pulse kicked up in rhythm from her nearness. "How else did I prove you wrong?"

"You could have gotten angry with Hans's behavior this morning. I've talked to him about it, but—" She shook her head helplessly. "You weren't angry."

"I have a lot in common with Hans." And it hurt to think about. "I didn't know my parents, so I guess my loss was a different one. But being a little boy hurting… I know something about that."

Gratitude made her eyes so bright and beautiful he swore he could see her soul. That tenderness unspooling in his chest went right on loosening.

The horses reached the end of the row and he turned them, standing full weight on the plow to keep the tooth in the ground. The decomposing wheat stalks caught and tangled, adding to the fact that the earth was trying to freeze on him.

"I sure appreciate this early snow. I always like my after harvest plowing to be challenging." He felt the metal groove twisting and he halted the horses. But it was too late, the old plow decided to pitch. "Great. That's just what I needed."

He wrestled the dang thing upright, sweating and trying not to cuss in the presence of his wife, and managed to get the contraption upright. Then he realized she'd been watching every move he made, and the corners of her mouth were twitching.

"Are you doing all right?" She was obviously trying not to laugh.

That made him feel more confident. "I was doing just fine until you came out to distract me with your promises of lunch."

"How many acres have you done this morning?"

"Ten. I've only got one hundred and fifty more."

"Lucky you. Here, you'll need this." She reached into the hamper and unwrapped the top half of a thick sandwich.

He took a bite. Hell, it was so good, it made his tongue ache. Moist seasoned meat, chewy bread, and some kind of white creamy stuff that he really liked. He'd never tasted it before, until he'd had one of her sandwiches. He figured there was a whole lot he had yet to taste when it came to Rayna. She'd only been feeding him for a short spell—

Wait up. Maybe he was liking a passel more than just her cooking. The woman walking beside him was his wife. And he wouldn't always be bunking down in a bedroll on the parlor floor.

The bed he'd put up in her room was for the two of

them. When she was ready. Ready to just sleep beside him. Not that lying beside her and not touching her was going to be a restful experience. But she'd married him because she'd had no better choice. It didn't take a genius to figure out she would need time.

But that didn't stop him from wanting her. He was dog-tired because he'd lain awake more hours than he wanted to admit last night, thinking of her in his bed. When he'd brushed his lips against her cheek, it had been the sweetest thing. He'd never known anything like that before. The tenderness pooled like warm light in the center of his chest brightened, filling him up. And at the same time a hunger for her thudded in that light inside him. He wanted to haul her against him and taste her satin skin. Kiss the graceful curve of her neck, feel her arch against him. He wanted to unbutton that pretty dress of hers—

Whoa there, Lindsay. He wanted what came after the wedding, but he'd never courted Rayna, never had the chance for her to come to know him. To know how safe she'd be with him. How treasured. So he had no right to a marriage bed. Not until he honored the natural progression of things.

He sunk his teeth deep into the sandwich, tugged back on the reins draped over his shoulders. The horses slowed a bit, which was making it easier to keep the plow in the ground one-handed.

"I didn't know food could taste so good," he told her when he was done eating. "What else do you got in that hamper?"

Soft pink blushed across her delicate cheekbones. She must have liked his compliment because she handed him another sandwich. Since he was hungry enough to eat worn-out shoe leather, he swore he'd found paradise on earth biting into a second sandwich thicker than the first.

Or maybe the paradise was having her at his side. He'd never realized how lonesome his life had been until this moment. It wasn't as if they were doing anything grand. He was simply doing his work. But she made everything different. The rustle of her petticoats, the faint scent of spring and the feel of her, it was as if they were linked. When she came near, his soul came on like a lantern on a dark winter's night, chasing away every shadow.

He shoved the last bite into his mouth, chewing as he handed her back the waxed paper. Efficient, she handed him a large cup and a spoon. Last night's stew, warmed and steaming. He could only stare, disbelieving. But the bowl didn't disappear, and the hot tangy gravy and juicy meat chunks had his mouth watering and his stomach growling.

It was just the thing he needed, for he was half frozen through. Rayna had taken care to warm the meal and it was only cooling in the bitter wind. He yanked back on the reins, stopping the horses, and took the bowl. It felt good on his hands. Even better in his belly.

He ate fast to the last drop. The good, flavorful stew thawed him from the inside out. Amazing what a difference it made. He felt ready to take on every acre that had been left fallow for too long—and that made plowing tough.

"You are the best wife." He couldn't hold back his feelings. They rushed through him like a dam breaking at high flood, rolling with a frightening force that no man could stop. He tried, but it just didn't work. Of all that he'd seen growing up, and what he'd imagined married life to be as a grown man, he'd never thought up this.

It wasn't the cooking or the food, not really. It was the woman. Thoughtful and diligent and just *nice.* Like those big fluffy clouds in a lazy summer sky he'd always imagined would be the softest place ever just to rest a spell, that's what Rayna was.

She blushed again, waved off his compliment, taking back the empty cup and spoon and closing the lid of the hamper. "I'll leave this at the gate. There's coffee and a couple more cinnamon rolls. I noticed you were partial to them."

"Everything you make I'm partial to."

"That makes it easy. Let me know if you need something. Or your coffee jug refilled. It's really cold out here. Just knock at the back door and I'll come, so you don't have to waste time taking off your boots." She glanced down at his muddy work boots with emphasis.

Her pointed look was about as fierce as a newborn kitten. "I'll knock," he promised.

Her smile was a sad one—he knew she was thinking of the man who by all rights should be plowing this field and missing him. Then the sadness was gone, as if she'd tucked it away willfully and lifted her gloved hand in a feminine wave.

His memories folded backward, too. Of households where he'd lived as a boy and witnessed the unhappiness and the arguments. Never a kind word was said between husband and wife. That's what he'd seen as a boy. The unhappy unions that were harsh, desperate and bitter—

He struggled to close his mind against the recollections of snarling fights between men and their wives at night. Nights when he'd been too exhausted from work to sleep, his belly growling and his hands, back and feet throbbing with pain. The threats and smacks and crying...

That was what made him be glad to be alone. And when he thought about marrying, he'd make sure it was to someone he could get along with. What he'd never imagined was a fancy two-story house with a woman that made his heart hitch and his soul ache with joy.

He watched her as she walked away, her skirts swishing, a few escaped tendrils of hair dancing on the wind, snowflakes clinging to her like a blessing. She knelt to leave the hamper, just as she'd promised, and continued on, growing smaller with distance. When she shut the door behind her, he could still feel the tug she made within him.

Chapter Fifteen

You are the best wife. Daniel's words plagued her all the way back to the house. It wasn't only his choice of words, but the emphasis in them. As if he'd been awe-struck. As if her bringing him a warm meal on a cold day was a miracle and not a simple thing she'd done for the past fifteen years whenever her husband had needed it and without his asking her to. It made her realize how empty Daniel's life must have been.

Her eyes stung as she let herself into the house. The fire needed wood, the outside chill was creeping into the room. But it wasn't the cold that was troubling her. Absently, she slipped out of her coat, hung it on the wall. *Daniel.* There he was, filling her thoughts. She pulled back the edge of the curtain, tilting so she could just see him hard at work, manhandling the plow through the stubborn earth. He was such a hard worker.

She respected him for that. For the good man he was, of honor and integrity. Had no one in his life before cared that he was cold and hungry? As soon as she wondered that, she knew the answer. Of course not. He'd spoken of his childhood as having been nothing but a field worker, indentured for food and a roof to sleep under.

She ached, watching as he turned the horses at the end row, treating them with care. If Kol were watching from Heaven above, what would he think? Would he be glad it was a man like Daniel Lindsay who'd replaced him?

As if Kol could ever be replaced. Rayna laid a hand over her chest, surprised to feel the beat of her heart.

"Ma?" Hans stood in the doorway, feet bare, his nightshirt wrinkled, rubbing his eyes with his fists. "I want some water."

He sounded fretful. She realized he knew what she'd been doing, whom she'd been watching. He was old enough to get a drink of water; they both knew it. He'd been doing so since he was two, but she realized it wasn't the water he was asking for.

"Come." She held out her hand. "Let me help you."

Hans ambled toward her, sleepy and frowning. She filled the dipper for him, the fresh water dripping as he slurped his fill. Dark circles ringed his eyes. Whatever sleep he was getting, it was not a deep sleep.

Hurting for him, she pulled him into her arms, pure love like a sun burning within her as she held her little boy, safe. He snuggled against her, holding her so tight. She held him tight right back.

The fire cracked and popped. The wash water cooled. The wind blew harder out of the north, bringing with it a fine veil of snowflakes.

Finally, Hans let go, wandering off to climb up on the window seat. Kneeling there, with his fingers gripping the sill, he watched Daniel working diligently despite the storm.

Hans's jaw grew hard. His breathing was ragged and angry-sounding.

Rayna sat beside him. She had lunch to get ready and the laundry to do, but it was not as important. She thought of Daniel, who'd been as little as Hans once, working in a field. That image remained with her through the rest of the day as she set out a warm lunch and as she scrubbed Daniel's clothes on the washboard in the lean-to. As she set supper to cooking.

Daniel was still out there working, a gray shadow against a world of white, with his head bowed and his back straight.

She kept sight of him until the fist of nightfall wrung the last of light from the sky. Until he was only a faint movement against the vanishing hues of gray and then nothing at all.

The temperature was dropping. She fed the fire and wrapped a shawl around her shoulders as she returned to the kitchen. She lit one lamp to see by as she warmed the lunch pails in the oven, for the air had condensed to frost on the metal. And warming the tin would help keep the food warm on the journey to the fields.

The wind closed in with a howl, and a thud had her turning around. The tall shape of a young man, so like Kol it took her breath, was shrugging out of snow-crusted wraps.

Kirk jacked off his work boots. "It's likely to blizzard. Daniel told me to come in and see to the fires. Make sure there's enough wood to get you by for a spell."

She'd refilled the bins herself. She hadn't been sure if Daniel would remember, with his work needing to be done before the earth froze too hard. But he had, and it touched her. It was a husbandly gesture, and it troubled her as she set Kirk's plate on the table and poured him a big glass of milk.

"What about your homework?" she asked as she cut the remains of the sweet apple pie in two and slipped it onto a plate. Then she added a napkin to set on the table.

Kirk was already seated and plowing through the chicken and dumplings as if he hadn't eaten in a week. "I'll get to it next. I got to know everything about the battle of Antietam by tomorrow."

"Then you'd best get started." She carried a lamp to the table and his book bag from the lean-to. "I'm wrapping up Daniel's supper."

"He said not to bother. He'll be in shortly." Kirk pitched in another forkful of dumpling.

Shortly? She glanced at the clock. The dark hands showed the hour. Almost seven. She had sixty-four minutes to go before Hans's bedtime. And what felt like an eternity before she could hide away in her own room and hope that tonight sleep would come swift and deep.

She already knew it wouldn't. In the other room, Hans's "whoo-whoo" echoed along the walls as his train traveled *chunkedy-chunkedy* along its tiny track. A normal evening activity for him. As Kirk dug into his pie, he hauled over his slate and books and began reading. The rasp of the page turning was another normal sound of an evening in the Ludgrin household.

No, the Lindsay household now. Daniel's ring felt strange and out of place on her finger as she drained wash water from the reservoir. She was Rayna Lindsay now. Life marched on, and she could hold on to the past with all the strength of her will and it didn't matter one whit.

It was autumn, and a harsh one at that. Wind pummeled the outside wall, shaking the windows in their panes. Snow scoured at the glass. An early blizzard come with the night.

She held the bar of soap in the palm of her hand, looking toward the door. "Was Daniel bringing the horses in behind you?"

"Nope." Kirk was staring at the door, too, his brow furrowed with worry. His book open before him. "Do you reckon he'll get in all right? Maybe I oughta—"

"No." Her harsh word sounded as bitter as the wind. Surprised at the sound, she gentled her voice but she couldn't hide the despair. "Daniel wouldn't want to put you at risk going out after him. Likely as not he is already on his way in from the barn."

Kirk slid into his seat again, but he didn't look happy.

It was something she never would have allowed, her son going out into the storm, even if it had been Kol out there. It wasn't safe.

She gathered Kirk's plates. He was only pretending to read. He'd been staring at the same page for the last five minutes. She looked to the door as she scrubbed each plate clean. Kirk was not alone in his worry.

She watched the quarter hour tick by and then the next. If Daniel had been putting up the horses, he would have been done by now. Sometimes people became disoriented by the whirling winds and were blown off course, only to be found when the storm was done, frozen to death ten feet from their door.

Daniel wasn't familiar with this land. He hadn't walked the fences and the fields enough to know them by memory. To recall every detail in his mind. Was he out there, freezing? She thought of the sharp bits of ice beating at the glass, making it impossible to see out. Or for Daniel to find his way.

Kirk stood with a clatter of his chair. ''I should go out there.''

''No. You could become lost, too.'' She laid a hand on his arm, feeling how fierce he was. Already Daniel had earned her son's respect. And hers. She remembered the man who'd worked without rest through the day. A man of steel. One not to be bowed by a winter's storm. ''Daniel is the most capable person I've ever met. He'll be in when he's good and ready.''

Kirk didn't like her answer, but he must have sensed her resolve. There was no way he was heading out into a blizzard. He returned to his book, but his gaze kept straying toward the door.

Another quarter hour had passed. Shivering when the wind drove ice through the wood walls, Rayna lit a second lamp and set it in the windowsill—to guide him home. She grabbed the scrap bag Betsy had lent her and began sorting through it.

Twenty minutes had gone by. Too long. Kol had ordered her never to head out in the storm, it was foolish because two people could pass within a few inches in such a blizzard and never know the other was there. Not even the light in the window could do much good, but it burned brightly, a cheerful flicker of flame in the bleak evening.

Finally she could take no more. She'd had enough of sitting and waiting. Of sitting like a good wife in the kitchen while her man handled the money, made the living and braved the risks of a merciless land.

Daniel was her husband. She needed him. She cared what happened to him. If he were lost, then she would find him. She'd lost one good man to the brutal heat. She'd not forfeit another to the bitter cold.

She grabbed her wraps, gave Kirk orders to watch Hans and took the lantern with her.

The blast of cruel cold struck her like a vicious body blow and stole the air from her lungs. Breathless, she struggled to pull the door shut behind her, wrestling until her arms ached. The lantern tipped and almost went out—then it did, leaving her in utter blackness.

How was she going to find Daniel in this?

She shouted his name. The fierce wind tore her words to pieces. She reached out and felt only the shards of ice that drove through the weave in her clothes and cut to the skin. "Daniel!"

Nothing.

She felt her way to the edge of the porch, but couldn't find the handrail. The blizzard felt as if it were a living thing, bent on confusing her, if it didn't freeze her first. Already she couldn't feel her feet. Her teeth rattled, so she clenched them. The door was safely at her back.

Did she turn around? Or keep going? Knowing everything she'd heard about being out in a blizzard was correct—she could pass right by Daniel and never know it.

Daniel. What if he was trapped in the barn, unsure how to find the house? If he was lost in the fields, there was no possibility of locating him in this. But if he was in the barn, then she could help him in. He'd be hungry and cold to the meat of his bones. She had to at least try.

The storm seemed to gather up more strength and hurled her hard, stumbling, against the door. Her back collided with the wood frame and pain bolted through her spine.

Daniel. Thinking of him gave her courage and she

lashed forward, fighting the hard blast of snow in what she thought was the direction of the steps. Her reaching hand found nothing but void. Off balance, she began to fall. The wind, like a snarling monster, caught her in its arms and dragged her up from the ground.

No, it was a man who held her up and not the roaring blizzard. A man's solid grip helping her to her feet, although she couldn't see him.

Daniel. It was Daniel! Not lost after all. She grasped his arms, grateful to feel the hard male strength of him beneath her numb fingertips.

Thank heavens, he was safe and she choked on her relief as he hauled her against the icy wall of his chest. She rested against him. Yes, it was definitely him.

Suddenly he was all around her, his arms enfolding her, his strong, hard thighs pushing against hers, walking her backward. Turning her so he protected her from the wind.

With his chin tucked over the top of her head, he guided her up. Once out of the main thrust of the storm, the snow drifted haphazardly over the steps and beneath the shelter of the roof and it was easier going.

The door opened and there was light, blessed light. Heat rose up before her as she stumbled forward. Her feet were gone, she couldn't feel them, but Daniel was helping her. Holding her up until the door slammed and the harrowing roar of the wind dulled to an angry howl.

She dropped into a chair, unaware of where it had come from, only of the tall, white-flocked man towering over her.

"What were you thinking?" Daniel yanked his snow-caked muffler off his face. "You have to know to never go outside in a storm like this. Let me see your hands."

He peeled off her gloves and knelt to rub her hands

in his. Kirk came running with a steaming cup of tea, the tea button floating in the steaming water, trailing amber color in its wake. Daniel gestured for Kirk to set the cup on the table.

She couldn't stop shivering. Vaguely, as if from a great distance, she heard the stove door open and the thunk and thud of wood being fed to the fire. The greedy snap and curl of the hungry flames. The pinging sound of ice shards tumbling to the floor as Daniel peeled off her wraps and then his.

"Thank God, you're all right."

His worried eyes, a beautiful shade of green and brown, almost gold in this light, studied her intently. Creases dug into the corners of his eyes and bracketed his mouth. His was an attractive, mature face. His movements as he unbuttoned her coat were clumsy but awkwardly gentle.

A warm heat took seed in her chest. Painful, for the seed was a tender one.

He had to be far more frozen through than she was, for he'd been outside all day. But he seemed unconcerned with his own condition as he lifted the cup in his big hands and held it to her lips as if she were a small child.

"Drink up. It'll help warm you." His voice came gruff, as if he were angry, but she knew he wasn't.

His tenderness enveloped her like the heat radiating from the stove. It curled inside her like the tea sliding through her, warming her from the inside out. Who knew this big, rough man was capable of this?

It wasn't the tea that was thawing her, she realized.

The cup was empty and he took it away. "Kirk, make another please."

She heard Kirk's gait approach, saw the cup disappear

from her field of vision, for there was only Daniel. Daniel crouching before her, wide shoulders as sturdy as the Rocky Mountain front she could see from her parlor windows.

Unyielding granite mountains so big and harsh they seemed like invulnerable shields thrust up at the sky. And at the same time so beautiful, they hurt to look at.

That was Daniel. Invincible. She should have known he could handle a Montana blizzard.

"Never go outside to find me again." His words were sharpened to a point, and yet the brush of his fingers at the curve of her chin was caring.

"I was afraid you couldn't know your way from the barn. Or—" She shut her eyes briefly against the image. "Or that you'd f-frozen to death in the field."

"I've survived more than one blizzard curled up in a hay mow. Or a haystack." The memory drew down his mouth and the light in his eyes dulled to a sad shadow. "I'm not so easy to kill off."

His attempt at humor wasn't funny at all. Her eyes stung. Maybe she cared about him more than she realized. "I would never want anything to happen to you."

If possible, the sorrow shading his eyes darkened. "Nor could I stand that for you. I knew it was going to blizzard. Why do you think I sent Kirk in when I did?"

She swallowed against a rising tightness in her throat. "And you started bringing in the horses?"

"As soon as I scented snow on the wind. The storm struck about ten feet from the barn, so I got the horses in. I rubbed them down and fed them and the cow, and tied a rope from the end post to my waist. I kept reeling myself back until I found your little backyard gate. There's a rope from the porch rail to the barn, so don't you worry about me losing my way."

Daniel heard the roughness in his voice, so thin, emotion shone right through it. Embarrassed, he turned away and jacked off his boots. Hanging his wraps up, ice fell everywhere. There had to be a broom somewhere around. Maybe in the pantry—

''Daniel.'' The way Rayna said his name was a way he'd never heard it before.

The effect rolled through him like winter thunder. Strangely drawing him around as if against his will.

There she was, a pretty slip of a thing, gazing up at him with those big golden lashes and a shine in her eyes that made him feel as if he were tumbling right off the edge of a cliff.

Behind her burned a lamp, seated against the glass panes, flaming brightly. A light to lead him in from the dark.

Undone, he took refuge in the dim pantry, chilled as it was closed off from the warm kitchen.

In the darkness, he wiped a hand over his face and waited until the roaring winds outside the walls drove in enough cold to freeze back up his heart.

Sleep eluded her. Rayna sat in bed with the thick blankets pooled around her and reached for the scrap bag she'd brought upstairs.

Maybe it was the wind blowing with hell's fury that troubled her this night. Last winter had been snowy enough but the storms blowing in had been more timid than savage.

Or maybe the truth was, she was alone with the storm. She'd had trouble sleeping without Kol as it was, and the blizzard tonight sounded like a living thing clawing at the walls, howling to get in.

It's just a storm. That was all. Nothing more. Yet the

noise kept her unsettled enough that she'd given up trying to sleep. Sorting through the rag bag, she figured it was just as well. She'd spent enough time not sleeping at night, just lying here, that she may as well be productive.

One thing she needed, if this weather held up through the season, was to replace her quilt. She wasn't cold beneath the pile of blankets, but she wasn't warm, either. Betsy had some lovely fabrics. Scraps left over from her sewing through the years. Rayna climbed out of bed, rummaged in the closet until she found the old pillowslip she kept her own scraps in, and began sorting through it.

The soft weave of cotton against her fingers felt familiar, soothing. She tried to concentrate on the colors and patterns, deciding what kind of fabrics she had that matched and what style of quilt she'd piece. Maybe an Irish chain. Or a nine-patch cabin. There were certainly enough calico scraps to make a pinwheel. Yes, that's what she'd do.

Sorrow rasped in her chest. That quilt she'd made as a young woman dreaming of marriage had covered the bed in this room for nearly half her lifetime. How sad, in replacing it, all hope was gone from her. That she was making, in the end, a quilt stitched not with a girl's dreams but with a woman's practical need.

Yes, this was a sensible quilt, not made with fancy fabrics special ordered from back East. But with the material at hand. She sorted through the calicos and plain cottons. She folded up anything that reminded her of the pretty pastel pinks and blues of her marriage quilt. That left the deeper colors, muted emeralds and rubies, marigolds and sapphires. More mature and sensible for it would wear well.

She didn't know why her eyes stung. Perhaps because this was another step away from her old life. From the way she'd lived as Kol's wife. Wanting to hold on and knowing she had to let go, she laid out the fabrics by color. Decided on the border colors of butter yellow instead of the white she'd used before.

It's not as if I've stopped loving you, Kol, she thought as the storm gathered up a new level of fury with which to batter the walls. As if in protest. *I'm simply... surviving.*

The ring on her finger glinted once in the lamplight. As if to remind her that she now belonged to another. A man she didn't love. A man sleeping downstairs. The memory of his touch on her chin remained like a ghost brushing against her. The hard shelter of his chest, the invincible band of his arms enfolding her, the way he'd held the cup to her lips—

He's your husband now, the wind seemed to whisper. There, at the edge of the shadows, further than the reach of the lamp, was a figure. A gregarious teddy bear of a man with merry blue eyes and platinum hair beginning to thin in front. He held out his hand to her and joy blazed in her heart. Then he was gone and the wind rattled the walls and she jolted awake.

Staring at the closed door where she'd sworn Kol had been standing, she was confused. Had she been dreaming? Her mind was fuzzy, she'd clearly been asleep. Of course it was a dream. There was no way to ever see Kol again, not on this earth, but even so, she'd dreamed of him. And, oh, to have seen him again in such vividness, brighter than any memory... She wiped the wetness from her eyes. She felt better somehow. And she knew what she had to do.

She put away the pieces of fabric, stacking them

neatly by color and replacing the scraps that would be of no use. With care she set the fabric on the closet floor and the scrap bags beside them.

Then she straightened, certain of her course, feeling the chill creeping through her long johns beneath her flannel gown. Wrapping up in her housecoat first, she eased down the hall and checked on Hans. Slumbering, he lay nearly hidden beneath extra blankets, so sweet and at peace—for now.

Frost clung to the banister and the small finish nails in the stairs. Snow dusted the floor in front of the parlor window, wetting her feet. The room was pitch-black and she felt her way. Her toe crashed into the leg of the sofa.

''Rayna?'' The blankets rustled. ''Is something the matter?''

Chapter Sixteen

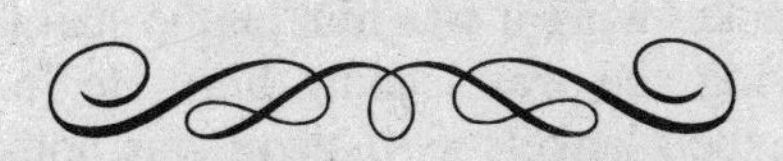

"No." She wrapped her arms around her middle, where the cold in the room seemed to settle. "Why don't you come up with me? It's so cold, neither of us can keep warm alone."

"Did my chattering teeth keep you awake?"

"Yes. I figure the only way I can get some sleep is for you to stop making so much noise." She continued the jest.

His chuckle flowed like warmed molasses. "Guess I'd better do the honorable thing and follow you to bed."

It was there in the air between them. The flicker of acknowledgment, of what went on between a man and his wife in private moments.

She swallowed against the uncertainty clumping in her throat. "I'm not ready for—"

"I know." As if he could see her perfectly, his hand found her shoulder in the dark. His touch possessive and reassuring all at once.

And it made her *feel.* The place so empty behind her breastbone ached like a broken tooth, and she moved into the shelter of his arms, sinking against his granite-like chest. Held on tight when she felt as if every part of her was falling.

His breath came warm in her hair and his words were muffled but sure. So sure. "I'm a patient man, Rayna. All I want is to take good care of my wife."

His words made it easier to gather up the blankets, which he took from her, and lead him up the stairs. It was strange knowing it was him on the stairs just behind her. Knowing she was leading him. He followed and spread out the blankets as if there was nothing to this. As if he was at ease being so alone together.

She helped smooth the blankets. The pile was thick. In the lamplight she realized the fine figure he made, the ripple of lean muscle and astonishing male strength. She couldn't help looking upon this man in his gray long johns, the fabric clinging to him like a second skin.

For the second time since they'd married, she gazed at him and wondered what making love with him would be like.

Tender. She shivered once, ashamed at her thoughts. She didn't love this man, and yet she was thinking about him as if she did. As if she would eagerly stretch out beneath him and invite his intimate touches, his kisses upon her breasts, that long, thick ridge outlined by his long johns hard and pressing urgently into her.

She'd gone without that kind of intimacy, that's all this was. Not a betrayal, because in her heart she would never love another. Just…a woman's need. To be held and cherished. To be lost in the need to bond with her mate.

Daniel stepped into the lamplight. Held out his hand. "Let me help you."

She was perfectly capable of getting herself to bed, but the part of her that had been so alone acquiesced.

She held her breath as he drew near, swept the housecoat from her shoulders and folded the garment carefully on the foot of the bed.

She couldn't seem to look away from the hard, inviting plane of his chest. If she leaned against him, she knew the comfort she'd find there from this man who was her husband. Who cared for her.

She didn't want to care for him. But he tipped her chin and covered her lips with his. A full kiss, brief, firm, gentle. The bottom fell out of her soul as he eased her onto the bed and held the covers for her.

The seed rooted in her chest unfurled a bit more. He covered her as if she were so precious to him. What passed for a hint of a smile touched his lips. The lips that had made hers tingle. And then he blew out the lamp.

An unfamiliar wanting swept through her. Not lust and not love. She didn't know what it was. Listening to the bed ropes creak and feeling the feather tick shift beneath his weight as he stretched out on his side of the bed, she fought the urge to reach for him. To find out if she held on to him, would it make the ache in her empty heart go away?

"Rayna?" His voice was a pleasant rumble that moved through her. "You're shivering."

"I'll warm up."

"I'm shivering, too." He pulled her against him, his strong arms enfolding her, and she settled like a spoon against him.

It was easy to relax into his body's heat. The chill slowly evaporated and the sheets grew warm. She could move away, but she didn't. It was nice to simply be held. To rest against the iron shelter of his chest and thighs.

And to feel that part of him, rigid and enormous against her upper thigh.

The want within her bloomed and she was no longer cold. The ache in her chest increased as he pressed a kiss into her hair.

"Good night, my wife. As long as you're in my arms, I'll keep you safe. Sleep well."

What did she say in return? That she was so grateful she wasn't alone? But that wasn't right. She could face her life without a man to hold her.

"I'm so glad that it was you who came that day to harvest the wheat. That the man I had to marry for my sons' sake was *you.*"

She didn't know if he heard what she meant. She wasn't certain if she could find the words at all. But Daniel's contented sigh seemed to signal that he understood in some way.

That of all the possible turns her life could have taken, she was deeply grateful that this man of stalwart goodness was holding on to her.

Daniel awoke to silence. Somewhere in the back of his mind he recognized that the blizzard had blown out in the night. But what he noticed was the wonder of waking up to find Rayna in his arms.

She was lilac sweetness. That was about to be his very favorite scent, for it would always remind him of this. Of opening his eyes to her relaxed in sleep, her hair like silk everywhere, her woman's softness tucked against him, her fingers twined in one hand. Her hand covering his other, which happened to be resting on her breast. He was stone hard against her lush bottom, and it was a great effort to keep his hunger from taking over.

One day she would trust him enough to reach out as

she was awakening. Opening to him the way a lover should, smiling and sated, to let him cover her. To love her the way he wanted to. *One day.*

For now, he removed his hand from her spellbinding softness. There was a good chance he'd be thinking all day about the way her supple breast had spilled over his fingers. Careful not to wake her or to let in the frigid air, he moved away from the faint lilac scent clinging to her hair and slipped out from the covers.

The cold nipped at his heels and slid up his leg as he grabbed his work clothes and stumbled into them—taking care to be quiet so as not to wake his wife.

She slept, her full lips slightly parted, her hair fanning out against the white pillowslip. Faint twilight crept through the part in the curtains, so he could take his time gazing at her. Letting the sight of her fill him up to get him through the day ahead.

The rooster was doing his best to raise the barnyard by the time Daniel pulled the back door shut behind him. He stepped out to find the boards bare at his feet.

The whole prairie lay in a thin coat of white, crusted and frozen and shining with the first piercing ray of a weary sun. The wind must have blown the snow right on to another part of the prairie.

One piece of good luck. Instead of spending his morning shoveling out, he headed with a whistle to the barn, where the cow greeted him with a welcoming low and the horses shifted awake in their stalls.

He milked the cow, left a fair amount in a cracked bowl in the corner for the barn cat. Then he fed and watered the animals and cleaned their stalls.

The sun was lifting up through the long streamers of fat clouds by the time he headed back to the house. The fire had been fed, judging by the thick plume of smoke rising up from the stovepipe.

And there was Rayna, framed by the frosted window, more beautiful in her work dress and apron, with her hair tied simply at her nape, than anything he'd ever seen.

Tenderness expanded in his chest. An odd, fragile feeling that left him feeling naked and vulnerable. But he welcomed it just the same. *This is what love must be.*

He could watch her forever. The way she moved, elegant and feminine. The line of her slender arm. The curve of her neck and shoulder. Her fairy profile.

His body remembered the alluring heat of her body. The enticing curves and sensual softness. He'd never had such a fine night of sleep.

The door flew open, stirring him. He leaped into motion so he wouldn't be caught staring like a smitten dunderhead.

It was Kirk, come to take the milk pail. "Ma said breakfast is ready. I think I can drive to school again, don't you?"

"You handled everything just fine yesterday."

A gleam of pride came into the boy's eyes. He liked being responsible enough to take care of his family, too. With a hint of a grin, Kirk disappeared the way he'd come. Daniel followed him into the delicious scent of fresh boiled coffee and sausage. Buttery pancakes steamed on the platter Rayna was in the act of setting on the table.

She looked up with a small smile. He could feel the warmth behind it in the vulnerable spot in his chest. A cup of coffee steamed on the table at his set place.

She must have seen him coming and poured him the first cup.

Before he could move to remove his boots and wash

up, he felt a tug on his pant leg at the knee. He looked down at the white-blond head of the little boy. Head tipped back, his big blue eyes stared up, mirroring pain and innocence.

"Ma said I had to tell ya. I'm sorry." He swallowed, as if that took a lot of gumption to say, and then glanced over at his ma.

Rayna nodded to him as if in encouragement as she set out the platter of sausages.

Hans took a shaky breath. "Fer yellin'."

"That's okay." He didn't know what to do with the little fella, so he ruffled his hair.

The boy grabbed his hand and glowered up at him again. Maybe that was something his father used to do. For a brief moment, they stared at one another, big man and little boy. In that moment Hans's fingers gripped his so tight, as if holding on. Before he let go and ran as fast as he could to bolt into his chair.

Yeah, Daniel knew how that felt. To be so little and helpless in a world too big and powerful. To have so many feelings to name starting a war inside you.

Most of all, just wanting a little protection and care.

Yeah, he knew just how it was. So he took care in sitting down at the head of the table. Took his time buttering up his stack of pancakes before sliding the butter dish toward Hans.

The boy didn't look at him, but he took the butter. And it felt as though a truce had been declared.

He sent over the maple syrup, too, real syrup that smelled as sweet as paradise.

Over the top of Hans's head, bringing the last platter to the table with her, he saw that Rayna was watching them.

And smiling.

* * *

The memory of Hans's quick goodbye kiss before he'd grabbed his mittens and run out the door remained with her.

As she hurried through her morning chores, she held the picture in her mind of Kirk holding the horse he'd saddled, one of Daniel's three saddle horses, books and lunch pail dangling on a catch from the saddle horn.

It felt so normal, somehow, the boys heading off to school as she went around the familiar routine of her daily chores. Dishes and sweeping and putting another pot of coffee on to boil, searing a roast Daniel had taken from his cabin's cellar and then setting it to slow cook. Rinsing the beans she'd set out the night before to soak and putting them on to simmer the morning through for noontime soup.

Now and then she looked outside, but she couldn't see Daniel. Only when she was upstairs, smoothing wrinkles out of the sheets and blankets, could she see him. A dark gray figure of a man against the brown wounds in the earth. The near perfect lines of furor broke the earth for nearly as far as she could see.

She plumped his pillow and smelled the faint scent of him on the pillowslip, the wonderful, comforting scent of salty male skin and wood smoke and leather. Was it wrong to have reached out for him last night? To have cuddled close to him when she awoke in the night instead of shifting away?

It was only wrong because she could not give him the love he deserved in return. And he did deserve to be loved. Look how hard he worked for all of their sakes. She took a few moments of idleness, when there was so much to be done, to watch him from the window.

Head bowed, shoulders braced, back powerfully set, he manhandled the plow through the stubborn prairie.

He'd done so much for her and her sons. He deserved all the kindness and affection she could give him—and more. She would do her very best for this man who wanted his life to mean something. Who had never been loved.

After changing, she went in search of boots that might fit. Kirk's were big, but they would serve. She checked the roast and beans, turned down the damper to keep the heat low while she was out, and filled the jug with coffee. That done, she buttoned into an old flannel work jacket of Kol's. Everything was too big, but she could make do, and hurried through the bitter chill to the barn.

It was fortunate Daniel had two sets of workhorses. The old curl-toothed plow was hidden in the back of the barn, a relic from leaner years, but it was small and not too cumbersome.

It took a while to figure out the harnessing and she nearly dislocated her shoulder lifting the heavy yokes over the Clydesdales' heads, but finally the task was done. She disengaged the metal tooth and took charge of the reins.

The huge workhorses both looked over their shoulders at her in unison, as if amused a woman was attempting this. But she was firm with them and they obeyed, ambling forward into the eye-stinging cold of the morning, steam rising from their nostrils as they exhaled and from the heat of their coats.

Rayna breathed in lung-burning air. The entire prairie lay in a crisp frozen hush as she headed out to join Daniel. As cold as it was, she refused to turn back.

It was a long way out finding him, but when she neared, she realized he'd spotted her approach and stopped his work. To stare at her with one arched brow as she pulled the big horses to a halt. He drew himself up like a bear ready for battle, his gaze darting from the horses to the plow to her dressed in a man's work clothes.

"I brought coffee," she said brightly, and handed him the jug and a cup. "Where do you want me to start?"

"You're going to use that thing?"

"I figure if a man can figure out how to do this, then so can I." Her chin up, she was ready for anything. She wasn't about to change her mind.

"A woman's place isn't in the fields." She couldn't tell if he was amused or angry, but the left corner of his mouth quirked as he thumbed off the crock's stopper.

"You accepted Kirk's help after school."

"Because these fields need to be turned over for spring planting. Before the next blizzard sets in."

"Exactly. Time is of the essence. Daniel, I never want you to think that your only value to us is this, the work you do."

The empty cup slipped from his fingers. "What did you say?"

Disbelieving, he watched her with his feet braced and jaw tensed, doubt crinkling in the corners of his eyes.

"You have a family and a home. You aren't hired field labor." She knelt before him and the wide brim of her son's hat hid what secrets could be read on her face. But her movements were confident and at ease as she retrieved the fallen cup, wiped it off and rose.

She kept her face tilted down and held out the cup.

The work gloves on her hands were too big, as was the hat and every article of visible clothing. It made his heart twist until his eyes stung.

His hand was unsteady as he went to pour the coffee.

Without a word, she took the jug and poured for him. Hot, rich coffee steaming, just like his entire being.

Awake and alive on this harsh autumn morning, he felt a part of him fall away, melt as the cool sun broke through the veiling clouds to touch the land.

White rays of light swept the earth and he watched, unable to breathe or to blink as the frosty earth responded. Tiny curls of dampness rose like the steam from his cup, like the frozen crust on his heart. Lifting up until the air was full of a wavering fog.

The horizon vanished. Then the outer fields of rolling land. The mist grew thicker until all he could see was Rayna. That was all. The way the brim hid her face, the bulky clothes disguising her lush curves.

He dared to place two fingertips beneath her chin and nudge gently. She didn't respond at first, and he could feel her pain. Feel how hard it was for her to let go of a past for this moment with him.

When she did tilt her head back so he could gaze upon her, her eyes were clear and dry. The secrets on her lovely face made the tenderness inside him swell like the mist on the plains. Obscuring everything: the past, his inadequacies, his fears.

Because it was there in her eyes, that she meant what she'd said. That last night, she'd chosen to stay in his arms. And this morning, she chose to work beside him.

It was a new thing, these fragile feelings. They were dangerous. He figured it was his heart that he risked as he set the mug on the plack, dropped the reins to the ground and cupped Rayna's face in his hands. The kiss he gave her came from his newly unburied heart.

With a softness he didn't know that he had inside him, but it was there, quiet like a light burning. He breathed her in, the soft wonder of her lips and the heat inside as he brushed deeper, tasting the coffee on her tongue. Sweet. So infinitely sweet.

Hours later, even after all the mist had burned away, she was all he could see. His wife.

His heart.

Chapter Seventeen

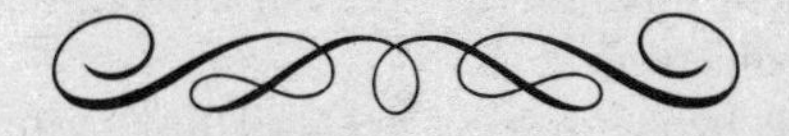

In the dark shadows of the kitchen, Rayna fetched the crystal lamp from the center of the table. The faint aroma of spiced roast and rich gravy and the cornmeal loaf she'd baked to go with it scented the air, making her remember the high points of a satisfying day....

Of working in companionable silence with Daniel. Plowing one end of the field while he plowed the other. Of how he came to wrestle the metal blade free whenever it twisted or became stuck on a rock. How she hadn't even had to ask. He'd kept an eye on her and the minute she had a problem, he was there.

Without words, he'd made one thing clear. He would always be there. Rayna struck a match, the tiny flame flaring to a brief life. As she touched it to the wick, it was as if that place so dark within her felt the spark of hope.

"Hey, pretty lady." Daniel's gruff voice knelled, pitched low and deep. She turned toward him when he stepped into the room.

It felt as if the empty void within her turned, too, a tender seedling seeking light in the complete winter of her life. How could it ever survive? She couldn't love again, could she? Her heart was gone, as barren as the endless plains. The most she could hope for was some sort of companionship with Daniel. A friendship.

He deserved so much more.

All she could do was her best. And she would. She shook out the match and carefully laid it in the stone tray next to the stove. Shrouded in darkness, out of the lamp's reach, he came to her. Put his big hands on her shoulders and rubbed.

"You've been on your feet all day, same as me." Intimate, that's how his voice seemed as he spoke against the shell of her ear. As if his words could dip inside her.

She let her eyelids drift shut and preened into the luxury of his fingertips rubbing at the searing knots in her muscles. "I can't think of the last time I was this exhausted. And that's saying something. I haven't been sleeping, except for…" She couldn't say the words.

"Last night?"

She nodded. She couldn't tell him why that was a sorrow, to have slept well for the first time since she'd been widowed. Sad because it was his arms. His perfectly wonderful, tender arms. The past life she'd had felt so far away, like the brilliant days of a hot summer when midwinter's eve draws the days dark and frigid.

"You're tired. Leave the rest of the work and come sit."

How could a man's voice be soothing and alluring at once? How could she think a man to be so sexually appetizing? She was not a woman of base vulgarisms, and yet his touch melted through her like warmed butter. Why was it this man who stirred her? She didn't want to be stirred.

"I thought about what you said this morning." Daniel

spoke as he drew her through the shadows. "We're family now. More than two people thrown together. There's caring involved. Right?"

The calloused roughness of his open palm rasped against the side of her face, and it was as if his tenderness flowed into her. She leaned into his touch, unable to deny it. In the shadows it was easier to close her eyes and to feel there was something undeniable that sparked between them, the same way the lamp's flame drew the kerosene along the wick. Burning and burning.

This was *not* desire she felt. It *couldn't* be. She was like the trees outside with no sap rising through those dark, barren limbs. Dormant for the long winter ahead. So why, then, did she feel need pulse in her veins? It was the need for his comfort, no doubt.

And not for a greater intimacy.

His lips touched hers with a wordless query. In the dark it was easier to surrender to the velvet seduction of his kiss. To the swirling tangle of pain and emptiness that disappeared when his arms banded around her and pulled her close.

There was no sorrow and no grief, only Daniel's solid chest and the caressing suction of his mouth on hers. Of the wonderful alive feeling of his hard muscles and harder erection against the curve of her stomach and the rising tide of need that drove harder against him.

She surrendered for one more long moment, and then it was no longer her need for comfort that kept them together. But the silent realization that he needed her. This good man who had taken on a father's burden. Because he needed to matter to someone.

And what value did life have without love in it?

Tenderness for this big, rugged man wrung through her, and she kissed him, his jaw, his face, his brow, and held him to her breasts when he sighed. Together, the lonesomeness was like the dark, ebbing away as the flame on the lamp's wick brightened.

It was a feeling she took with her when he led her into the parlor's light and warmth. A feeling that survived and took root as she settled in to sort through the fabrics she'd brought down from upstairs, earlier, when the potatoes had been baking for supper.

Daniel eased the lamp he'd taken from the kitchen table onto the windowsill at her side. Golden light pooled on her lap and the small, flower-petal-shaped calico pieces she was pinning together.

"A quilt?"

"For our bed." She said no more as she bent to weave the silver straight pin through the edges of fabric.

"I noticed you took away the quilt that was there."

He knelt, unaware that Kirk in the corner had looked up from his history book. That Hans's clattering train had crawled to a stop. Rayna searched for the right words and then realized there was only the truth to tell him. "That was the quilt my mother and I pieced when Kol was courting me, for our marriage bed. I just couldn't—"

Apology filled her face and she glanced toward her sons, who were watching them. It hit him like a sucker punch. He was a foreigner here as surely as if he'd emigrated from another country.

He didn't understand the life Rayna had lived. Where a mother and daughter sewed with high hopes for a happy marriage. Where a new husband and wife made love and conceived children and welcomed them not as burdens to feed, but precious in their own right.

He couldn't begin to understand all that she'd lost. But he was starting to see. The fragile swell of tenderness in his chest, this was just the beginning of it. Of the love he felt for Rayna, a bond that would deepen and grow with time.

It was also a caring she did not feel for him.

He cradled his hand, so big and rough, against her delicate jaw. "So you are making a quilt for our marriage bed."

She nodded, her eyes so huge and luminous he could see straight into her heart. So bleak and wounded. The power of it stunned him, for she'd kept it so well hidden.

What manner of closeness Rayna and her Kol must have shared, a magnitude Daniel could not imagine. He'd only seen the outward appearance of those few couples he'd seen in town who, after years of marriage, still looked upon one another with respect and affection.

He could see, feeling the tug of love in his very being for this woman, what marriage must become in so much time.

It surprised him when her hand covered his, holding him against the side of her face. "You are my husband now, and I owe you so much."

"No more than I owe you."

"What could you possibly owe me?"

No, he realized, she really didn't know. And how could she? She'd always been loved. He waited until Hans's train was busy making noise again and Kirk had at least returned to the appearance of studying before he answered.

Even then, he pitched his voice low, so only she could hear. "You have given my life meaning."

"Oh, Daniel, you make it impossible, don't you?" What could only be agony showed on her face.

An agony he felt move surely through him. Worry creased deep into his chest as he caught a breath.

"What? What did I do? I don't ever want to make you unhappy."

"You, Daniel Lindsay, make it impossible not to care for you."

"You care for me?"

"Like I said. You make it hard not to."

"And that's a bad thing?"

"You are such a good man. You are breaking my heart, and here I was so certain that I didn't have one left."

"How am I breaking your heart, pretty lady?"

"I don't know." She closed her eyes, leaning into his touch.

Maybe he knew what she meant. The tender places in his chest hurt something fierce. Not from a wound, but from the way the frozen prairie aches when dawn's light touches it.

She cared for him. That was a miracle, wasn't it? It wasn't what she'd had; it didn't take a smart man to know this marriage was hard for her. But they were making a decent life, the two of them.

Being cared for was a fine thing, and the tired cramp of every muscle he owned didn't trouble him a bit as he sat in the chair by the fire. He took up his knife, intending to whittle, and caught Hans glaring at him.

Well, they had a long way to go, but one step at a time.

He hadn't noticed how lonesome he'd been. But the hush of Rayna's needle as she sewed, the scratch of Kirk's stylus on his slate and the clunk of Hans's shoes as he stormed out of the room and up the stairs.

Why, it was a far sight better than anything he'd ever known before.

"It's nearly his bedtime anyway." Rayna set down

the work she'd practically just started, looking at the ceiling overhead where Hans's stomping ended with a loud groan of bed ropes. "I'd best go get him settled."

He nodded in acknowledgment, working the willow limb he'd brought in when he'd fed the fire. He wished he knew how to make this easier for Rayna. It was something to know that Rayna cared for him—something he'd never been able to say before.

When she breezed by him on her way upstairs, he swore his soul moved. She left the room and he could still feel her softness, her presence, as if she'd opened up a room in his heart and walked right in to stay. Her steps on the stairs and then the gentle cadence of her gait overhead keened through him.

If only he could forget the sadness he'd put in her eyes. She hadn't said a thing, but he knew.

He knew, somehow, as if he could hear her thoughts. She was sad because he wasn't another man.

"Daniel?" Kirk held his book and slate in the crook of his arm, looking as if he was going to head up, too. "Hans doesn't understand. I tried to tell him. He's just a little kid."

"I know. I'm not mad at him."

"Good. Just so you know. I'll help you in the field again after school. But should Ma be working like that?"

"It was her idea. I don't like it, either. But your mother is one determined woman. I figure it means something to her, that she helps to take care of you boys, too. Hell, it'll take you, me and her to make it through the winter."

Kirk swallowed hard, a boy struggling with heavy burdens. "You can count on me."

"It's nice to know you're a man I can count on, Kirk.

Trust me, I've promised to do my best, and that's what I'll do. I won't let you or your ma down. You've got my word on that.''

Some of the worry seemed to let go of the boy as he moved away, and his gait seemed lighter as he pounded up the stairs.

Daniel set aside his work. He'd worked damn hard, and his vision was starting to blur. Exhausted, he watched the fire burn, the logs turn to embers and ash. That only reminded him of his responsibilities.

What was left in the woodshed out back wouldn't see them through half the winter. It was late, but he could take Kirk hunting with him. Besides the pig he'd bought last spring and the steer getting fat on the summer's wild grasses, a few deer would help.

As for the bills due the grain and seed and grocery stores, he'd have to sit down with Rayna after the plowing was done and decide what could be paid. He'd have Kirk stop by the newspaper office. The boy could write up a good ad for his cabin, empty now. Rent income would help, if he could find someone who wasn't moving East after losing everything.

It wasn't a burden he minded, he realized as he banked the coals and locked the doors. He turned down the lamps until only darkness and shadows kept him company as he groaned up the stairs.

Rayna. She'd be watching for him. He knew it as he cleared the last step. Hans's door was open and the path of light guided his attention to the little boy tucked in bed, struggling to keep his eyes open as his mother read to him.

Oh, but she's a beauty. It was her spirit he saw, that part of a person that was harder to see. Gentle words and spring light, that's what she was. Her soft alto a low hum as she read of a moon watching over a sleeping child, and the rise and ebb of her voice tugged at something deep within him.

There were no memories of a mother's loving voice at bedtime unraveling the mysteries of those letters on a printed page. But the yawning emptiness no longer felt so vast.

It was hope that breathed through him as he left mother and child alone. Hope for visions he'd never much counted on coming true. But as he walked into their bedroom, with the pile of wool blankets covering the sheets and mattress, he wondered what would come of this practical marriage.

If love, like the quilt Rayna was pinning and sewing, could be made. From the scraps and scars of two peoples' lives to make something whole and good.

He knew she was coming even before he heard her step in the hallway. He felt her presence as surely as the soft fragrant scent of her. Desire like a banked fire glowed within him. Her eyes widened, her gaze spearing to his bare chest.

He'd embarrassed her? He hoped not. But it was a cute thing, how busy she suddenly seemed, paying close attention to the tasks of shutting the door and unbuttoning her shoes. He wondered why there were only the two boys. If Rayna had ever wanted another baby.

Either way, he shrugged off his shirt and went to toss it in the basket she kept in the corner for laundry. Her shocked gasp fired up his adrenaline. He spun around, reaching for the Colt he wasn't wearing—it was folded up in the holster on the highest shelf in her kitchen—only to find her coming toward him with her eyes bright.

"Your back. Turn around."

What was wrong? He glanced over his shoulder.

There was no spider or anything, was there? He felt her touch move through him before her hands lighted on his shoulder blades. Brighter than anything he'd known before spiraled through to the very deepest part of him. Places where he'd stored up his boyhood of sorrow and worse.

Places that could not take such illumination. He went to step away from her touch, to keep those places buried within him.

She stopped him. The press of her hands, the brush of her gaze on his bare skin. The faintest warmth of her breath that he seemed able to feel as if it were a spring breeze. Then came the gentlest brush of her lips. One kiss after another in a curing lash up to his nape.

Hell. It was his scars. He hadn't meant for her to see them. He'd just forgotten. They'd been a part of him for more than half his life. "Don't, Rayna. That happened a long time ago. I don't think about it anymore."

Another kiss was her answer. So searingly sweet, it made every part of him ache.

The caress of her fingertips was painfully soothing, as if she could take away the little boy's pain. It was too late, it was impossible, but he appreciated the gesture. His throat closed up and he squeezed his eyes shut. Feeling. Just feeling.

That hurt, too.

"Oh, Daniel. What made these marks? A belt?" Not repulsion. Not censure.

He expected both. Maybe even deserved it. "That just shows you've never been beaten. A whip did that." And for no reason at all, because there was no way she could understand he just opened his mouth and out it came. The truth. "I was eight."

She sagged against him. ‘‘Hans will be eight this spring.’’

One little boy spared the harshness of this world. He’d make sure of it. The little boy with Rayna’s chin and button nose.

He didn’t tell her why he’d been punished. He’d been so thirsty in the blazing August fields, he’d just given up, hungry and exhausted and hopeless. The foreman had not particularly liked his refusal to work.

‘‘There is nothing a sweet little boy could do to deserve such treatment.’’

Her comfort was so powerful, it crept inside him, from her soul to his. That’s when he knew how alone he’d been all his life. It wasn’t the solitary way he lived, or the lonesomeness of a boyhood without a family of his own. No, it was this. The way his love for her had taken root inside him. Growing in a place where there had once only been shadows.

Everything he believed, everything he’d ever done to keep this part of him safe, fell away. And he was hopeless and helpless as a wave of emotion rolled through him like the shock through the earth after a dynamite blast. Shaken, he wasn’t aware that he’d turned in her arms until his mouth was hot on hers. Until the wrenching aftershock rocked through him.

Need. It burned inside him. Not the need of a frightened child, but the yearning of a man’s heart for its match. Rayna. She was all he was, everything within him that was good and strong. Her kiss, her hands small on his shoulders, her body welcoming him as he walked her back until she was against the bed and he came over her.

Driven beyond himself for this need to love her, he eased her onto the sheets. She seemed to feel it, too, for she was kissing him fully. Arching against him in silent need, her cheeks wet with tears.

The tenderness he felt for her was powerful enough to make the world disappear around him. He cherished her, just as he'd vowed to do, with loving words and pleasing touches. He honored her with his hands and mouth as she unbuttoned and slipped out of her dress and corset.

And when they were naked together and moonlight tumbled through the window to cast her in silver wonder, he entered her slowly, carefully, and cradled her head in his hands as he made love to her. Gazing into her eyes the entire time, so he could see into her soul.

So joined, he loved her until she surrendered, until pleasure broke through her and into him. They came together, and that's when she shuttered her eyes and pressed her face into the hollow of his throat. When he was done pouring himself into her, he kissed her brow until she let him gaze upon her one more time.

And he said it truly, so she would know how he felt beyond doubt. "I love you. With all I am. With all I will ever be."

Then she wrapped her arms around him tight, clinging to him. He held her safe until sleep claimed her. His woman who gave him value. He didn't know love could do that, but now he did. He kissed her brow while she slept, even in her dreams holding him, holding on.

Chapter Eighteen

Rayna woke with a start. It was still dark. Surprised she'd been able to sleep at all, she looked to the window. The moonlight was gone. It had to be well into the early morning hours.

Daniel, what a man he is. Her soul broke watching him sleep. He lay beside her on his stomach, arms flung up over the pillow. The dark shadows played along the contours of his muscular back and shoulders. The covers were pooled low on his hips. The long, lean, hard look of him made her yearn to wrap her arms around him and hold on. To kiss a long string of kisses down his back and reach beneath the covers. But if she gave in to those impulses, he'd come awake, pulling her to his chest, already hard and needing her. She wanted him to come inside her again, so she could lose herself with him. Until there was only him.

It's also what she didn't want.

He slumbered peacefully, his dark hair tousled, his breathing even and untroubled. She resisted the urge to reach out and slipped from the bed instead. Trembling with emotions she dared not name. Regrets she could not erase.

The cold air was a shock on her bare skin. She searched for her nightgown in the dark, found Daniel's nightshirt and had to go to the corner of the room where it had landed. Teeth chattering, she slipped into the warm flannel and found her socks.

What she wanted was away from Daniel, away from here, in this room where they'd made love. But the house was too cold, and so she grabbed the extra blanket from the foot of the bed and wrapped up in it at the window.

She pulled aside the curtains, but frost etched the glass so thickly, she couldn't see out. There was only the vast feel of black night and the hushed tap of snow against the glass. The storm arrived not with a howling crash but a tired inevitability. As if there was no other choice.

Exactly how she felt. She gave in to the frigid draft rushing through the wood and glass as if it were paper. Let the icy air force her eyes to water. Let the cold sink deep into her bones. Maybe it would numb the pain of her soul.

It didn't. The faint chime of the kitchen clock, muffled by the floorboard and distance, marked the passing of one hour to the next. The storm moved in, as it was destined to do, the wind whipping along the eaves was a particular sadness.

It was an affliction she shared. With Daniel, she'd felt something she'd never had with Kol. No pleasant loving joy, but something so intense it scared her.

Daniel had devastated her defenses. Every last one of them.

In the solemn hours before dawn came, she felt revealed. Her soul was open and exposed, and every emotion quivered. Sorrow at the man she'd lost. Affection for the one she'd gained. Fear at being so close to another man again.

Anger at her weakness.

I want him again. Over and over until she could lose herself from this world and let Daniel overtake her senses, her body, her soul. The overwhelming experience of being joined with him, clinging to his brawny shoulders, slick with sweat, as he stroked in her, pushing her to her surrender.

Until there was only the pure joy of him inside her and the crash of pleasure roaring from him and into her, the rare bliss of her shattering release as he emptied into her with a hot rush that could change everything.

She could feel the evidence of his seed. How could she have forgotten? The cap lay in her box in the necessary room. It wasn't going to do any good there. Without it, she had no protection against Daniel's seed taking root within her.

This was not the time to be forgetting such an important precaution.

Daniel murmured in his dreams. Indistinguishable sounds, and he rolled onto his side. Thrashing in absolute silence as the bed ropes groaned beneath him.

Dreaming of his childhood? A single moan tore up his throat, the sound of absolute suffering and he fell still. *The poor man.* She wanted to go to him, to trail her fingertips through his hair. To stroke comfort across his brow.

She was hardly aware of having crossed the room, but she was there, at his side like a guardian angel in the dark watching over him. He was at peace now, breathing slow and deep. His big body sprawled on his side, his arm flung over the pillow. Naked, she could just make out the shape of him in the dark, and he was stunning.

Tenderness, unwanted and unbidden, blazed through her. The empty place in her chest gave a painful hitch. She reached out to twirl a shock of his hair around her fingertips. Mussed from their lovemaking.

She let his hair fall away from her touch. Undisturbed, he slept. She felt the uneven lay of scars and skin as she drew the covers up over his thighs. Sweat bathed his skin from his dream.

What misery had he known?

She remembered the scars marking his back as her fingers grazed his side. Sympathy swelled within her for this man so strong. He could never be hers. Not truly.

Sadness crashed over her, as strong as the tenderness that made her tuck the blanket beneath his chin. He was safe and warm now, yet she couldn't make her feet carry her away from his side.

''Hmm, Rayna,'' he sighed in his sleep. So much love rumbled in those words.

Her soul broke a little more at the sound. *What am I going to do with you, my husband?*

For it felt as if now, this night for the first time, he was her husband truly. They'd finally had their wedding night. The vows promised between them were sealed. *What a wonderful lover you are.* Her lips tingled in memory of his deep, passionate kisses. Her body felt renewed, alive again, pleasantly sated from his incredible touches.

Her entire being *felt.* The emotions she'd tucked away in her heart with Kol's loss had been sparked to life again. Like eyes kept too long in the dark burned and wept at a sudden light.

I love you. With all I am. With all I will ever be. Daniel's sensual baritone rumbled through her. Even in memory, her body responded. Her breasts ached, her thighs parted and she craved him like a hunger that came not from her flesh but from her soul.

After making love, he'd said those words with unwavering love and honesty, and she'd given up the last of her resolve and clung to him, both relieved and troubled that she'd surrendered to him.

While she watched, he rolled onto his back with a moan, exposing a wide wedge of his iron chest. Her body clenched with desire. She wanted him. Still. She wanted to slip into his arms and to experience him again.

"Rayna." He eased up on his elbows, groggy and sleepy. "Come here. Come to me."

She should argue. She couldn't give in to her weakness, her needs. That was exactly what she wanted. One more time. One more joining. The night was not over. Morning had not yet come.

She let him draw her over him. Felt the covers fall over her and his arms enfold her. The heat of him, the texture of his skin and wonderful body burned the chill from her soul.

Like flame joining flame, she let him guide her onto his shaft. Let his heat spear into her until they were both burning. Until there was only their heated coming together and release.

And sweet, sweet bliss.

Daniel woke with Rayna in his arms. His heart swelled, filling him with gratitude, and he held her, afraid to move.

Maybe if he didn't breathe or move or think, he could make time stand still long enough to soak in this wonderful moment. Nothing in his life had ever come close to the joy of opening his eyes to a new day, with the woman he loved wrapped against him, skin to skin.

Sated from a night of lovemaking, she lay boneless against him. Using his chest for her pillow.

I love you, my wife. Tenderness flowed through his blood, more intoxicating than any liquor he'd ever known as he gently cupped the back of her head and held her to him. His heart beat with the unwavering truth.

He was hers, body, heart and soul.

But the faint chime of the downstairs clock heralded the hour, and there was no holding back the coming day. It had already begun. But to leave Rayna? No, he didn't want to do that. For the first time in his life he wanted to stay late in bed. For the first time in his life he had a reason to.

Oh, she was beauty. He hurt with love for her. How perfect the slope of her nose and the lush curve of her lips beneath. Just parted and relaxed. He knew intimately the feel of those lips on his. Her hand rested, slightly splayed against his belly. Remembering her tender touches and her secret caresses from last night made him ache for more.

There would be time for that come nightfall. When he could have her all to himself again. Smiling, he stroked the satin strands of her rich hair, a wild tangle from last night. Who would have thought prim and proper Rayna could—

She moaned, snuggling against his chest, exposing the soft pillows of her breasts. Hell, she was perfection. He watched as her lashes flickered and she gazed up at him sleepily.

"Good morning, beautiful." He cradled her head and came over her. She was beneath him, all soft woman's heat. A hard punch of love rose up from his soul.

Her answer was a kiss, and she felt so relaxed and

supple beneath him. He loved knowing he'd pleased her last night. The shadows in her eyes were still there, but she closed them as they kissed.

As if it was too much to feel, she tore her mouth from his and buried her face in the crook of his shoulder. He feared for a brief moment that she was going to push away from him, but he was wrong. She opened to him again, searching to take him into her, and he was only happy to oblige. For he belonged to her.

With a growl he wrapped his arms around her, filling her deep. He felt her need as she wrapped around him tight.

Oh, she was his love. His first and his only. He didn't know how to tell her.

So he showed her.

The entire morning through, the memory of being intimate with Daniel did not leave her. Nor, she realized, did that memory leave him. Through breakfast he watched her intense and steady. As she helped wrap Hans into his muffler, she could feel Daniel's gaze like a tug on her soul.

Just where she didn't want to feel him. She turned her back to him but it didn't help. Every movement he made—pulling on his boots, feeding the fire, finding the warming potatoes she'd put on to heat for the cold ride into town—grated along every inch of her skin.

It made her even more aware of the man in the room with her. The man she shouldn't have turned to last night.

''Ma, I can do it.'' Hans fretted, pulling away.

She had to fight to get the muffler close around his ears. She was persistent because it was cold out and she didn't want him getting sick. Once she was satisfied, she pulled his hat over his ears and kissed the tip of his nose. Not much of her little boy showed. "Now you're snug as a bug."

"Ma, I'm not a baby, you know."

"I know." Sadly, he was growing up far too fast. "Do you have all your homework?"

"Kirk has the books and stuff." Hans squirmed, overwarm in his layers of clothing.

She tugged his cap down. "What about your slate?"

"Uh..." Hans rolled his eyes upward. "I guess I forgot that."

"I'll run up and get it. You get your lunch, okay?"

On her way through the kitchen, she had to pass Daniel. Daniel, who made her nerve endings stand up like flowers to the sun. That intensity pricked and crackled through her and no distance seemed to diminish it. Every step away pulled at her very being.

As she walked past her open bedroom door, she caught sight of the bed made, without a wrinkle on it, and the pillows fluffed and in place, just the way she'd made it earlier. But it was so neat and tidy, and she remembered how mussed the covers had been after a night of passion spent in Daniel's arms.

She squeezed her eyes shut until she was safely past, but she could not close off her thoughts as easily. Or the recollection of Daniel's touch, Daniel's words, of Daniel's heat fusing with hers.

By the time she returned to the kitchen, glancing at the clock fearing the boys would be tardy, she didn't see him at first. Not until she cleared the edge of the table and there Daniel was, crouching on the floor so he was eye-to-eye with Hans, who glared at him with eyes filled with all the hatred his grieving heart could muster.

Hans yanked down his muffler. "I can help Kirk take care of Ma."

"I know you can help take care of your ma. But someone has to take care of you, little boy."

"Nuh-uh. You go home."

Rayna's jaw dropped as she watched her son tug his muffler back over his face as if he hadn't said anything so hateful. The slate nearly dropped from her fingers as she took a breath to scold him.

But Daniel beat her to it. He didn't seem angry. No. It was hurt that brought his voice so low. "This is my home now, too."

Hans's eyes flashed and he opened his mouth, but then he spotted her. Perhaps deciding against whatever it was he wanted to say, he ran. The door slammed so hard, the windows rattled in their panes.

Daniel rose, pain etched on his chiseled features.

"Daniel, I'm sorry. He should not speak to you like that. I'll—"

"No." He caught her by the wrist. His hold was not angry. Nor was his voice as he took the slate from her. "Hans is hurting enough. All he sees is me trying to take his father's place."

"He was h-horrible to you. *My* son. I don't know what to say."

Daniel supposed she couldn't understand. On one hand, she was right. The little fellow had behaved badly. But Daniel knew something about being that young with a shattered heart. "You stay in here where it's warm. I'll give this to your son."

It was an odd thing, feeling her regard for him. It filled him up, so that the wicked north wind had no bite to it. It was as if a part of her soul was his now. Wasn't it a fine thing, for he wasn't alone anymore.

He grabbed Hans, who struggled to climb onto the waiting horse, and deposited him handily onto the gelding's back behind his brother. Hans rewarded him with a hard glare.

It's okay, little guy. You get this hurt out, so it's good and done with. Daniel buckled the slate into place with the other school things. *Then you and I will get along just fine.*

"Daniel?" It was Kirk, who'd pulled down his muffler to speak, and both muffler and boy were already covered with thick snow. "You figure another blizzard is heading this way?"

"No, the wind's blowing straight as could be. There's no mean in it. If it gets worse by afternoon, you boys come over to the rail station."

With a nod, Kirk pulled his scarf back over his face. Hans kept right on scowling over his shoulder, Rayna's little boy, who looked so much like her.

"Daniel? I've got your lunch." It was Rayna come out on the porch, the affection in her voice the best part. He had someone who cared about him. Who worried if he was cold or hungry or troubled. "I'm sorry—"

"It's all right." He kissed her, and the satin-soft heat brought back the memories of last night. Of loving her. Of the privilege of being loved in return. She probably didn't know all that it meant to him. "You have a good day."

"You, too."

With two steps away, the thick gray-white curtain of snow closed around him, stealing her from his sight. But not from his heart.

He took up the reins of his mare, wiped the snow off the seat and hunkered down into the saddle. Snow beat at him as he joined the boys by the gate, holding it open for them. Hans was still glaring at him.

One day that would change, too.

For now, Daniel was content to ride, his bigger horse breaking a trail for the smaller one the boys rode. He was truly happy for the first time in his life. It wasn't something he was comfortable with. Happiness, and the hope for more of it. Things looked pretty good from where he sat.

Yep, it sure made a man, even one as skeptical as him, dare to dream—just a bit.

Rayna knew her stack of work was waiting, for Betsy would be by before noon for pickup, but she lingered at the window. Foolish it was, because the thick snowfall hid all sight of Daniel and the boys. The shadows made her think she saw the flank of a horse.

No, it was merely shadows. Even if it hadn't been snowing, she couldn't have seen them anyway. They were down the driveway and on the main road to town. Even so, she rose and locked the door.

It was the image of Daniel, kneeling before Hans, that had her staring out into the shroud of tumbling snowflakes. Daniel, who'd let Hans's cruel words slide right off him. Daniel, with the scars on his back. He'd been Hans's age. His words came back to her. *If I can keep you and your sons from the kind of hardship I've known, then I guess that makes my life mean something.*

Rayna sank into the cushions on the window seat. How could a man who'd known such cruelty have such a flawless heart?

She had no notion how she was going to stop from falling in love with him. Just when she couldn't take any more feeling, any more risk, he went and made it impossible for her not to care.

He'd breathed life back into her when it wasn't what she was ready for. She didn't know if she would ever be able to risk so much of herself again.

Chapter Nineteen

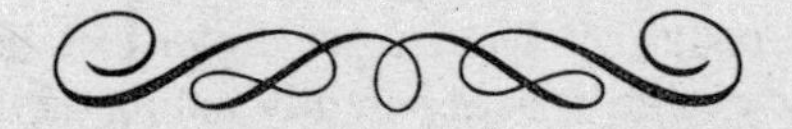

"Daniel!" Milton Danzig's bellow sliced through the afternoon's chill. "Put down the shovel and come in!"

Daniel wiped the snow out of his eyes, his breath rising in great clouds. What could that be all about? He jammed the shovel into the coal and tried to see the back door, but Danzig had already gone inside.

Maybe that wasn't a good sign. Daniel loped through the rail yard, the cars lined up in need of unloading. There looked to be enough work. He wasn't about to get fired, right? He was the last man hired, and no doubt would be the first to go when the work was caught up.

Just another couple weeks, he prayed as he stomped coal dust and snow chunks off his boots. A few more paydays and he'd have that November first payment made. And if not... *Hell, I can't think about that.*

Danzig looked up from his desk. "You got someone to see you."

There, by the red-hot potbellied stove, sat two boys. Kirk, who hopped to his feet. Hans sat with his head down and face hidden, not moving.

Daniel was across the room in three strides. Something had to be wrong to take them away from school. "What is it?"

"Hans is sick." Kirk lowered his voice. "I asked the teacher if I could take him over to Doc Haskins's, but the doc's out on house calls."

"Take the little feller home," Danzig called from the corner. "Go on. I know you'll work late to make up the lost time."

"I appreciate it." Daniel got down to take a look at the little boy, who was apparently acting as if he wasn't there. The little tyke did look flushed. His breathing came louder than it should. Daniel stripped off a glove to feel the boy's brow.

Hans jerked away, but not quick enough.

Yep, the boy was burning up. "You did right, Kirk. You head back to school now. I'll make sure he gets home."

"What about the doctor?"

"I'll go fetch him. Don't you worry."

It was hard, getting used to a stepfather, Daniel figured. Kirk was nearly grown. It was a good thing he felt a responsibility for his brother.

When he saw Kirk nod, he understood. Trust took a long time coming, even under the best of circumstances. But it was something Kirk was learning to do.

Daniel reached for Hans's mittened hand, to help him stand, but the boy went to his brother instead. The little boy clung to the oldest as they headed outside.

The wind had a howl to it, and Daniel didn't like the sound. A whiteout wasn't far away. Since he had no time to waste, Daniel swung up on his mare, without bothering to saddle her. Then he held out his arms.

Kirk lifted Hans up, and the little fellow struggled at first, but he was too ill to do much more than make a show of it. Daniel tucked the boy against his chest, beneath his coat to keep him as warm as possible.

It was a new feeling, as he headed out, nosing the mare toward home, leaning low to urge her to go all-out. There was a new spot of tenderness twinkling to life in his chest. Hans held him so tight.

You just hold on to me, little one. Daniel felt his responsibilities weighing on him mightily.

Rayna recognized the bright blue cap, snow-dappled though it was, and the riot of bouncy brown curls. She opened the door. ''Hurry, before a gust blows you away!''

''I hope you don't mind, I just helped myself to your barn. I didn't have the heart to leave poor Bernie standing out in this.'' Betsy tumbled in with the driven snow. ''Oh, whatever you have in your oven smells divine.''

''Baked beans and a venison roast.'' Rayna shut the door with her foot, reaching to help unwrap her friend from layers of wool. ''Are you hungry? You arrived just in time.''

''Oh, I shouldn't. With this weather, I wanted to try to get done with my route early, but you know I have a weakness for your cooking.''

''As if you aren't the better cook!'' She shook the ice from Betsy's pretty coat and hat and hung them near the stove to dry. ''The pot of coffee isn't fresh, but it's hot.''

''That sounds heavenly. Hot is all I care about right now.'' Betsy helped herself to a cup from the drainer. ''Tell me you got Mrs. Mendelson's mending done. Please?''

''It's done. I just have one button to fix. It's coming loose, and if I leave it, it'll be something I'm replacing for you next week.''

"This is such a help!" Betsy brought the pot with her to fill Rayna's mug on the table. "Let me get a good look at you. You look…content. No, that's not the right word. Something put the color back in your cheeks. Could it possibly be that fine new husband of yours?"

"Betsy!" Rayna nearly dropped the bean pot. Had she heard her friend right? "What goes on between a husband and wife in the privacy of their home is none of your concern, Betsy Hunter, but—"

"Ha! I'm right. You've made the marriage official, right?" Betsy reached for the sugar bowl, looking as happy as a cat in a creamery. "As if you weren't going to tell me anyway. Was I right?"

"I'm not going to dignify that with a response." But Rayna was laughing as she searched through the drawer for a ladle.

"This is the only romance I get, hearing about my girlfriends' wonderful love lives."

Rayna loaded two plates with steaming molasses flavored beans and crisp strips of salt pork. "You were right. Daniel is a wonderful lover. And wanting him that way feels like a weakness."

"How can that be? He's your husband now."

"He's a man deserving of all the love I can give him. But after all these years of being married to a man I loved more than my life and giving birth to our children, my heart is gone. And so holding on to Daniel that way is just…holding on."

Ashamed, she laid the plates on the counter. In the long seconds between the ticking of the clock and the snap of the fire and the agony she felt between one breath and the next, she heard Betsy's chair scrape on the floor as she stood.

Betsy's hand landed on her shoulder. Betsy's voice

rich with empathy. "There are many kinds of love. There is certainly no greater love than that of two people working together to protect children. What a special man your Daniel must be, to take on so much responsibility."

"You understand." Rayna twisted the slim gold band on her hand, reminding her of her promise to honor Daniel. Not that she needed reminding. "It feels like a betrayal to Kol."

"Not a betrayal. He would want you to find happiness." It was in Betsy's eyes, her special understanding. For her marriage had been one of great love, too. "You and I both married our first loves. It's a rare thing, to have the gift of a love so pure and wonderful and passionate. I wish that this new marriage of yours grows into a love that is rich and rewarding, my dear friend."

That is my wish, too. "Have you ever found your heart again?"

"No. But I have hope."

Hope. Was it enough? Maybe it was for now, she thought as she and Betsy placed the food on the table. Bringing fresh butter and thick slices of sourdough bread, Rayna settled across the table from her friend.

Already Daniel had added to the memories in this room. Of how he'd come the morning after she'd found all the bank notes. How he'd looked through the papers he obviously couldn't have read, but understood what they meant.

Surely happier times were ahead for all of them, right?

"I don't have the knack for baking that you do. Oh, this bread is delicious." Betsy, always effusive with her compliments, reached for another slice. "It always surprised me that more men weren't lining up to marry you. Daniel must be the envy of a lot of men in these parts.

Marrying you and getting the best section of wheat land in the county. Of course, we all know you are the greater prize.''

''Prize? Oh, I think providence was looking out for me in sending Daniel into my life. He's...wonderful.'' One hundred percent. Everything that was good and true. But she couldn't love him.

Then why did it feel as if a part of her innermost being missed him? Yearned to be in his arms again? ''Oh, I've started sewing my squares together.''

''Oh, your quilt. Let me see!''

Rayna put aside her spoon and rose to fetch her sewing basket when a shadow outside the window snagged her attention. That was definitely not her imagination! The shadow became a man pounding up the porch steps. Daniel, and in his arms was—

''Hans?'' She had the door unlocked and open before Daniel could knock. He blew in, carrying her son safe against his wide chest. Hans coughed, a horrible rasping sound, and Rayna wiped the snow off his dear face.

''Ma.'' Hans's eyes filled. Oh, he was so ill. Why hadn't she noticed this morning? This time when she brushed a kiss to his brow, his skin was overheated.

Rayna's knees went weak. ''It is your throat, baby?''

Hans could only nod and reached for her. She lifted him out of Daniel's strong arms and cradled him against her, the big boy that he was.

''He'll be all right.'' Daniel said the words as if they were a promise he could keep.

''Want me to carry him upstairs?'' As if he were made of mountain, unshakable and commanding, Daniel stood before her.

''No, I can do it. Just, please, get the doctor. Get him now.'' Rayna leaned her cheek against the top of Hans's sweaty brow, fighting to keep calm even as the little boy began to quake with chills.

"I'll bring him as soon as I can." His hand settled on the back of her neck, meant to comfort her.

And, amazingly, she felt the current of his strength filling her. It would be easy to lean on this man. To let herself need more than his comfort. More than his passion in the night. His broad chest was right here for her to lean on.

All she had to do was take a step forward.

She took one back, away from all that he offered her. Wishing, just wishing she was naive enough to make a different choice.

Home. There it was, lit windows blazing bright through the darkness. Daniel shut the barn door good and tight before drawing down his hat to keep the flakes out of his eyes as he trudged through the accumulation of snow. A good six inches had fallen since Kirk had been this way to do the evening chores.

His home. Where he belonged. Where he was loved, and in the case of Hans, if not even liked, then at least needed. That was, all around, a pretty fine feeling, to know that when he opened that door, his loving wife would welcome him. Just being with her, why that alone was more than enough to make him happy.

It gave a man a sense of satisfaction, yes it did. Filled up a part of him he didn't even know was empty. All day he'd been feeling as if a chunk of him was missing. And now, as he broke through the heavy snow toward the back porch, that gnawing pain plaguing him the evening through stopped.

Hell, he'd never been like this before, all bent up inside from missing her and the boys. He'd been thinking of nothing else but this house and the people in it. Hoping that Hans was feeling better. That Kirk wouldn't be next to fall ill. Wondering about Rayna. He'd bet money that he would find her up and attending to her little boy, even though it was well past her bedtime.

Yeah, being with her was what he'd been daydreaming about. What had made him desperate all afternoon and the evening through, just to look upon her lovely face. Just to hear the alto sweetness of her voice. Simply to pull her to his chest and know that he was loved. That *he* mattered. Him. And not because of what he did for her, but for who he was.

It was amazing how one event that hadn't taken five minutes in front of the preacher had changed his life. Suddenly he was a husband, a stepfather and an extensive landowner. All in one fell swoop. His chest twisted all up inside. He'd never had so much before.

He'd never had so much to lose.

As he hopped up the back steps, there she was, wrapped up in a huge gray shawl, opening the door for him.

"Come in out of the cold, stranger." Her welcoming smile made him fall in love with her all over again.

It was something to see he'd been missed, too. So he swaggered in and shucked off his snow-driven layers. Getting her clean floor all messy. She didn't seem to notice as she hung his things up to dry, efficient as always.

"I had the chance to work late making a few deliveries. Teaming pays better, so Saturday's paycheck ought to give us a little breathing room." He ignored the growl of his stomach and the half-frozen stiffness of his body. What he couldn't push aside was the craving for holding her in his arms.

Love was an odd thing, not the companionable link he'd imagined of two people getting along. It was scary, that's what it was. To feel his heart stripped bare and his soul exposed.

But it was awe-inspiring, too. Grateful for this gift, for the chance to be loved, he gathered her against him tenderly, although she had her back to him and was shaking out his muffler. Ice tinkled to the floor and her lean muscles bunched and pulled beneath his hands and he hugged her tight.

Lilacs. He loved the smell of her, spring flowers and warm woman and home. He'd do anything for her, anything, because of the way she surrendered to him with a strangled moan.

It was hard for her, too, this unveiling of the self. But feeling her against him, not just body but soul, brought a gratitude so powerful, it made his throat ache and he closed his eyes against the brightness.

The time between one heartbeat and the next froze, and he treasured it. Kissed the delicate dip of her neck, right behind her ear, and felt. Simply felt love spilling through him. A perfect moment.

A perfect love.

Then his heart beat again and Rayna stiffened. She broke away from him as if she'd felt nothing at all. Back straight, shoulders tensed, head up, she grabbed a hot pad and fetched his supper plate from the warmer.

His chest twisted—with disappointment or longing, he didn't know which. Maybe both.

"I've got to change Hans's poultice." Politely spoken, the way she'd been when he'd first come. When he'd been a stranger and not the man who'd made love to her in the dark intimacy of night.

Daniel pushed aside whatever emotion was building

within him. It was only right that Rayna was concerned about her sick child. He was worried about Hans, too. "How is the little guy?"

"He's not improving." Rayna's voice was clipped.

Worry, that was all. He understood that. "Is the doc dropping back by?"

"Any time now. When I heard a horse, I first thought you might be him. You'll keep an eye out for him?"

"Yeah. I'll get this grub down me, and I'll be up to help. Tell me what you need, pretty lady."

I need you to stop breaking my heart. It seemed she had one after all. The pieces of it, broken and sharp. Nothing whole to give him. And even if it was, she wasn't a sixteen-year-old girl any longer. She'd learned the cost of loving with all her heart. She couldn't do it again.

Not even for a man as deserving as Daniel.

Leaving him to his supper, she took the stairs two at a time. If she could get away fast enough, maybe she could also escape the pull he had on her soul. Like the mountains to the prairie, the sky to the earth. She could not hand over so much.

Hans was awake and waiting for her, his face flushed above the pile of blankets. "M-Ma," his voice scratched painfully, and his eyes filled.

"Do you want some more water, sweet boy?"

He nodded, looking so miserable as she filled his favorite tin cup. His fever had yet to break. And until it did, he was in danger. Life was so fragile. A gift that could be taken away at any moment.

She held his cup to his lips. He sipped. Struggling to swallow, he teared up anew. Her poor baby. She wrung cool water from a cloth and folded it in thirds so it would fit across his little brow.

''That m-man.'' Hans sniffed.

''Yes, Daniel's home.'' She settled the cloth in place, hating the hot feel of his fever. Hated how small and vulnerable he was. ''He's watching for the doctor.''

''Can't he g-go?''

So much pain filled his eyes. ''No. He's going to take care of us the way your pa did.''

''He's gon-na l-leave, too.'' One tear overflowed, falling along his baby-soft cheek to tap against the pillowslip.

''No, my baby. He's here to stay.''

''N-no.''

She smoothed his hair away from his sweaty brow, wishing she could hurt for him, too.

''Rayna.'' Daniel. He was standing in the hall.

He had to have heard what Hans had said about him. How did she tell him that she understood far too well? There was no way to spare Daniel's feelings from the truth. It wasn't easy trying to let another man close. Not with wounds so deep.

And Daniel, incredible Daniel, held his chin up and his shoulders back. No anger showed on his face or in his stance as he ambled in, bringing the doctor with him. It was with concern that Daniel studied his stepson from the far corner of the room.

Concern and compassion.

And she knew the truth. That in marrying her, it wasn't the land he'd wanted. Or her, as loving as he'd been to her and as well as he'd treated her.

He was here for Hans. For the little boy living a life Daniel never had. In saving Hans, Daniel was saving himself, too.

A rush of emotion tore through her so powerful, it brought her to her feet. Agony for the small boy alive somewhere inside Daniel who'd endured beatings and neglect. Who'd gone to bed hungry. Who'd never been tucked in or cared about or sent off to school with a lunch pail full of good food and books to read from. Who had worried over him when he was ill? No one.

A sorrow beat at her, driving her from the room. Every piece of her soul cried out to hold the man who needed her. Who'd put aside lifelong lessons of neglect and rejection to risk loving her. Daniel loved her with the same intensity that she'd loved Kol so long ago. It was with the ideal passion of a first love.

Not knowing, or understanding, that to love wholly was also to lose wholly.

She couldn't love him the same way. She could *never* love like that again. She refused to need someone so much. She wouldn't lean on anyone ever again.

It was the surest path to heartbreak and desolation. Love was a falsehood. It made a person seem safe and sheltered, but from what?

Not life, not the world. Her faithful and complete love for Kol hadn't saved him from collapse and death. She didn't even get to say goodbye. He was taken from her, and her life…it hadn't been stable and it hadn't been secure.

She'd built her life on a young girl's dreams of happiness. She'd been wrong.

She was a woman with scars of her own. She wasn't about to depend on another man so she could close her eyes and hide from a world that was not safe or particularly kind. She would take care of herself. She had a job, she helped in providing for her family. She wasn't about to cling to a girl's whimsy of what love and life should be.

"Rayna?"

It was Daniel, following her into the dark shadows of the parlor where the fire writhed and twisted in the grate. She knelt in front of the wood box and chose a good cured piece of fir. It would burn clean and hot. She stacked the two-foot chunk of wood into place on the crumbling skeletons of burning logs. The orange flames flared, greedily lapping at the moss and bark on the wood.

"Rayna." Daniel, with love in his voice and his heart on his sleeve, crouching close, as if he belonged beside her. "That's my job. Let me handle this. You go upstairs to be with Hans."

That was Daniel, always helpful, always good and kind and strong. Always. And it was killing her.

Stubbornly she grabbed another log with her bare hands and winced when a sliver gouged into her palm. But the pain didn't matter. It was a small thing compared to the torture coming to life within her.

It wasn't her heart that was breaking, she realized. It was her soul.

"Here, sweet lady." His rugged hands, calloused and scarred from a lifetime of hard work covered hers with an uncommon tenderness.

She felt his love move through her like a light so pure it could dispel any darkness. She grabbed another chunk of wood, fighting him, struggling against the part of her that wanted to close her eyes. To lean against his chest. To breathe in the luxury of being in *his* arms.

It was too much to lose. Her heart was gone. Did she have to risk her soul, too? "I can't do this."

"That's why you should let me." With care, he wrestled the log chunk from her grip. "You're tired. Let me watch over Hans for a few hours while you nap. I can apply a poultice and keep him cool."

"No. No, I can't let you—"

"Yes you can. Just trust me. I won't let you down, Rayna. I'd die first. You have to know how much I treasure you."

She twisted away so she wouldn't have to look at him and see the adoration in his eyes. The depth of love she could not return. She could not allow it. What words could she use? Anything that came to mind would hurt him, and hurt him deep. He didn't deserve that. Not Daniel, his hand steady as it came to rest on her nape. Possessive and affectionate and, oh, the soothing balm of his touch.

She had to move away. Had to stop this before he could invest any more of his perfect heart. There was no kind way to do it. No easy way. Only the truth.

When she turned to him, she wasn't aware of the tears welling in her eyes. Or the rent beginning to crack through her soul. Only that she had to save both of them. It was the truth of this world. This merciless world. "I will take care of my son, Daniel. He is not your son."

"Well, now…uh…" Confusion dug deep into the corners of his eyes, his honest, beautiful eyes. "He's my stepson, too, and the child of the woman I love. I—"

"Daniel, you have to stop this. You have to. I'm begging you." Breaking apart, that's what she was, shattering from the inside out.

"What am I doing, sweetheart?" His hand cupped her chin. His fingers eased away her tears.

She wanted to grab on hard and hold on to him and never let go. "You are loving me. And I can't take it. I've lost the love of my life. I can't do it again. I just can't. We can be friends, we can even be lovers, but I can't l-love you."

"You can't love me?" His jaw ground tight. His eyes

filled. He stepped away from her as if he'd been slapped. His hurt resonated in the darkness and in the shadows.

"*I* can't love. It's me, Daniel. Not you."

"I see." He turned away, the darkness in the room seemed to cling to him. And the hurt remained. "I'll go bring in more wood."

He was gone with the even knell of his boots. The outside door swung closed, not with a slam or a bang, but a small, final click. A lonely sound in a hopeless winter's night.

Chapter Twenty

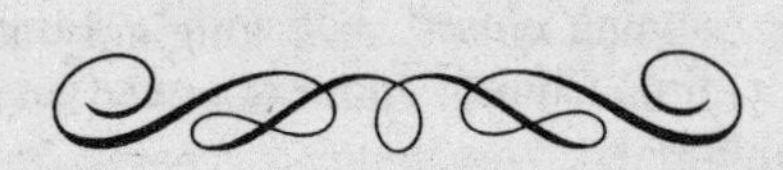

I can't l-love you. Daniel let the bitter wind cut through his clothes, chilling him to the bone, but not to the soul. Rayna's honest confession had numbed him to the bottom of his soul.

Nothing, *nothing* had ever reached so deep inside him, not since he was seven years old.

Not until Rayna. Until he'd been foolish enough to put aside those hard-learned lessons in his life and believe he could belong somewhere. And mean something to a woman so good and fine, she made his spirit stronger.

But now, he didn't feel strong at all. He felt tired and frayed. All the memories stored up and locked away, uncoiled in his mind. Images of the dismal winters when he was very young spent in the dormitories of the county orphanage in Little Rock, Kentucky.

He'd been one little boy in a cot shivering in the dark, alone in a crowded upstairs with too many cots and boys crammed into every available space. Trying to fall asleep with his teeth clenched to keep from chattering because there were not enough blankets to go around.

The nights were the worst, what he dreaded most. Too

cold to sleep, stomach growling, he'd lain awake listening to the other boys' misery. Some wept for their dead parents, others for the pain of being unwanted every day. Others for the hope they'd thrown away, making the night a time for despair.

Sometimes, during the day, married couples would pay a visit to look at all the children. Some were childless and the women would gaze longingly at the pretty little girls with their curls and wide-eyed sweetness.

He never blamed them much for being chosen. Even when he'd tried his best to be quiet and good, wishing, just wishing, a kind motherly lady would see what a good boy he would be.

That's what this reminded him of. He'd learned a long time ago to shut off the pain of wishing. That only led to certain disappointment. Just as the boy he'd been had learned not to even hope he'd be adopted, the grown man he was now should have been wiser.

Pain cannoned all the way to his soul. Rayna could explain her feelings all she wanted—that she wasn't able to love, that she couldn't lose her heart again.

It didn't matter. The truth was, she didn't love *him.*

He loved her. To the bottom of his soul, with all the strength of his spirit. She was the only love he'd ever had. The only real home he'd ever known.

Whatever he was to her, he wasn't enough. Not for her to love.

Love wasn't a decision. It wasn't something made out of duty and marriage vows and practicality. It was like the night. It just came. Without struggle or uncertainty. Day turned to night. That's just the way it was.

Love either grew or it didn't. It was as simple as that.

The snow tinkling from the sky to tap like music against the endless plains calmed him. Made him draw in a deep breath and see that the only mistake made had been his. Like the little boy he'd been so long ago, he tucked away the corners of his heart. And the edges of it. Until there was nothing open or exposed or able to feel.

He had a job to do. As with all the families he'd been with before. He'd wagered his freedom for the chance to matter.

It was a bet he'd lost. The truth was, he had more to lose. Much more. As he loaded up his arms with heavy cured wood, he knew there was more at stake than just his heart. This land, and the homestead he'd earned with his sweat and blood.

That's why he was here. That's what he ought to be worrying about. Not whether a good-hearted and incredible woman loved him or not. Because that was a proven fact. She didn't, she wouldn't.

She couldn't.

He was here only to work. Yeah, he understood that now. He dragged his feet on the way back to the house. Not so much because of the heavy wood he carried, but because he'd have to look Rayna in the eye and act as if he hadn't made a fool of himself. And the pain of her rejection…why, it reminded him of the little boy still inside him somewhere crying out in misery.

And knowing that no one cared. No one ever would.

By the time he made it beneath the shelter of the porch roof, he took one look behind him. The snow was falling so hard that it was already filling in his footsteps. Almost as if he'd never been.

Rayna had been holding every muscle tight, but seeing his shadow on the porch, standing as invincible as ever, made her sigh with relief. *Thank heavens he's all right.* She'd been afraid...

No, she should have known that Daniel, incredible Daniel, was doing as he'd said he'd do. His arms were loaded with stacked wood for the fires.

She opened the door, the draft icy enough to freeze her breath. Shivering, she felt him pass by her like the click of a telegraph line. A tangible, electrical current that she couldn't help responding to.

Daniel, covered with snow, disappeared with his load into the parlor. Without a word.

She felt his hurt inside her like the darkness and the cold. She gripped the door frame, leaning against it for support. Watching as he knelt to empty his arms, moving methodically and fast, as he did everything. She studied the long line his back and neck made as he knelt in the shadows. The way his dark hair fell forward to hide his face as he worked.

He was dear to her. She admired him. She cared for him far more than was prudent. She'd risked more than she could lose already. Last night, open beneath him, she'd welcomed him into her body and more. So much more. And she had to stop this now. Life was too fragile.

"I'll be all right, Rayna." Daniel, steady and stoic, rose to his full six feet. He kept to the shadows, as if lost in darkness. "You go on up and take care of your boy."

"I need to know that you're all right. That you understand. You are so wonderful, Daniel." Emotion caught in her throat and stopped her. She had no more words. None. Only feelings, and that was some place she didn't dare go. A place beyond need and affection and companionship.

A place where lovers whispered their affections, from one heart to the other.

His gloved hand bit into the round of her shoulder joint. She melted against him. Lost, so lost. Clinging to his leather coat. The ice stung her skin, but she held on. She had to make sure he was all right.

She kissed the spot on his chest above his heart. "I just can't rely on another man. I just can't lose like that again."

"It's all right." His assurance rumbled through her. His arms banded her tight. "A heart can take only so much grief in this lifetime."

He understands. Grateful, she moved into his kiss. Savored the tender caress and suction of his loving caress. Her soul beat with a pulse of its own. As she reached out for more, he slipped away, leaving her wanting.

Leaving her alone.

Daniel heard the pad of Rayna's gait on the floor overhead. The rasp of the door's hinges. The muffled groan of the bed ropes adjusting to her weight.

She was getting some sleep, was she? That must mean Hans's fever had broken. Daniel knew without having to ask that she wouldn't have left his side otherwise. The doc had come a second time and said if the boy showed no improvement by midnight to come fetch him.

The kitchen clock struck eleven. An hour to go, and the little boy was on the mend. Good. Daniel covered the embers, so they would be ready to go come morning, and stood. Stretched his aching muscles.

He had a long day of work ahead. And if he didn't settle enough to sleep, then tomorrow would only be the harder for it. He checked the locks and took a last look outside from the wide kitchen window. Nothing out of place, although it was hard to tell with the snow still falling.

His thigh muscles were stiff. Too much lifting yesterday. He took his time. Hans's door was open, probably so Rayna could listen for him. Sure enough, he spotted their bedroom door cracked open a notch.

Daniel hesitated, wanting to make sure he'd given Rayna enough time to fall asleep first. He couldn't help glancing in the little bedroom, where shadows upon shadows masked the toy train and cavalry and soldiers scattered across half the floor. Hans murmured in his sleep and rolled over. In the dark, he was nothing but a faint outline small and helpless.

Feel better, little guy. Daniel had vowed to keep the boy safe, and he would. Except for an act of God, it looked as if the note payment would be covered. Two more paychecks would do it, and with no time to spare.

The coal yard was busy; Danzig was pleased with how hard he worked. And with Rayna's extra income, yeah, they would be all right until spring planting. He'd sweat through the growing season and pray for a good harvest. That's all they needed. A good harvest. And just in case, he planned to keep his job in town.

There was one little boy who was going to grow up the right way. With plenty of blankets on his bed. A doctor when he fell ill. A stomach that had never known hunger. Toys on the floor and a mother's love.

Yeah, he was a lucky kid. Daniel's throat ached as he turned. If nothing else, he could still make a difference. It mattered.

It had to be enough.

A small voice called out in the dark. "M-mister?"

"You can call me Daniel. Want me to get your ma?"

"I'm awful thirsty."

''I can get that for you. Stay under the covers where it's warm.'' There wasn't enough light for him to see by, so he lit the small tin lamp on the bedside table before filling a little tin cup with a horse painted on the side of it.

Hans's hands shook with weakness, so Daniel knelt and held the bottom of the cup steady. The boy's blond hair was sticking straight up. His eyes were troubled as he finished up and collapsed into his pillows.

''That enough?'' Daniel asked. When the kid nodded, he left the cup on the corner of the table, within easy reach. ''In case you get thirsty again.''

''Mister?''

Hell, he could see the boy wasn't going to call him anything familiar. ''Yeah?''

''You better leave now.''

Feeling better, was he? Daniel figured that was a good sign. ''No, Hans. I'm not going to leave. Not now. Not later.''

''Yes, you are.''

''I know how it is. You're hurtin' over your pa, but I'm here for good. Like it or not. It's nothing to be worrying about tonight. You go to sleep, all right?''

'''Kay.'' Hans's frown was a deep one and his troubled sigh was full of burden. ''Mister? You're not gonna leave?''

''No.''

Hans studied him with sad eyes. Eyes so like his mother's. ''Okay.''

Daniel turned down the wick and darkness reigned once more.

Rayna knew the instant Daniel entered the room. It wasn't the hush of the hinges or the pad of his socks as he crossed the floor. In the dark, with the wind beating at the eaves and with her entire will fighting it, the light within her grew.

"How's Hans?" Her question startled him.

He froze and the hard line of his shoulders, just visible in the dark, tensed. "He needed water. I filled his cup. He's fine."

He's fine. But Daniel was not. Rayna held out the covers to welcome him in. There was only one bed iron—she'd given Hans all but the one at the foot of the bed. Only enough to take the chill out of the sheets.

Daniel took his time, lost in the utter blackness on the far side of the room. His clothes rustled, his belt buckle thunked against the floor, and then he was climbing in beside her. A hulk of a man so close.

And so distant.

He did not turn to her. He did not draw her into his arms.

It was just as well. She closed her eyes, but sleep didn't come.

She doubted if she would ever sleep truly well again. Not with her heart gone and her soul in pieces.

Daniel lay awake, too. Silent, with his back to her. Until the clock downstairs struck four and he rose to take care of the livestock. It was another day of hard work for them both.

Rayna waited until he was outside before she rose, washed quickly and dressed. The boys were fast asleep and so she hurried downstairs to start her chores.

Daniel squeezed the last of the milk into a bowl for the barn cat, who curled around his ankles in thanks. Leaving the calico purring in contentment, he clipped the lid on the pail and wrapped up for the trip back to the house.

Not that he was looking forward to it. The thought of sitting at the breakfast table with Rayna…his guts coiled up good and tight. No, he wasn't over the pain. Although humiliation had set in. To think that he'd ever had a chance in the first place.

Maybe it was the way of things. A man who'd grown up alone was meant to be that way. Truth was, he'd never come across a woman that made him think it would be worth the risk.

Until Rayna.

I can't l-love you. He could still hear her words thick with apology and raw with truth. She didn't have the heart for it. Sure, he understood that. Because he'd just used up the last of his.

He was as alone as he'd ever been. He'd survived loneliness for all of his thirty-five years. He didn't need Rayna. He didn't need love.

And if that wasn't true yet, then by God he'd make it true. Anything was better than living with his heart torn out and bleeding. Nothing he'd ever known had hurt so fierce or cut him so deep.

Two more weeks, he thought as he shoved the barn door open against the resistance of the drifting snow. Two more weeks and the first payment made—that was the hardest. If he kept his job in town through the rest of the winter and into spring, even if he had to harrow and seed the fields at night by lantern, then that's what he'd do.

With an angry shove, he propelled the barn door closed with a definitive bang. Puffing great clouds of warm air, he let the snow fall everywhere around him, tapping on his face and thudding on his shoulders, covering the tops of his boots as he went. He wasn't ready to go in yet, but it was too cold to stay out. Somehow he would walk into that house as if he hadn't suffered more than a mild disappointment.

Instead of being knocked to his knees.

The storm had only gained fury through the night and when he saw a tall, lanky figure moving through the blinding whiteness, he held up the pail. Kirk, no doubt, come for the milk. Daniel knew he'd spent too much time in the barn and Rayna was probably cooking breakfast, by now in need of the milk.

"Kirk!" He shouted, cupping his mouth with his free hand. "Head on in. I've got all the chores—"

A muffled explosion resounded through the dense snowfall and something struck him in the chest. The force was powerful enough to rock him back on his heels. The bucket slipped and tumbled to the ground, rolling with a faint metallic clatter out of sight. Daniel looked down. The front of his jacket was dark. A dark red stain flowed like a creeping ink spot. Blood. His own.

He'd been shot? He oddly felt nothing. Nothing at all. And then he couldn't breathe. Pain blinded him and he was falling. The icy snow pelted his face and he didn't know which way was up. Kirk had shot him? No, that couldn't be right—

His knees hit the ground and the impact ricocheted through his torso. The shadow before him darkened until it was Clay Dayton emerging from the veil of snowfall. Daniel didn't remember reaching for his revolver but the six-shooter was in his hand and the bang and flare of the bullet firing was all he saw as death pulled him down.

The shock on Dayton's gnarled face told Daniel his

shot was true as the light drained from his eyes and he surrendered, knowing that even as he died, Rayna would be safe.

Thunder. That was Rayna's first thought as she rescued the fresh cornmeal muffins from the oven. It was certainly snowing hard enough and lightning and thunder were not unheard of in near blizzard conditions.

But the second shot that followed in a few seconds' time couldn't be thunder. It was more like gunfire. *Daniel!* She turned down the damper, left the stove and ran, pulling on her coat as she bounded down the steps. The storm tore at her, pushing her back as she struggled forward.

"Daniel!"

No answer but the howling wind. She couldn't see anything but snow—at her feet, falling into her face, tumbling straight down from the heavens. Something had happened to Daniel, she knew it, for she could feel the agony in her soul.

And then color broke through the world of white. Crimson red streaked across the ground at her feet and she saw Daniel's gloved hand still clutching his revolver.

"Daniel!" She fell to her knees, wiping the snow from his face. He didn't move. His eyes were closed. Was he breathing?

His chest was sticky with blood. The accumulating snow was stained, too. His blood was everywhere. She pressed her hand down in the center of it and the warm gush through her fingers told her he was still alive. But for how long?

"Rayna?" A voice came out of nowhere. A man—

Doc Haskins—broke through the curtain of snow. ''Oh, God. It's Daniel. Move aside. Let me see.''

The competent doctor knelt beside her, mindless of the conditions. His ministrations were cloaked by the gusts of snow. As if the winter was not bleak enough, the downfall turned torrential, so that she could only see snatches of Daniel's face.

She wiped away the snow and lifted his head onto her lap. Her dear Daniel. He was dying, she could feel it. How could she endure losing him, too? Not Daniel, so good and honorable. He didn't deserve this, he didn't.

Her own heart stopped beating as she pressed her cheek to Daniel's and whispered in his ear so he would know. ''Your life means something to me.''

She didn't know if he could hear her or if he was already lost to her as the blizzard shrouded them.

Chapter Twenty-One

"Rayna, you need to eat something." Mariah emerged from the dark hallway with a tray. The faint tinkling of ironware and the fragrance of chicken broth gave away the contents of the ironware bowl.

"You know I'm not hungry. I can't eat."

Rayna twisted on the wooden chair she'd brought up from the kitchen. Her bones were stiff and her fanny ached from sitting for the better part of two days. She set down her sewing hoop, and the deepest part of her being cried out at the sight of Daniel so still beneath the pile of blankets.

Deathly still.

"I can't eat until he's well." She said it stubbornly, as if she could will it to be true. With every ounce of her soul, she wished it, although the doctor told her to prepare for the worst.

Her throat ached with grief.

"You have to keep your strength up. It's only sensible." Mariah's firm tone was gentled by affection as she placed the tray on the edge of the bed. "It's hard, I know, my dear friend. But try."

Rayna merely nodded. How could she get even Mariah's delicious chicken soup with her homemade noodles and thick chunks of meat past the grief wedged in her throat? She could hardly breathe as it was.

Mariah studied the sewing clamped in the big wooden hoop. "This is beautiful, Rayna. You're almost done."

"It gave me something to do while I've been watching over Daniel. And worrying."

Mariah nodded approvingly and it took no words for the understanding that passed between them. The love of a good man was worth anything and should never be taken for granted.

Rayna waited until she was alone again to brush a kiss against Daniel's cheek. His dark hair tickled the side of her face. Love, keen and bright, welled up from her soul. She'd been lucky to love Kol. To have had the chance to live and laugh and share her life with her first love. She wouldn't trade those years for anything. Because loving him was worth the fall. The pain of grieving him was a small price to pay.

Daniel moaned, low in his throat, and she stroked his forehead until he calmed. She'd been wrong. She hadn't known until she'd held his head in her lap, watching the doctor frantically trying to stop the blood loss, that she did love Daniel. Her heart was whole after all.

"Please live," she whispered over him. She hoped he could hear her somewhere. That he could feel her in his soul, the way she could feel him.

With hope, she picked up her sewing and nipped the threaded needle through the border seam. For the second time in her life she was piecing together a wedding quilt. She was no longer that young girl with stars in her eyes. She was a grown woman, strong and experienced, but now she knew the value of a good man's love.

She sewed long into the night, until she was too tired

to see. When the quilt was done and the backing tied in neat knots, she realized this quilt, too, was stitched with hope for a happy future.

A future that could only be possible if Daniel lived.

Hell, he was hurting. Way too much to be dead. Daniel fought to open his eyes, and it was like swimming to the surface of a deep lake. Fighting, he opened his eyes. The bright light stung.

The shadowed figure moving to the bedside was too big and brawny to be anything but a man. Kindly Doc Haskins's stubbled face came into view—a little blurry, but Daniel wasn't one to complain. He was glad to be alive. Except for the pain streaking and throbbing through his chest that nearly had him passing out again.

Haskins looked plenty relieved. "You have one of the strongest wills I've ever seen. I didn't think you'd make it. Dayton sure didn't and his wound was as bad. Let me take a look at your incision."

"What? You cut me open?"

"Had to. The bullet was lodged deep. But you'll be just fine now. After a little bed rest. Build back up your strength. You'll be as good as new." The doc reached for his stethoscope.

"Wait, Doc. I don't have time for bed rest." His vision was clearing now. He was in bed alone with blanket and quilts covering him. Snow fell at the window—it was day. He could see the storm was still raging. "I've been down for—what?—a few hours. It's got to be—what?—just before noon."

"Going on three days after I took that bullet from your chest. You're just lucky I was on my way to check on your little boy."

"No. That can't be possible. I haven't been asleep for

three days. I have a job. I can't lose that paycheck.'' He looked around again. The doc was the only one in the room. Rayna? Where was Rayna?

And then he knew. *She's not going to come see you, man. You let her down.* He had to get up; he had to talk to Danzig. He had to see, maybe, if there was any way, he could work. They were so close, so damn close to making it. Maybe the doc would hold off on his bill. He had to get up, that's what. Get up and—

Damn it. He was still lying on his back. Wheezing as if he'd run five miles with his boots on from doing nothing more than trying to lift up off the pillow.

''Lie still or you'll tear out your stitches and be in a worse mess than you're in now.'' Haskins wasn't a bad sort, as far as a sawbones went, but the doc didn't understand.

He had to get up, he had to— Pain dug like an ax blade through his ribs. His vision blurred and he shook from the exertion. Weakness flowed through him like water, and it didn't do him any good.

Especially when he heard her familiar gait at the doorway. He felt her like a warm summer breeze moving through him. Turned toward her as if she was the very air he breathed.

Rayna. Her hair was down, caught in a ribbon at her nape. Shimmering locks and flyaway curls and, hell, the sight of her, settled him. Made him feel calm down deep. The pain seemed a small thing when she gazed upon him. Her sorrow, her exhaustion, her worry, that's what hurt more.

How could she stand to look at him? Shame filled him. It took terrible effort, but he managed to turn his head. There was no way he could endure seeing the disappointment on her face.

Maybe even hatred.

He'd known most of the sorrows that life had to offer. Hunger and neglect and despair and cruelty. But he'd never known the sorrow of failing the person he loved more than anything. It was a despair so black and choking, it felt as though he were drowning with no one to save him.

''Daniel?''

He couldn't answer. He didn't move.

The pad of her shoes on the wood stilled. Her dress rustled to a stop, her petticoats whispering. ''You sure had me worrying.''

''I truly am sorry about that.''

Rayna glanced at the doctor, who was closing the door to leave them alone, and then back at the man on the bed. Her invincible husband with the bandaged chest. The man she'd sat next to for almost every moment of the past three days. She'd bargained with God, she'd replayed every conversation that had ever happened between her and Daniel. She'd willed him to live.

And yet here he was alive and he felt lost to her. Maybe she'd failed him too completely by not loving him enough. By not being enough.

She loved him now. And it was too late. She could feel it. Why else would his sadness fill the room like smoke? Why else would he refuse to look at her?

What should she do? Walk away without telling him the truth? The only truth she knew for certain? That through the waiting for him to live or die, she'd found something astonishing.

Her love for him.

''Just go,'' he said tonelessly. As if he didn't care for her anymore. As if she'd lost him for good. ''As soon as I'm able to get out of this bed, I'll get out of here. You'll never have to see me again.''

Oh. He doesn't love me anymore. Rayna wrapped her arms around her middle, feeling bereft. As if she'd had a second chance for happiness and she'd destroyed it.

There was no reason he would forgive her. Why would he? She'd broken his heart. She'd told him she wasn't able to risk so much. That she couldn't love him. He'd been shot because of her.

What did you say to the one man who was more than your heart, but your entire soul? She didn't know. After so many hours of waiting and praying for this chance, she fell short of words.

But not of love.

His hand was hot and so male—bigger and rougher and the skin tougher. Calluses marked his knuckles and paraded across his palm. She ran her fingers down the center lines of his palm. Wishing she could make this right for him. Did she even have a chance?

''Your quilt. You finished it.''

''I had plenty of time while I was sitting in this room with you.''

''You were here?''

''Yep. I'd never worried over anyone the way I did you.''

''You worried over me?'' Daniel couldn't believe that he'd heard her right. There's no way she could still care about him. ''I failed you. You're the only person I've ever loved and I let you down. Why are you here? I lost your land. I lost my ranch. And your boys—''

He fought to stay calm because the next thing she was going to say was that she was done with him. She wanted him out. She wanted him gone. And he'd honor that. He'd abide by her wishes.

He couldn't blame her. He'd failed her. It was as simple as that, and he was going to handle it with dignity. "I let you down, and I know you don't want me. But I promise you this. Once I'm back on my feet, I'll get back to work. Give you the money you need to help you keep your boys with you."

"What did you say?"

"I'll help you keep your sons. Maybe I could take a railroad job and send you what you need."

Rayna stared at him, her mind a jumble, not knowing what to say. Even completely defeated, Daniel's first thought was of her sons. Of her. She'd never met a more noble man. "I appreciate that, but I'm going to keep this place."

"But how can you do that? There isn't enough money. I can't work. I can't meet the payment."

"Mariah's husband worked the last two days at the coal yard. And Betsy's brother is working your shift today. They plan on trading off with Katelyn's husband until you are strong enough to work again."

"What? But I don't know those men. Why would they help me?"

Didn't he realize the truth? "Because you are a good man and they wanted to help. It's a blessing to have friends, Daniel. It's not good to be alone, as you have been. You're not alone anymore."

"What?"

He looked so confused. Was it that hard for him to believe he was a wonderful man? "I told you, you have immense value to me, and not for the work you do. For who you are."

"Me?"

"You, Daniel Lindsay, are impossible not to love. I

fought it, I refused to surrender to it, and I even believed my heart was incapable. But you made me love you."

"How did I do that?"

"With your goodness and your integrity and your heart, Daniel. Your wonderful, loving heart."

"You love me?" Daniel had to wonder if he was in heaven after all. He was loved. His chest felt near to breaking apart, and not from the bullet wound. Happiness filled him, buoyant and sweet. "I love you, too, my beautiful wife."

"I guess this means I'll be needing you right here in my life. I don't want you taking a job far away from me. What do you think of that?" She laid her hand on his shoulder.

Her left hand with his ring gleaming on her fourth finger. She was still wearing it. He couldn't be dreaming. He just couldn't, although it felt like a dream because nothing this good had ever happened to him before.

He studied the quilt covering him. The rich jeweled colors of fabric pieces now whole. Whole. Like his life. He smiled up at the woman who was his first love. His only love. "You went to the trouble of finishing our wedding quilt. I might as well stick around. It would be a shame to let all that sewing go to waste."

Joy shone on her lovely face. "It's just my good luck I'll be stuck with you for…what, twenty or thirty years?"

"That's my plan, darlin'. Longer, if I can manage it."

Rayna felt as if she were breaking into pieces, but not from grief. Not any longer. For when Daniel held out his arms to her, the last of her sorrow faded like the ice of winter giving way to a green spring.

With a full heart, she climbed beneath the quilt she'd made and snuggled carefully against the man she loved.

Epilogue

May, one year later

''There, little one. Mama's here.'' Rayna lifted her infant daughter from the cradle. Looking like a little rosebud with her pink dress and socks, Ruby Danielle Lindsay stopped fussing and gave a wide toothless grin.

''You just wanted to be held, didn't you, love?'' Nestling her sweet girl against her heart, Rayna grabbed the cookie plate with one hand and gave the screen door a shove with her foot. The hinges whispered and the warm breeze sifted over her, smelling of sunshine and growing grass and lilacs blooming.

''There are my two favorite ladies.'' Daniel took their daughter into his big strong arms, love etched into the corners of his eyes. The emotion looked good on him. The past year had been a hard one, but the rewards were many. Having him at her side was the greatest.

''Ma! Just in time.'' Hans dismounted from the pony Daniel had bought and taught him to ride. ''I'm starving.''

''Be sure and share with your brother.''

Kirk, grown taller and broader, the very image of Kol, looked up from his schoolbook. His studies interrupted, he let the wind batter his textbook as he took the plate of cookies and held them out of Hans's reach. "Gee, thanks, Ma. They're all for me, kid."

"Those are for me, too." Hans shoved at his brother and they wrestled affectionately, the plate of cookies set aside as the boys took off to race in the sunshine.

Kirk in his last year at the town school was studying for his graduation exams. He was to attend college in Oregon in the fall.

"Come sit on the porch with me." Daniel held out his free hand.

The moment she twined her fingers through his, she felt the surge of pure love moving through her like sun through the maple trees. She had to be dreaming, for how could anyone be so joyful?

But this was no dream, just hopes for a happy marriage come true.

With supper roasting in the oven and a temperate afternoon to spend with her husband, Rayna let him lead her to the porch swing he'd built. When he settled in next to her, Ruby gurgling against his chest, she could feel the affection in her heart double, as it seemed to do every time she felt his hand in hers.

He must have felt it, too, because his fingers tightened around hers and he leaned against her to brush a tantalizing kiss across her lips. "Have I told you lately I'm in love with you?"

"Only twice today."

"That's not nearly enough. I love you."

"I love you."

Like all dreams come true, there were no words that

could describe the depth of her feelings. The depth of her feelings for this man she'd married.

It was enough to let the dappled sunlight filter through the maple trees to warm them. And to gaze out at the endless blue sky and their fields of green growing wheat.

To know that all she needed to be happy was to spend her days beside Daniel. The man she would treasure for this new season of her life.

* * * * *